WHEN I DISAPPEAR

AMANDA MCKINNEY

Storm
PUBLISHING

Previously published in 2023 as *The Stone Secret*, an Independent Publisher Book Awards Gold Medal Winner – 2024. This version includes updated plot and new content.

Ebook ISBN: 978-1-80508-887-5
Paperback ISBN: 978-1-80508-889-9

Cover design: Lisa Horton
Cover images: Arcangel, Shutterstock

Published by Storm Publishing.
For further information, visit:
www.stormpublishing.co

ALSO BY AMANDA MCKINNEY

A Marriage of Lies

The Wife's Silence

The Perfect Murder

The Stranger in My Bed

The Anti-Hero

Mine

Steele Shadows Mercenaries

Her Mercenary

Her Renegade

Steele Shadows Investigations

Ryder

Jagger

Steele Shadows

Cabin 1

Cabin 2

Cabin 3

Phoenix

The Road

Rattlesnake Road

Redemption Road

On the Edge

For Henry and Mama

ONE

Who are you pretending not to know?

Perhaps it's the other man or woman in your marriage. Or maybe it's your psychiatrist who signs off on your monthly Xanax prescription, a dealer your husband has no idea you've been seeing for five years.

We all have that person in our lives, don't we? Our dirty little secrets, their purposes justified one way or another. Some of these individuals are harmless, discreet deceivers, others far more sinister.

I, personally, am privy to the latter.

Picture this:

It is three o'clock in the morning, the time of night when everyone is asleep. The nocturnals have finally succumbed to exhaustion. The drunks have passed out, one hand clutching a bottle of Jim Beam, the other a grease-stained wrapper from the dollar menu. Even the early risers are still asleep, desperately clinging onto the one remaining hour of being comatose before they force themselves out of bed on the promise of a good day.

The world is asleep.

Except for you.

You are sneaking through the woods.

It is late summer in the foothills of Vermont, in the middle of a heatwave. Despite the early morning hour, the humidity is thick in the air, heavy in your lungs. The black long-sleeve T-shirt you're wearing is damp, sticking to your skin like papier mâché. Your hair is sweaty under the balaclava you are wearing like a beanie. It is too hot to pull over your face just yet.

Overhead, a full moon hangs in a cloudless sky. Moonlight dapples the forest floor beneath your black boots—oversized to throw off investigators should it come to that.

You are calm, steadfast, resolute in your step. A laser-like focus, determination in your eyes.

There is no hesitation in your purpose, no second-guessing. In fact, it is the opposite. For the first time in your life you are absolutely certain that you are exactly where you are meant to be. It's unnerving, really, how calm and confident you are. How easily you banish the little red flags that creep into your subconscious.

Finally, you spot your destination through the trees, a red, weathered two-story farmhouse with faded white shutters.

Your pace quickens.

The property is washed in silver light. Long, black shadows stretch across the backyard. The house is dark, save for the dim, orange glow of a table lamp from somewhere inside. A night-light of sorts, you assume.

A dog barks somewhere in the distance as you stride across the yard.

You pull the balaclava over your face.

Gloved hands and a lock pick are used to quietly break into the farmhouse. The door squeaks as you open it, a slow, tired groan of metal against metal.

The scent of garlic and tomato sauce permeates the air as you step into the kitchen, along with a pungent artificial potpourri that makes your stomach churn. Moonlight streams through the windows, pooling onto a stained linoleum floor. The light dimly illuminates a small, unimaginative kitchen with rows of cabinets on each side and dated appliances below them. Tools, stacks of lumber, and boxes scatter the floor. The kitchen is undergoing a renovation of sorts.

Three blue digital clocks glow through the darkness. The microwave reads 3:02 a.m., the stove 3:04 a.m., and the coffee pot 3:11 a.m. You wonder how someone could live with three mismatched clocks in one room.

The door catches on something as you try to close it behind you, a welcome mat that reads *Wipe Your Paws*. Funny, because there is no sign of any animal in the house.

You turn and begin to toe the mat out of the way when you hear the soft creak of a floorboard behind you.

You are not alone.

Your body stills, a rush of excitement tingling with this new plot twist.

Just as you start to turn back, you hear the *whoosh* of the bat a split-second before it comes crashing down on the back of your head. Pain explodes in your skull, a wave of nausea washing through your body at warp speed. You're grasping at anything to steady yourself, eventually finding the counter for support. Your world goes temporarily black, only to reemerge in blurred waves of color. You stagger, not recognizing the moan that comes out of you. Your voice sounds disconnected from your body.

You are struck again, this time in the ribs.

It isn't until the metal bat slams into your kidney that something awakens inside you. A searing, electric pain that flips a mental switch, igniting that human instinct to survive. In an instant, white-hot anger replaces the pain, and like a superhero gaining his powers, you are suddenly invincible.

Jaw clenched, eyes wild, you unfold yourself from the defensive position.

You are ready to fight—to live.

You spot a kitchen knife poking out of the wire dish rack next to the sink. You lunge forward and grab the knife that seems perfectly placed just for you.

It is not your time to die. After all, you have been here before. You remember this, an all-consuming boil of rage that replaces common sense.

You spin around, dodge the next attempted blow by a mere inch. The bat whizzes past your ear. You feel the soft puff of air against your skin.

You release a guttural scream and plunge the knife into your attacker's stomach.

She stills, her bat raised mid-waist, the silver twinkling in the moonlight. An aluminum Louisville Slugger.

Your eyes meet.

The world seems to stop around you.

"Oh..." she says in a breathy whisper. The bat drops from her hand, clamoring onto the tile floor.

You watch the old woman die at your feet.

So, back to my initial question: Who are you pretending not to know?

For me, it is myself.

I am pretending not to know myself. This dark side of me. A part of my personality, my genetic makeup, that makes me do evil, vile things. No matter how hard I try to suppress this person, their ugly face arises unexpectedly like a virus coming alive after lying dormant for years.

Yes, I am pretending not to know this side of myself.

The side of me who murdered Marjorie Stone.

TWO
SYLVIA

Twenty Years Later, Present Day

"Hand me that bottle of wine over there, will you?"

Shirley looks at me from her perch on the armrest. Lazy black beady eyes, one milky with blindness, the other heavy with boredom.

We engage in an overly dramatic stare-off, me and my half-blind cat, whom I have recently started having full-blown conversations with. My cat does not talk back, I should be clear; it's just me, vocalizing a tangled mess of jumbled half-thoughts laced with curse words... Well, this is not entirely true. Shirley does talk back, in her own way, of course. The saunter of annoyance, the tail-flick of I'm-only-*kind-of*-interested, the slow look-away of dismissal. Yes, Shirley has much to say—and quite the attitude for a hairless runaway missing half of her vision.

Shirley breaks eye contact first, bored with my childish antics. Per usual.

"Fine." I fling my feet off the coffee table and, using every bit of energy I have left in me, push to a stance. My hips groan in protest, my lower back pops. A dizzy, heady feeling swims through my brain. Likely from the half-bottle I've already consumed.

It's two-thirty in the afternoon. A bleak, cloudy day, the crisp autumn air bordering on frigid. Thorncrest, the quaint little Vermont town I call home, is in the middle of a cold snap. Daily temperatures are projected to reach only the mid-fifties. A sign of a bitter winter to come.

I stumble while my body adjusts to being upright, much like waking on a cruise ship after a long night wasted at the bar.

The screams and accusations from the reality show on the television pull my attention as I bend forward and deftly weave around a stack of books, a stained coffee mug, and a pile of used tissues. I grab the wine bottle from the far side of the table. (Funny how rising from the couch feels like an act of God, but retrieving a bottle of wine? Suddenly I'm as quick and nimble as a gold-medal gymnast.)

"You're nothing more than a dime-store slut," one housewife spits at another.

"Hey, I'm not the one with a box full of second-hand dildos under my bed."

"Oh, how dare *you..."*

Eyes locked on the television, I sink back down on the couch and refill my wine glass, splashing a few drops on the rug beneath my feet. I wonder what second-hand dildos are. Surely not *used* dildos, right? Is that even a thing? Do people recycle their sex toys? I am just about to Google this very question when Shirley raises her head at the sound of tires on gravel outside.

I frown, look at the clock, a forgotten commitment tickling the fringes of my memory.

"What day is it?" I ask Shirley.

Outside, the vehicle rolls to a stop.

I surge off the couch, tripping over my blanket as it tumbles to the floor. I sprint to the kitchen, the sudden burst of energy sending my heart rate surging. A reminder that I need to move more.

I pull open the pantry door. One shutoff warning and one delinquent credit card glares back at me. I push them aside and squint at the *Friends* calendar tacked on the back of the door. Scribbled under today's date:

Hair, 3 p.m.

"Shit."

I totally forgot.

My house is a wreck. I haven't washed my hair in four days. I have no makeup on, and I'm half drunk.

A car door slams outside.

I run to my purse, grab my wallet, and empty the contents. Heart racing I count the cash. Barely enough to cover it—which means no groceries this week.

Shirley saunters past the doorway as I walk out of the kitchen, flashing me the side-eye of disapproval—well one of them, anyway.

I open the front door as Ginger Dubois is raising her swollen, veiny hand to knock. Per usual, the sixty-something's short hair is fluffed to perfection, not a strand out of place. The color is lighter than I remember, a shimmery silver that highlights a round, ruddy face with a pair of aggressively stenciled eyebrows. Her leathery skin is at least two shades darker than last time I saw her, suggesting either a recent beach vacation or a nap under a spray-tan gun. She is wearing a paisley-print shawl over a fitted black T-shirt with a yellow peace sign in the middle. White capri pants and blinding white sneakers complete the look. One cool cat.

Ginger Dubois is a bit of a legend in Crest County. People either love her or hate her, there is no in-between. The eccentric spinster's claim to fame was being owner of the only reputable beauty salon in the area, which she named Dye Hard. Clever cat. Dye Hard had a good twenty-year run, before the failing economy forced Ginger to close her doors. Now she makes house calls.

I find the woman absolutely fascinating.

Ginger steps inside, a bag in one hand, a bejeweled to-go mug of wine in the other. Her perfume makes my eyes water.

I sneeze.

"Jesus, woman," she says, looking around my house, "you've got to get either a housekeeper or a husband."

Sniffing, I close the door and lock it. "I know, I'm sorry, it's a mess. I forgot you were coming today. And, by the way, last I checked husbands don't clean."

"No, but you will in order to keep him."

"That's pretty antiquated."

I grab a chair from the kitchen and drag it into the living room while Ginger lays out her box of tricks on the ironing board I leave out like a piece of furniture. Next to it is an old bike I bought from a thrift store a few months ago. I take it for a spin down the driveway on occasion, after a few glasses of wine.

"It's not antiquated," she says when I return. "It's love. When you love someone you want to do things for them—like keep the house clean. That's how it works."

"Well therein lies the problem."

She glances at me. "You don't love anyone?"

No one loves me, I think, but don't say it.

I take a seat in the chair next to the living room windows. It's an awkward, open space that I have no idea what to do with. Besides place an ironing board and bike in it.

"That's why I'm here, dear," Ginger says, draping me with a plastic cape. "To make you look your best so that you can go out and get yourself one of the only two single men living in this town."

I laugh. She isn't joking.

"Okay, what are we doing?" She runs her fingers though my hair.

I consider the women on the television. "I'm thinking about going lighter, maybe. And maybe add a little body up top."

"Ah, lovely. Okay, we'll do blonde highlights and I'll add some layers to the back."

"Keep the length."

"You got it, sister. And I'm going to bring by a deep conditioning treatment later this week, when I get the shipment. You need it."

I study the reality stars in front of me, and contemplate going fully blonde as Ginger mixes the color. They all look the same: bleached blonde hair, skeletal botoxed faces, long skinny fingers garnished with ten carats of cubic zirconia. Society's definition of perfection.

I couldn't be more different from these women.

I have boring brown hair, the color of poop. Though I've cut it many times, it is now midway down my back. Long, straight, and boring.

Ginger begins smearing color through my hair. I stare blankly at the television. I used to be good at small talk, but years of living alone has slowly eliminated that skill.

"You know someday I'd like to put makeup on you, give you a full makeover," she says eventually. "You have round, beautifully hooded eyes and big lips. Both very sultry."

"Well thank you, Ms. Dubois. Your tip just doubled."

She laughs a breathy wine-fueled laugh right above my face.

I grab my wine, take a big swig to catch up.

"You know," I say, hanging onto the glass, "I don't want to brag, but I have been told that I look like Gisele Bündchen."

"Brag away, dear. There is absolutely nothing wrong with it."

"It's true," I continue. "Those are the exact words from a

drunk homeless man that confronted me outside of a coffee shop in Dallas."

"Your hometown, right?"

"Right. His exact words were: Has anyone ever told you that you look like an ugly Gisele Bündchen."

Ginger bursts out laughing.

I'm tickled by her boisterous response. I used to be funny, I think. Both intentionally and unintentionally. Now, I just look pissed all the time. I was cursed with a perpetual resting bitch face. A constant downward turned mouth, the pink corners drawn to the floor like magnets. I've put a ton of work into changing this unfortunate condition. I've tried to train the muscles upward by doing face exercises I found on the internet. But no matter how many repetitions of "kiss and smile" I do, my mouth always turns back downward.

"You have the same hair color as your mother," she says, ripping me from my thoughts.

THREE

SYLVIA

"I remember when she moved here after Gerald died. Your mama was the talk of the town, having returned after so long."

My grandfather, Gerald Stone, was a hard man. Cold, callous. Though I didn't know him well, I don't think I ever saw him smile. At least not after his wife, my grandmother, passed away in a mysterious house fire. After he passed, my mother inherited his multiple properties, including this house, and decided to move back to her hometown.

I followed shortly after.

"I think it's wonderful that you decided to stay in Thorncrest after she died. I'm sure it would warm her heart to know you're keeping her legacy alive in her hometown."

I am completely dumbstruck by the conversation. I don't want to talk about my mother, or her death.

Ginger picks up this hesitancy and switches topic, to one only marginally less depressing.

"So have you found a job?" she asks, as she always does since she learned of my lay-off from the *Crest County Newspaper* six months ago.

"Not yet." I pause. I know I haven't put as much effort into hunting for a job as I should. Truth is, I've got too much ego to accept just any job available. I'm picky, this girl who doesn't wash her hair for four days, lives in a pigsty, has spent almost all her inheritance, and sleeps with a hairless cat.

"Remind me what you did there? At the newspaper?"

"My official title was associate-editor-slash-journalist. I was responsible for coordinating story planning, and also for managing our social media outlets. But really, I did whatever was needed at the moment."

In a large, bustling city my position would be highly coveted. In a town of only 2,700, a blip in the middle of miles and miles of untamed wilderness, not so much. I enjoyed it, nonetheless.

I did everything from interviewing the Best in Show winner at the annual Crest County livestock contest, to reporting on the 150 varieties of apples sold in the area, to drafting help-wanted ads, and finally, my favorite part of the job, chasing down leads and doing real groundbreaking, investigative work within the county. I, Sylvia Stone, was the lead investigative journalist on two of the most viewed stories in the county: Old Man Merkle's Tractor Thief, and the Kinky Kids—an unruly group of teens responsible for spray painting gangly penises on the side of the middle school. Yes, I, Sylvia Stone, was on it.

Pay: A whopping fourteen bucks an hour. Now I'm a thirty-nine-year-old woman who makes nothing.

Ginger jerks her chin to the women arguing on the television. "You could always marry a rich man like the housewives," she winks.

"Maybe after these highlights, I'll go for it," I wink back.

The local news cuts into the program. The headline: *Local Man Missing*.

It's been years since someone went missing from the area.

The last was a teenager ran away to join a traveling sex club. The girl turned up five days later, with four new tattoos, a shaved head, nipple piercings, and a severe case of chlamydia. (So says the receptionist at the hospital who illegally viewed her medical record).

I grab the remote and turn it up.

"...*Crest County Police still have no leads on the missing twenty-eight-year-old man we reported on yesterday. Please take a look at your screen. If you have seen Jesse Taylor—that's his image on the screen—please call the number listed below...*"

Ginger scoffs. "That boy."

I perk up, sensing incoming gossip.

She delivers. "Jesse Taylor, son of the town doctor, a spoiled misfit with chronic failure-to-launch syndrome. I can't stand the kid. You heard about that group of teens who tried to break into a jewelry store a few months back? Jesse was the ringleader of the crew. Kid refuses to grow up, enabled by parents who allow him free rein of their fancy, lakefront home and bottomless credit cards."

"I think I heard about the break-in at the jewelry store."

"I'm sure you did. His parents did nothing and everyone knew about it. His dad, Dr. Harris Taylor, paid off the owners so that they wouldn't press charges. Total enablers, they are. I used to cut his mother's hair. Janet, her name."

"Yeah? What's she like?"

Ginger hesitates. This surprises me.

"Strange... There is something odd about that family," she says and I get the vibe she's holding back.

But I don't press; instead, I zone out as she combs my hair, sending me into a trance-like state.

Forty-five minutes later, I look marginally more like the women on the television. This pleases me. I'll go all blonde next time, I decide, as Ginger packs up her things.

I bid Ginger farewell and watch her sportscar disappear down my driveway, pondering on her comment about the Taylors and their missing son.

There is something odd about that family...

FOUR
RHETT

Twenty Years Earlier

A beam of sunlight cuts through the trees, spotlighting the saw bench. I reposition the two-by-four. The loud trill of the saw breaks the silence of the nature around me, waking me up and heightening my senses. Wood chips pelt my safety glasses, instantly coating my hair, my shoulders, my T-shirt, and my boots.

A clean cut.

I stack the piece, grab another. Measure, cut.

Again, and again.

There is nothing like the smell of sawdust in the morning. Nothing like the satisfaction that comes from creating something from nothing with your hands.

Nothing like a cool, spring morning.

Tango, my Rottweiler mix, leaps out of the woods and shakes the dew from his coat. Strings of slobber fling into the air, sparkling in the early morning sun.

"Find any breakfast?"

He trots up to me and nudges my work bag.

"I'll take that as a no. Okay, okay," I perch my safety glasses on the top of my head and kneel down. "I should have named you Jabba the Hutt."

I toss him a few dog treats, then scratch behind his ears. Tango has an insatiable appetite—for both food and my shoes. Not just any old shoe though; it's the left shoe of my only "nice" pair. Never the right, and never my jogging shoes, or my work boots. Just that left damn shoe.

Satisfied, Tango darts back into the forest. A smile catches me as I watch his black furry body fade into the brush.

My attention is pulled to a silhouette passing by the windows. I pause, straighten, and squint into the blurred glass a few yards away. It's definitely not my client, the homeowner, Marjorie Stone. This person is much too quick and agile as she moves from window to window.

She disappears upstairs.

Ten minutes later, I dust myself off and make my way into the kitchen to refill my coffee and open the boxes that were delivered yesterday afternoon.

When Marjorie Stone hired me to update her kitchen cabinets, she made it clear that she didn't want to have to maneuver through clutter while I worked. I understand why. Mrs. Stone wears nothing but house dresses, at least an inch too long. It's a miracle she hasn't broken a hip already. Mrs. Stone also made it clear that I needed to know Jesus. I assured her that I do, and we've been off to a good start since then. I'm pleased because I need this job. Badly. When I opened my carpentry business earlier this year, I didn't realize what it took to run a business, especially on your own.

I take a second to savor the fresh, warm coffee, then slide it onto the counter and grab a knife.

The moment it punctures the packing tape on the first box, I feel someone behind me.

I straighten, turn.

The woman standing in the doorway is a younger, much prettier version of Marjorie Stone. She has brown hair, doe-like brown eyes, and long feathery lashes. She's short, like Marjorie —much shorter than my six-foot-three frame.

We stare at each other for a beat, lingering just long enough to make it awkward.

Her gaze flickers to the knife in my hand.

I quickly slide it onto the counter.

"Hey, there," I say, "I'm Rhett Cohen, with Cohen Carpentry."

"Good to know. I almost called 911."

"Oh," I shrug. "They know me there."

Her brows pop.

"I'm joking." I wink.

She grins, sets a coffee mug in the sink, then surveys the mess surrounding me.

"This is hardware for the cabinets," I tap a box with the toe of my boot, "and this the liner for the inside, and a few extra tools."

She nods, studying the frame of what will be a row of six cabinets. "Looks like things are coming along."

I fist my hands on my hips and take in the progress. "So far, we're ahead of schedule."

Just then, Marjorie walks in, a fresh coat of makeup on her face. The woman goes through several shades of blush a day, I've noticed. This morning, she's chosen a reddish tint and yellow eye shadow to match the yellow daisies on her white house dress.

Her eyes round. "Oh! Sylvia, I thought you already left. Good—you two can meet." Her wrinkled eyes twinkle and it's painfully obvious what's going to happen next.

"Sylvie, this here is Rhett. Isn't he the most handsome thing you've ever seen?"

I grin at Sylvia whose cheeks are on fire.

"Mama, stop."

"But isn't he, though?" She begins twisting the stone pendant she always wears around her neck. "He's single, too, you know. Can you believe that? And he owns his own business!"

"*Mama—*"

"Oh, and he's got this cutest dog. Well, terrifying at first, but after you get to know him, he's so sweet." She leans in to Sylvia's ear. "I've been feeding him hotdogs when Rhett isn't looking. A business owner *and* a dog lover. I mean, couldn't you just—"

"*Mama.*"

Marjorie winks at me and I can't fight a laugh—which Sylvia doesn't appreciate.

"Well, I'll let you two..." Sylvia stammers, flustered. "Get back to work or whatever. Bye."

Sylvia spins on her heel and hurries out the front door, sending it popping on its hinges.

Majorie and I laugh, then she sighs.

"That girl," she shakes her head.

My gaze shifts to a framed picture on the wall of two young girls. One brunette, one blonde.

"The brunette is Sylvia," Majorie says.

I study the little girl, grinning from ear to ear. She's proudly lifted a bloated bullfrog she must have just caught. Her brown hair is so tangled she looks like she spent the morning with her finger stuck in an electrical socket. Her face is streaked with dirt and one shoe is missing from her foot. (I wonder if Tango had a brother).

"And that's Anna." Marjorie's voice is different when she introduces me to the blonde in the picture. Softer. More emotional.

This little girl is starkly different from Sylvia. Not in facial features or body shape, but in appearance. In contrast to the tomboy next to her, Anna's long blonde hair is perfectly curled. She's wearing a white dress and holding a pink purse. There is not a speck of dirt on her.

FIVE
SYLVIA

Present Day

I awake with a start. My torso propels forward, popping off the pillow like a Jack-in-the-Box doll. I blink, the wine I'd consumed with Ginger now a ball of haze in my brain. The smell of chemicals in my hair makes my stomach turn.

The room is ice-cold. This is the first thing that registers.

The second is: Someone is here.

I look at Shirley, curled in a tiny ball on the armrest, her ears perked as she stares at the front door.

Yes, someone is definitely here.

I look at the clock—2:37 a.m.

A flutter of fear sweeps through my body. Who would be visiting me at two-thirty in the morning? Or is "visit" even the right word? Is someone about to break into my home?

I take a quick inventory of my surroundings. I'm on the couch, Shirley on the armrest. The television is on, illuminating the dark room in a flickering blue light. The curtains are open. *Shit.* This means that whoever is outside my house likely saw me through the window as they walked to the front door.

I suddenly feel extremely vulnerable. Are they watching me now? Am I supposed to pretend like I'm not scared? Feign strength and confidence? Instead, I am frozen in inaction, over-thinking the situation, like always.

I try to recall the active shooter training I'd taken for a story written earlier in the year about school safety. Unfortunately, however, my brain is a vacant warehouse of dead air. Besides, even if I could remember the self-defense protocol, I don't own a gun. But I do have a bat, and not just any bat, an aluminum Louisville Slugger.

"It's okay, Shirley," I whisper as I push myself off the couch. Thank God I am dressed—if you consider "dressed" a pair of gray sweatpants, an oversized brown sweater, and rainbow toe-socks.

Feeling extremely exposed, I grab my cell phone and dial 911, but I don't connect. Instead, my finger hovers over the call button, prepared to tap. I kneel down in front of the couch, and with my other hand, search through the dust motes until I feel the cool, sturdy metal of the slugger. Weapon in hand, I stand.

Shirley is gone, of course. Likely hidden under the bed ensuring her safety—hers only.

On an inhale, I stride to the door, chest puffed, a steely expression on my face. It's the most badass I can get.

I pause to listen before turning on the outside light. I peek out the window next to the door. A torch of yellow pools on the porch, hardly illuminating any farther than the front steps. A handful of leaves flutter down from the red maple out front. A blanket of crispy, dead leaves coats the driveway.

There is no car. No human lurking outside.

I consider that perhaps the noise was from the family of raccoons that live under my porch.

But... maybe not.

After sliding my phone on the windowsill, I open the door, brandishing the bat as a weapon.

Lying on the welcome mat is a long white envelope. There is no name, address, stamp, or return address. Just a blank envelope.

Someone delivered me a letter at two-thirty in the morning?

After a quick scan of the woods that surround my yard, I pick up the envelope and step back into the house. I close and lock the door, testing it twice before backing away.

"Shirley!" I whisper-hiss, demanding my partner in crime be a part of this creepy new adventure that has just appeared on my doorstep. When she doesn't come, I set out to find her. Shirley is going to be a part of this whether she likes it or not.

I find the wrinkled ball of skin in the kitchen, curled on top of the microwave. One of her favorite spots—which, for some reason, kind of grosses me out.

"I'm okay," I mock, rolling my eyes. "Thanks for checking on me."

After closing the curtains, I click on the overhead light and raise the envelope. "We got a delivery."

Shirley cocks her head, mildly interested.

I notice my hands are unsteady as I examine the envelope.

Inhaling, I slowly rip off the corner.

Inside is a single sheet of white paper. Typed across the middle are three numbers:

3:02

SIX

RHETT

I wait until the guard passes before pulling the crumbs I confiscated from the kitchen from my jumpsuit breast pocket.

I sink onto the cot, and bend over. *"Tsk, tsk, tsk..."* I whisper under the bed.

A minute passes.

"Tsk, tsk, tsk..."

Finally, a tiny black nose and wiggling whiskers appear next to my palm.

"Here you go, Nacho," I whisper. "Don't tell anyone."

I watch as the mouse picks the crumbs from my palm, one by one.

I met Nacho five years ago. Fifteen years into my twenty-five-year sentence. He was just a baby. I began sneaking crumbs from my meals and feeding him daily. Soon, however, I realized the only thing this little jail rat would eat was corn chips—hence the name Nacho. This amused me. The rodent would rather starve than eat something he didn't like. I admired this steadfast allegiance to self.

I have no idea how Nacho got separated from his mother, or how he made his way through the tiny crack in the corner of my jail cell. All I know is that little rodent saved a tiny piece of my soul, in a time I needed it the most.

"We've got a big day ahead," I whisper, stroking his little black head. "My parole meeting is today." My voice cracks before I can finish the sentence, punctuating how nervous I am.

I've been denied parole twice due to the brutality of the crime I was convicted of. After each rejection, however, I've remained hopeful. Because a life without hope isn't one worth living. I realized that very quickly after being locked in the state penitentiary.

At the sound of boots on the floor, I surge to a stance.

"Go," I whisper to Nacho.

He looks up, blinks.

A knot forms in my throat, and to my complete shock, tears spring to my eyes. I don't want to leave him, this little dirty jail rat.

How ridiculous, I scold myself and remind myself of my goal—my purpose. The plan I've spent the last twenty years outlining.

On a deep inhale, I lift my chin, square my shoulders.

The guard, Mitch, unlocks the cell.

I wait until I'm invited out.

We don't speak as he walks me down the corridor, his hand gripping my elbow. I close my eyes, blocking out the hoots and hollers from the other inmates.

My heart begins to pound as I'm led through one, two, three heavy steel doors.

We pass the visiting room. My mom's face flashes behind my eyes. Her warm smile, her milky white skin. Then my father's face.

I glance down at my naked wrist, the sudden onslaught of flashbacks making my stomach sink.

. . .

"Dad," I look up from the saw bench. "I didn't expect you today."

Smiling, he surveys the garage, the makeshift office of the company I just started—Cohen Carpentry. He's wearing his usual threadbare khakis and worn orthopedic sneakers, but today, he has on a colored short-sleeved shirt.

"What's going on?" I ask, sliding my protective glasses onto the top of my head and dusting off my pants.

He swallows deeply, and I realize that this isn't just a regular pop-in.

"Is Mom okay?" I frown, meeting him in the center of the garage.

"Yes, yes. Everything's okay."

I gesture to the two folding chairs in the corner. "Sit, Dad. Tell me what's going on."

I settle in next to him. He puts his hand on my knee. If Mom isn't sick, then he is, I think, because my father rarely ever touches me.

"I want you to know..." He clears this throat. "I want you to know how proud I am of you for starting your own business. For making something of yourself. I know we—you—didn't grow up with much, but I did the best I could."

I am dumbstruck. Speechless at both the display of emotion and the praise. My father has always been a very stoic man.

As I struggle for words, Dad pulls something out of his pocket and grips it tightly in his palm.

"I want to give you something."

"Dad, no..." I gawk at the vintage Rolex that has been passed down by his father. It's the only thing of value that our family owns. Grandpa won it in a poker tournament in Chicago in the '70s.

"Yes, son," he cuts me off. Then he does something I've never seen before.

*My father smiles so widely that his eye sparkle. "A busi-
nessman needs a nice watch. It's yours now."*

Sweat beads on my forehead as the guard opens the door to a small conference room.

Behind the gleaming wooden table sit three people. Two men in suits, and one woman in a blue dress. Her hair is swept into a bun and a pair of owlish glasses sit on the tip of her nose.

A single plastic chair has been positioned in the center of the room.

"Mr. Cohen, please, sit."

My knees feel like they're going to give out as I lower into the chair. I study the panel in front of me. The three people—whom I've never met and have never met me—who hold my fate in their hands. If I am granted parole, I know that it can take up to two weeks to be officially released. But that's fine with me. I can handle two more weeks.

The meeting begins.

I can hardly hear their questions through the blood rushing through my ears. I answer the best I can while trying to conceal the nerves simmering underneath it all.

We reach the final, arguably most important, question of the meeting.

"Mr. Cohen, do have any intention of causing anyone harm once you're released?"

"No," I lie.

SEVEN

SYLVIA

The following two nights I receive two more letters, both delivered in the same manner as the first, both around two in the morning. The second letter reads:

3:04

The third:

3:11

Night four, I am ready. I am prepared.

I took a sleeping pill at dawn, and slept all day, ensuring I would be alert and ready when night came.

I have my baseball bat. I have Shirley's attitude, and I have an entire pot of coffee on tap.

I am *totally* sober. There is not a single drop of wine in my body. A victory in itself.

As if reenacting a scene from a movie, I've set up the living room to look exactly as it did the two previous nights. The television is on, the light flickering over the dark room. The curtains are open. I am even wearing the same sweater and sweatpants. (Different underwear.)

I am a producer in my own little scary movie, a gripping mystery, surely to earn an Oscar nod. It's a bit over the top, I know, but I can't help it. I'm bored. Also, I have a natural tendency to solve mysteries. This is why I loved my job at the newspaper so much.

I sit on the couch and wait.

And *wait*.

Finally, at 2:57 a.m., a rapid, *tap, tap, tap,* on the door breaks the silence.

This time, I am crouched, like a cat ready to strike, on the other side of the front door.

Gripping a can of mace in one hand and my cell phone in the other, I fling open the door, ready to confront whoever or whatever is at the center of the mysterious letters.

My late-night visitor is too quick, however. He is already gone and I see nothing but the outline of a dark silhouette sprinting across my lawn.

"Wait!" I lunge out the door, sliding on the white envelope in the center of the welcome mat.

Letter number four.

"Wait!" I yell again. "Stop!"

I sprint after him, mentally cataloging the height, weight, every detail I can of the silhouette running away from my house. He is wearing a black sweatshirt with a white skull and crossbones on the back. And he is extremely fast, which suggests that he is both young and very fit.

The stranger darts around the house, trampling over my beloved vegetable garden.

I can't keep up. The silhouette disappears into the woods.

I skid to a stop at the tree line. Chest heaving, I stare into the black mass of trees, listening to his heavy footfalls fade into the night.

The world goes silent once again.

"Dammit."

I glance up at the moon just as a cloud drifts over it.

Something is in the air tonight, more than just the chill. Something ominous that sends a ball of dread twisting in my gut. I don't like it. It feels like something is coming.

I've felt this before.

Once back inside, I carry the white envelope to the kitchen table, and open it as carefully as the ones before it. This time, however, something tumbles out. I recognize it instantly. It is the necklace my mother used to wear every day, a long gold chain with a stone pendant attached to the bottom. Except now, the pendant is speckled with dried blood.

The letter in this envelope reads:

You are next

Ice-cold fear trickles up my spine.

You are next...

I cup the necklace in my palm, stare down at the memory.

You are next...

My gaze shifts to the picture hanging on the wall next to the window. It is of me and my mother, one month before she was brutally murdered.

You are next...

I study the letters, one by one.

3:02

3:04

3:11

You are next

My heart thuds in my chest.

There is no question now. I know exactly what the letters mean.

He's back.

EIGHT
SYLVIA

It is a cold, wet day. Not rainy—wet. A thick, cloying cloud of moisture hangs in the air, a deceptive mist that tricks you into thinking you don't need a raincoat but then saturates you the second you walk out the door.

A storm blew through sometime in early morning, stripping the trees almost bare. The streets are covered in heavy, wet leaves. It's the kind of day made for curling up on the couch with a cup of tea and a good book, not for pulling into the Thorncrest Police Station with a purse full of mysterious letters.

My windshield wipers drag across the blurred windshield, squeaking loudly against the silence. One is worn bare and does nothing to wipe the rain. My stomach clenches. I feel like I'm going to be sick. I consider a quick run to the gas station bathroom across the street before going in.

No, I tell myself, *you are not going to be sick.* I know this because I haven't eaten a thing all day. I'm just nervous.

Extremely nervous.

My palms are slick as I slide into a vacant parking spot under a sagging pine tree. I hesitate, considering the chance that a dead limb might fall on my new Jeep Wrangler that I can't afford. And then I remind myself that a dented hood is the least of my worries at the moment.

My heart pounds as I force myself through the motions: Turn off Jeep, put keys in purse, check face in rearview mirror—gasp in horror. Thanks to the humidity, my limp, straight hair is now a puff of frizz, the strands neither straight nor sexy-beach-wavy, but more of psychopath-chic, like Doc Brown in *Back to the Future*. My mascara is smudged under my eyes, highlighting the dark circles I'd awoken with.

I take my time pulling my hair into a bun at the nape of my neck and fixing my face.

I am stalling.

I am a freaking wimp.

Banishing my nerves, I grab my purse and push out of the Jeep. I've already made my decision. I am already in too deep.

This is happening.

I slam the door, sending a blast of raindrops into my face.

A car drives by. I turn my cheek against the spray of water.

My heels echo on the wet pavement as I stride across the parking lot. Yes, I have totally done myself up for this visit to the police station. Conservative two-inch black pumps, dark skinny jeans, and a silk blouse under my favorite tweed jacket that I haven't worn since being laid off.

It felt good, pulling myself together. Like I had a purpose. Like I had money.

I take in the building as I approach, a new location for the Thorncrest Police Station. I remember when it was a Walgreens. A few years ago, the city bought the building using government funds intended to revitalize the community. They removed the awnings, added bulletproof windows and a large brick wall around the perimeter and called it the new (and improved) police station. To me, it still looks like a Walgreens.

The front doors slide open as I approach. The waiting room is blinding white and smells of paint and stale coffee. A row of plastic chairs line the room. A few awards and news articles hang crookedly on the walls, a not-so-subtle reminder of the station's excellency.

I am not alone.

A haggard-looking woman sits in the corner of the room, her skinny, frail body vibrating with nervous energy. She reminds me of a poodle, one of the miniature ones. For a second, I wonder if she's high. The woman is on her phone, hunched over, elbows on knees, long, curly blonde hair falling over pointy shoulders. She's wearing a wrinkled, white blouse tucked haphazardly into a pair of khaki slacks. A Louis Vuitton handbag sits next to her foot, a diamond ring, almost as large as the bag, on her finger.

I recognize her but can't quite place her.

A loud, frantic voice echoes from the other end of the phone. The woman is shaking her head, waiting to respond.

Naturally, I eavesdrop when she speaks.

"...the day before yesterday. He seemed normal... No, he didn't seem off, or anything weird—weirder than usual anyway... No, I don't know why he would leave, or where he went, or, hell, even if he's okay." Her voice shakes. "I swear to God when I find him, I will kill the bastard myself..."

I clear my throat and look away. A domestic issue. Thank God I've never married. I have absolutely no desire to be involved in that kind of crap on a daily basis.

The receptionist looks up from under fake eyelashes as I approach, chomping like a Clydesdale on a massive wad of pink bubblegum. There is no friendly smile as our eyes meet and I assume I've interrupted her Tinder scroll.

I step up to the little silver speaker box in the middle of the glass, the letters feeling heavy in my purse.

"Hello. I'd like to speak to an officer on duty please."

"Okay," *chomp, chomp,* "what's this about?"

"I, ah, received a few... odd letters on my doorstep."

Her painted brows lift in interest. I now have her full attention. *Ha. See? I'm interesting.*

"Name?"

Nerves tickle my stomach. "Sylvia Stone."

"What kind of letters, Miss Stone?"

I'm relieved when she doesn't recognize the name. "Well, that's what I would like to speak to an officer about."

The woman studies me for a minute, waiting on the rest of the story so that she can gossip with her girlfriends later. When I don't oblige her, she picks up the phone. Indicating *"one minute,"* she lifts a long, skinny finger with an acrylic nail hanging on for dear life at the tip. Baby blue, just like her eyes.

She must have muted her end of the speaker because I can no longer hear her, but I watch as she relays my request to the officer on duty. Likely a sixty-something overweight beat cop with a handlebar mustache.

The jittery blonde woman in the corner is now texting ferociously on her bejeweled phone.

Dammit, I *know* I know her. I just can't place a name with the face.

A few minutes later, the steel door opens and the on-call officer steps into the waiting room.

My assessment of him was off by about forty years.

The tall, painfully skinny twenty-something looks like he's just stepped off the set of the Andy Griffith remake. A modern-day Barney Fife, right here in the flesh. Big, wide brown eyes, a nose far too large for his face, and a downturned, skeptical mouth which I'm guessing he knows is his only form of intimidation. The officer's uniform is at least two sizes too big, his pants cinched at the waist. The only physical altercation this man is capable of handling is in *Call of Duty,* where I have no doubt he holds at least one record.

The blonde surges out of her seat, addressing Mr. Fife. "Have you found my son?"

Her son?

"Detective Stroud will be out in just a second," the officer says in a jarringly deep voice that doesn't match his skinny body.

Then, it hits me. The woman is Janet Taylor, super wife of Harris Taylor, the town's OBGYN. Her son is Jesse Taylor, the missing twenty-eight-year-old man I saw on the news.

Interesting.

Fife refocuses on me as Janet sinks back into her chair, displeased with her continued wait on the detective.

"Miss Stone, my name is Officer Marino." He stretches out his hand. I clasp the long, bird-like fingers, and shake firmly. "Come on back."

NINE
SYLVIA

I'm led through the steel door and into a small room with a folding table and two plastic chairs on either side. An interview room, except it is the exact opposite of what I expected. There is no blinding white paint, no bleach smell, no heat lamp hanging down from the ceiling, inches from your sweating forehead. Instead, the walls are painted a dark beige and the recessed lights are rather dim. The room has a calm, soothing feel and I wonder if that's intentional. After all, gone are the days of intimidating detectives asking tough, in-your-face questions and leading accusations. Instead, it's a new age of hand-holding and coddling. Honestly, I'm not quite sure how I feel about this.

Officer Marino sits opposite me, the table between us. As I lower onto the cold plastic chair, he folds his hands confidently on the table, his back pin-straight.

I'm beginning to think I have the wrong impression of Officer Marino.

"Okay." His tone is dispassionate, with a touch of boredom as if he has done this ten times already today. "Tell me what's going on."

In a calm, even tone (despite my racing heart) I lay out the last four days of my life, detailing the evening I received the first letter, the second, third, and the fourth. By the time I tell him about the necklace tumbling out of the envelope, I have Officer Marino's full, undivided attention.

"Do you have the necklace?" he asks.

"Yes, and the letters." I pull the envelopes from my purse and slide them across the table.

"I'm assuming you handled these without gloves, correct?"

"Yes—sorry."

He nods, expecting this response. Instead of immediately opening the envelopes, Marino studies me for a minute.

"So, you're Marjorie Stone's daughter."

The tickle of nerves in my stomach turns into a sinking ball of grease. I force myself to hold eye contact.

"Yes. I am—was."

"I remember hearing about the case."

"Most people around here do."

"You worked at the newspaper a while back. Right?"

"Yes. I was laid off."

"Sorry to hear that."

"Thanks." I look down, but quickly correct this obvious show of nerves. *Never look down. Chin up, shoulders back.*

My eyes lock onto his.

"I joined the force about a year ago," he says. "I think I saw you a time or two, working a few stories."

I nod, unsure where he is going with this.

He looks down at the letters. "May I?"

"Of course."

Marino pulls a pair of blue latex gloves from his pocket. With the delicacy of an explosives expert, he carefully removes each letter from the envelope and lays them out, one by one, much as I had done on my kitchen table the night before. However, instead of reading the letters first, Marino focuses on the necklace. I watch him closely as he studies the piece of jewelry, paying extra attention to the tiny blood spatters on the stone pendant.

My pulse starts to pick up.

Then, he shifts his focus to the letters, reads them one by one. Once finished, he looks at me.

"Let me ask first: To confirm, you did *not* see the person who delivered these letters, correct?"

"That's correct. Only the backside of them—him or her—as they ran away."

"What about a vehicle?"

"No. I didn't see one." I notice the necklace is still clutched in his gloved hand. This bothers me and I'm not sure why. "My guess is that they came up through the woods."

"And you said the person was wearing a black sweatshirt with a skull and crossbones on it, correct?"

"Yes."

"Were they carrying any kind of weapon? A gun, a stick? Anything like that?"

"No, I don't think so."

"Miss Stone, do you mind if we hang onto these items for a bit?" he asks, referring to the letters and necklace.

"No, of course not, please."

"Thank you. Excuse me just a moment."

"Uh—okay..."

Marino steps into the hall, necklace still in his gloved hand, and closes the door behind him. My heart pounds as I attempt to eavesdrop on the hushed conversation on the other side of the door. Though I can't make out the words, there is no mistaking the sense of urgency in the officer's tone.

He returns, the necklace now gone.

"Firstly," Marino settles back into the seat across from me, "I want to say you did the right thing by coming to us."

I nod.

"Has anything like this happened before?"

"No."

"Not after your mother's death?"

"No."

"Do you have any kind of security at your home?"

"Locks on the doors and windows; that's it."

"I'd like you to consider getting a home security surveillance system. They're relatively cheap. The cameras hook up to the internet and connect to an app on your phone. Put one above every door that leads to the outside. This way if he comes back, we can get a clear image of him."

"Okay, I'll look into it," I lie. I have exactly zero dollars for that.

"Good. I'm going to have Darla bring in some paperwork for you to go through and sign before you leave so we can open an investigation on this immediately."

My stomach rolls. "An investigation?"

"Right. At the very least you can charge whoever did this with criminal harassment, once we find him."

"Wait—I don't know if I want to go down that route just yet. I'm more concerned about what the letters mean."

"I understand, but we follow protocol, Miss Stone. For now, this will be filed under harassment." He shifts back to the letters. "Now. Tell me what *you* think the letters mean."

I shift in my seat. "Well, considering the letter that reads '*you are next*' was delivered with my deceased mother's necklace, it appears to be a threat. Like, I am the next to die. Or it's a horrible, horrible joke."

"Right—harassment," he schools me. "But what about the other letters? With the numbers?"

"Well, I'm not sure how much you remember of my mother's case, or how familiar you are with the details, but, I think..." I lick my lips. My mouth is dry. My nerves are getting to me. "Well, each letter appears to highlight a specific time of day, right? Three-oh-two, three-oh-four, three-eleven, right?"

Marino nods.

"The coroner's report indicated that my mother died—was murdered—sometime between two and four in the morning."

When he doesn't respond, I continue. "My mom's clocks in her kitchen—where she was killed—were always off. And it always bugged me. I told her to fix them so many times and she wouldn't. Anyway, I remember two of the three clocks were always exactly two minutes apart, and the other was way off..." I pause, wanting him to finish my thoughts and confirm that I am not totally crazy.

He doesn't, so, I press on. "Well, I'm—I'm thinking these letters might signify the exact times that were on the clocks in the kitchen when she was killed."

The officer's eyes narrow as he processes the information. Marino is very comfortable in silence, I note.

"Do you have the crime scene photos?" I ask, feeling anxious under his stare.

"We do."

It isn't lost on me how quickly Marino answers the question. Considering he wasn't around during my mother's murder, I figured he'd have to check. Had he been looking at my mother's case file recently? If so, why?

"I was thinking," I say, "we could look at the crime scene photos and see if the clocks match up, and also check for the necklace. You see, my mother wore the necklace that was in that envelope every day. If it's not on her body in the crime scene photos, then it's safe to say her killer took it... and *her killer* is now sending it back to me—along with the threat, *you are next*."

Marino stands. "I'll be right back."

TEN
SYLVIA

What feels like an eternity later, though I'm sure it's only a few minutes, Marino returns with a thick brown folder in his hand.

"Is that it?" I ask.

"Yes, Marjorie Stone's case file, yes. Are you sure you want me to do this in front of you, Miss Stone?"

My heart flutters. "Yes."

The officer removes the thick rubber band holding the file together and pulls out a stack of reports. Interview transcripts, evidence logs, photographs. What remains of my mother's memory, right there in his hands.

He flickers me a glance before filtering out the crime scene photos. Like a magician at a card table, Marino fans out the horrific images that changed my life forever.

I swallow back the emotions, and force strength, poise.

Chin up, shoulders back.

No words are spoken as we study the pictures, both zeroing in on the grotesque image of my mother's stabbed dead body.

There is no necklace around her neck.

Marino then pulls the evidence log and coroner's report from the stack. There is no stone necklace noted anywhere in the logs, meaning the necklace was *not* at the scene—or on my mother's body—at the time of the responding officer's arrival. Meaning, whoever killed her, took the necklace.

Then, we filter through the photos, laying out the ones with the clearest pictures of the appliances in the background.

Microwave clock: 8:14 a.m.

Stove clock: 8:16 a.m.

Coffee pot: 8:23 a.m.

3:02

3:04

3:11

"The clocks are exactly as you said. The times in the letters align with each clock." The officer meets my gaze. "You have one hell of a memory, Miss Stone."

"It's hard to forget. Trust me."

"When did you put it together, assuming your theory is correct?"

"Last night. After the fourth letter. I really think these times signify the exact time she was murdered."

"Okay, so let me get this straight." Marino stands from his chair, begins pacing. "The last four nights in a row, someone leaves an envelope on your doorstep, each envelope containing the—*presumed*—exact time Mrs. Stone was murdered, marked by three different appliances in the kitchen. The last letter however, appears to be a threat, and included with this letter is your mother's bloody necklace, which we now know was taken from the scene."

I nod.

Marino stares at the photos.

"The person who sent these letters has to be her killer,

right?" I say. "Who else would know about the clocks, and who else would have the necklace? He took it from the scene, maybe thought it was valuable or something. It's him, it's got to be."

"Rhett Cohen is still in prison."

"He was sentenced to twenty-five years and it's been about that. I heard he's up for parole soon."

"But not yet."

I begin picking at my hem. "Right."

Marino tilts his head to the side. "You're suggesting that Rhett Cohen removed your mother's necklace after he killed her, and then either A: Somehow smuggled it into jail, where he has sat on this piece of evidence for twenty years, and has now, for no apparent reason, decided to mail it back to you, along with a handful of creepy letters. Or B: Hid it somewhere before he was arrested and has paid someone to uncover it and deliver it to you, *twenty* years later. And somehow was able to communicate these instructions to this unknown person without the prison guards catching on."

"Sounds impossible, I know."

"Yes, it does." He crosses his arms over his chest. "Let's just start from the beginning—who else knew the intimate details of your mother's case? Enough to know the timeframe of her TOD?"

"Not many people at all aside from me."

"Did you tell anyone that specific information? Her time of death? What about the mismatched clocks? Did you tell anyone about that?"

"No."

"No friends? Boyfriend? You're sure?"

I nod. "I'm sure."

"Think on it for a few days—it was a long time ago. Memories fade."

"I didn't have many friends then and I don't have many friends now. I didn't tell anyone that information, I'm sure of it."

"Okay, then we look at who had access to the coroner's report, which indicated her estimated time of death."

"Lots of people had access to it, right?"

"Not as many as you'd think. The coroner, the responding officers, the detective on the case, the DA, the defendant's attorney, the judge." He thinks for a minute. "If I recall, the case didn't drag on, correct? It was closed rather quickly."

"Correct. Rhett Cohen was arrested just days after it happened."

Marino pauses, then seems to decide something. He gathers the images, taps them against the table then stuffs them into the folder. "Alright, I'll speak to everyone who was involved in the case and we'll go from there. Anything else?"

"W—wait. That's it?"

His brow cocks.

"Hang on…" I exhale loudly, my impatience evident. "What if Rhett Cohen *didn't* kill my mother? Do you remember how much he proclaimed his innocence? What if he was right? I mean who else would have this necklace? Only the killer—right? And you yourself just agreed that it seems impossible that Rhett Cohen could have been in possession of this necklace for the last twenty years and just randomly decided to send it back to me. It doesn't make sense, does it?"

As I say it, I realize the magnitude of the words coming out of my mouth. Am I implying that an innocent man was charged with murder? That an innocent man—who *I* testified against—has spent twenty years locked in a state prison for nothing?

My God, what am I doing?

As if reading my thoughts, Marino states the obvious. "You just said a whole mouthful there, Miss Stone."

"I know. I just… I'll never forget how adamant Rhett was that he didn't do it. It always stuck with me, bothered me. And now… this. Her necklace, and weird letters with intimate, detailed information only the killer would know."

Marino scrubs his fingers through his hair and begins pacing again. Now I know why he's so skinny.

"Okay, let's imagine for a minute that you're correct. Cohen is innocent and the real killer is still out there. Why in the *hell* would he, the real killer—the man who got away with it—walk right up to your front door and drop a piece of evidence from the crime scene that would unquestionably reignite the case?"

"I don't know the motive. But maybe he wasn't the one who delivered it. Maybe he paid some idiot to do it." I gasp, my eyes rounding with epiphany the moment the words leave my lips. "Mrs. Taylor's son... Jesse.... He went missing just before I got the letters, right? What if it was him?"

By Mario's lack of expression, I realize he's already put this string together.

"What was Jesse wearing when he was last seen?" I ask. "Do you know if he owns a black sweatshirt with a white skull and crossbones?"

"Yes, he does, Miss Stone. That is the description of what he was wearing when he was last seen. The information was released to us and the media."

My jaw drops. "It's him, then. That's the same clothing the man was wearing who delivered the letters. It's got to be him. What else do you know? Have you—"

"I'm not at liberty to discuss other cases we have going on."

"But, do you know why, or where—"

"Ma'am—"

Marino slides the case file under his arm, signaling that he is done with this conversation.

He gathers the envelopes. "Darla will meet you in the lobby with your paperwork. You can leave once you've signed every- thing. If you get another letter, I want you to call me immedi- ately. Don't touch it, just leave it there on your doorstep and call the police."

"Okay."

"Also, whether it is innocent or not, please act accordingly as if you have received a real threat. The last letter is a clear threat to your safety and well-being. I want you to document everything. Anything that feels odd to you or out of place, write it down and let us know. And mix up your daily routine, check your mailbox at a different time than you usually do, take a different route to the grocery store, etcetera. Lastly, remember there is strength in numbers. If you go anywhere, take a friend or family member with you."

I don't bother to tell him that I have neither.

He continues. "I'm sure I'll have some follow-up questions—is that alright?"

I'm upset that the officer is not giving me more time, but I don't want to push it. I've done what I came here to do.

"Of course that's fine. Do you have a piece of paper and pen I can write my number—"

"I've got it, don't worry about it."

"Oh."

We stare somewhat awkwardly at each other for a minute, and I get the vibe Marino has much more information than he is offering up.

I force myself to stand and accept that the meeting is over. "Well thank you. Keep me updated, will you?"

"Of course."

Marino opens the door, gestures me into the hall just as Detective Stroud is walking by. I almost walk face-first into the doorframe. The detective is wearing a blue dress shirt, sleeves rolled to the elbows, suggesting a tough day, and khakis. I've seen the detective around town a few times, but not this close since the day of my mother's murder, twenty years ago. I do a quick estimate in my head: Stroud was only in his mid-twenties when he worked my mother's case, which would make him mid-forties now. He has aged beyond what would be expected, with sunspots, crow's feet, and frown lines marring his face. His sandy blonde hair is cut into a severe buzz that shows a scar running along the side of his head. He's grown a beard since I last saw him. Despite all this, he is still handsome—he was extremely handsome in his younger days, in a bashed-up kind of way. He has new tattoos, I also notice. A large Celtic cross on his left forearm.

Detective Stroud nods at Officer Marino and glances at me. I can't tell if he recognizes me or not.

"Call me if you need anything," Marino says, though he has already turned his back to me. He hollers at Stroud.

I make my way down the hallway slowly, listening to the conversation behind me.

"Is Rhett Cohen out of jail yet?" Marino asks Stroud.

"No, not that I'm aware. I don't think so."

"We need to confirm that. I'll have Darla call the warden. We need to see who he's been communicating with, who has visited him, mail, emails, phone calls. I want to know it all..."

I push through the thick steel door.

Janet Taylor, Jesse's mother, is no longer in the waiting room. She's outside in the parking lot, sobbing, her head buried in the arms of her handsome husband, Dr. Harris Taylor.

His eyes meet mine as I look at them out the window.

A small smile crosses his lips.

ELEVEN
MARJORIE

My therapist said I should keep a journal. So here it is. She said I should write down what I'm thinking about, at least once a day. She told me not to overthink it, just write.

Today, like every day, I am thinking about Anna. I am thinking about her little blonde curls and how they always smelled of strawberries from the shampoo she loved so much (and tried to eat once!). I'm thinking about the tip of her nose, and how I would lightly tap it with my finger when I reminded her how much I loved her.

I'm thinking of her laugh, her giggle, the way her cheeks would blush when she was tickled. I'm thinking of all the times we were snuggled under the blankets watching a replay of a Disney movie we'd seen a hundred times, and how she would mindlessly rub her little feet against each other under the blankets.

I'm thinking of my love for her...

This morning, I caught myself reminiscing on my childhood. On that one day.

It was winter, incredibly cold. I was thirteen years old.

My mom was passed out on the couch. She was drunk

again. My mom was a terrible, terrible drunk. Mean and hateful. But she was nothing compared to my father. Gerald Stone, I know now, was a very ill man. I'm sure he would have been diagnosed with a slew of mental disorders if he had gone to the doctor, and likely been prescribed a handful of drugs to cope. I'm sure my life would have been different if he had sought help, as I am doing now.

I was abused as a child. I can finally admit that. For most of my life, I wasn't able to admit it. I didn't consider myself an "abused person." But my therapist opened my eyes.

I don't even remember what I did wrong that day. Probably left something out or forgot to put something back in its rightful place. My mother and father were neat freaks. Everything was organized, not a single spec of dirt anywhere.

I only remember Gerald's voice that morning. The hair-raising tone of his scream. He and my mother were fighting, I'm not sure what about. Her being drunk? Or one of them having an affair? I don't know. I'll never know.

I hid in my closet where I eventually wet myself. I needed to go when I went in, and then was too scared to come out. Even all these years later, I use the restroom incessantly to ensure I never find myself in a situation like that again.

Soon, however, Gerald found me and dragged me out by my hair. I remember feeling like someone had poured piping hot acid on my head as he dragged me across the room, ripping the tiny strands from my skull. I remember the cigarette between his lips. The smell turned my stomach. I remember the way he looked at me when he realized I had wet myself. I remember the shame I felt.

I begged him to let go, which he eventually did, but instead, he grabbed my arm. I couldn't keep up as he pulled me through the house, out the back door, to the shed. I lost a shoe somewhere along the way. I never found that shoe.

I was shoved inside the shed. I fell to my knees, careful to avoid the stained bucket in the corner, which would serve as my bathroom for the night.

Before locking me inside—this was always my punishment—Gerald kneeled down in front of me. His body was backlit from the porch light outside, his face hidden in shadows. The tip of his cigarette glowed in the darkness.

He reminded me of a monster.

After blowing a stream of smoke in my face, he removed the cigarette from his lips and put it out in the center of my forehead.

He said, "Now you have a scar to match the ugly pock marks on your cheeks."

I still have that scar.

Anna used to run her little finger over it sometimes.

TWELVE
SYLVIA

I can't sleep.

I'm tossing and turning in my bed, my vision plagued with flashbacks, my mind racing with memories. Not just the bad ones, but all kinds of memories. Weird, pointless memories, like remembering the scent of the foundation my mother always wore. It had a very distinct fake-perfume odor and she wore it so thick that the scent lingered in the room after she'd apply it.

I never saw my mother without makeup. Not once. Multiple times a day, she would reapply this thick, mask-like foundation. It was a shade too dark, and I wanted to tell her, but never had the courage. As Mom aged the foundation would sink into her wrinkles, but still, she wouldn't stop wearing it. One day, the neighbor commented on her blush. That didn't go over well, although I think it had more to do with the rumor that my father, while Mom was pregnant, had sex with our neighbor in the back of her minivan before he left us. I've never met my father.

For someone who loved makeup so much, you'd figure she would have taught me how to apply it. I didn't start wearing makeup until I left Dallas, my hometown, and moved to Vermont.

I was just nineteen years old.

A year earlier, my mother had received the deeds to my grandfather's properties (after he had passed), and left Texas (and me), and moved to Vermont. I was eighteen, which, according to her, was a totally appropriate age to live in a city by myself with no family.

Once there, Mom sold two of the properties, used that money to pay off her debt, and then moved into her childhood home, a large, red farmhouse in the middle of twenty-four wooded acres. One property remained. An old, two-story craftsman home, less than five minutes away. I asked if I could rent it from her, after realizing that living on my own wasn't all it was cracked up to be. She said yes. I packed up and moved the next day with the intent to jump head-first into my adult life by applying for a position at the local newspaper once I arrived. There I would work my way up the ladder and eventually become a journalist—my dream. I blame Nancy Drew for my love of mysteries. I was hooked after reading my first whodunnit book.

In its heyday, my new home had been featured in a regional architectural magazine. Now, however, the thing is practically falling apart. The foundation has cracked and settled, creating uneven flooring (you literally walk downhill to the master bedroom). There are cracks in the stone walls, and the roof leaks like crazy.

I spent my entire first week in Vermont learning how to fix a leaky faucet, a whistling furnace, how to remove popcorn ceiling, and the best way to exterminate an entire village of mice. When I became overwhelmed with home repairs, I gave up, and got a job at the newspaper and my life as an active Thorncrest citizen officially began.

Honestly it really wasn't that bad at first. Thorncrest is a tourist town, lots of good people-watching. And I enjoy the outdoors. I even went on dates with some decent men in the first few years. There was Craig, the local insurance agent, who suffered from a serious case of Loud Cellphone Talking Syndrome. I was unsure if Craig was simply one of the unfortunates whose voices carried like the wind, or if his masculinity demanded such a grand display of importance... Come to think of it, there is no winner in that scenario, is there?

And then there was Kevin, a former Thorncrest High Mathlete turned traveling water filter salesman who conveniently misplaced his credit card(s) when it was time to pay for dinner. Neither relationship amounted to much, but I enjoyed the compliment of a date, nonetheless.

It was also nice to live without having to pay rent, I'm not going to lie. I didn't even have to cook. Marjorie and I had a standing Sunday dinner date and I left each visit with a box of leftovers that fed me for the entire week. Everything was just easy... too easy.

Then she died.

I went into a shell after. My life became an endless cycle of wake up, shower, go to work, go home, eat, drink, and pass out. Wash, rinse, repeat.

Not two weeks after the murder, I was approached by a Los Angeles based literary agent. According to her, several big-time publishers were interested in signing me for a book deal to follow me through the trial and retell the story.

I declined. A stupid, stupid decision. Had I known then what I know now, I would have jumped at the chance of a big payday.

This is when I started binge watching TV and drinking way too much. I found an escape by watching self-righteous train wrecks self-destruct on national television. And then when I got sick of the news, I turned to reality television. And just like that,

I became addicted to watching other people make a mess of their lives.

This is also when Shirley entered my life, a stray Sphynx cat lost in the woods, likely abandoned. When I first saw her hairless wrinkled body sniffing around my porch, I thought she was a demon risen from the depths of Hell, the final sign of the end of times.

Nope. Just a hairless cat with a bad eye.

The next day, I bought Shirley a dress. The next day, a bejeweled collar. The next day, a pink bed. The day after that, I randomly decided I wanted to build a garden and grow my own vegetables. That was big purchase.

This is when my impulse buying began.

In no time at all, I blew through the savings account and found myself completely broke. Like, clipping coupons and having to decide between electricity or running water, broke.

I'm in a rut, there is no question about it. Bored, numb, broke. And now, on top of it all, it feels like I've been grabbed by my shoulders and yanked backward twenty years, awakening all those horrible feelings and emotions from the weeks surrounding my mother's murder.

Although two decades have passed since that fateful day, I remember it like it was yesterday.

It was mid-August, hot as hell. I was on my way to work. It was one of those rare mornings that I was running early. I remember noticing the world around me that morning—a stop-and-smell-the-roses moment. The sky was an electric blue, the dew-covered grass an emerald green. Funny, isn't it? The color of the sky and grass are as strong a memory as the moment I walked into the kitchen.

THIRTEEN
SYLVIA

Twenty Years Earlier

"Let's go through what we know of your mother's last twenty-four hours. Can you do that for me?"

I swallow the knot in my throat. "Yes, what I know of it, yes. Um, well, my mother doesn't work; she stays home. So I assume she was home all yesterday."

Detective Stroud scribbles in his notebook. "What does she do during the day?"

"Mostly bakes for the church, watches television, not much."

"You're not sure if she left the house, for any reason, yesterday or today?"

"No."

"No, she didn't, or no, you don't know?"

"No, I don't know..." My voice is shaking from the adrenaline, causing me to stutter. "But, I don't think so. She's a homebody."

"How often does she leave the house?"

"Not often. Only to the grocery store on Saturdays, on Sundays for church, and for the occasional errand."

"Why is that, do you know?"

"Why is what?" I ask, my gaze flicking to a white van that just pulled up outside. *County Coroner* is written on the side.

"Why doesn't she go out much?"

"She's kind of an introvert. Like me, I guess. I guess I got that from her."

"Nothing wrong with that. What church did she go to?"

"The one across from the post office. Cross something."

"Cross Life, yes, I know it. Did you go to church with her?"

"No."

"When was the last time you spoke with her?"

"Yesterday afternoon."

"Do you remember what time?"

"On my way home from work."

"What time is that?"

"Five o'clock—well, specifically, probably ten after five."

"Did you call her or she call you?"

"I called her."

"And what was she doing at that time? Can you replay your conversation?"

I wring my hands on my lap in a desperate attempt to expel the anxiety that's making me feel like I'm about to jump out of my skin. "Yes, she'd called earlier in the day to ask if the strawberries in my garden were ripe. She wanted to make strawberry rhubarb pie for Sunday dinner. I told her yes, then she asked how my day was. I told her good, and we hung up. And then, she called again later in the evening, but I was already asleep. When she didn't answer my return calls this morning, I got worried. And that's why I came over."

"Can you tell me about your mom's love life?"

"Uh..."

"That's probably an awkward question, I get it, but did she

have one, that's what I'm asking. A romantic interest in her life?"

"I don't think so."

"Ms. Stone is a widow, correct?"

"No. Where did you hear that?"

"That was the rumor when she moved to town last year. It's incorrect?"

"Yes. My father left her when she was pregnant with my sister."

"Ouch. Where is your sister?"

"She died a long time ago."

"I'm sorry to hear that. Is that your only sibling?"

"Yes."

"Okay. What about friends from church? Did she have any there?"

"I don't know."

"Can you think of anyone she interacted with lately? Anyone at all?"

"No, I—wait, yes. You saw the mess in the kitchen. She is—was—having her cabinets redone. Someone, a carpenter, has been here working on them for the last few days."

"Who?"

"I... I can't remember. I don't know the guy, but I think the company... Cohen's, yes, Cohen's Carpentry."

An officer walks in the room. He looks at me, but addresses Detective Stroud.

"Mind if we take Miss Stone up to the bedroom real quick?"

Stroud frowns, taking a second to consider. Am I not allowed to go up to my mother's bedroom?

"No," he says finally. "I don't mind."

I follow the officer out of the sitting room, with Stroud close on my heels. Quick pops of light flash from the kitchen where my mother's dead body is being photographed.

It's like I'm in a dream.

I'm led upstairs, to my mother's bedroom, and to her armoire. He motions to the jewelry box sitting on top, crookedly positioned as if it had been pushed around. The top is standing open.

"Do you notice anything that looks abnormal here?" the officer asks.

"Yes. Half of her jewelry is gone."

The officer glances at the detective; the detective looks at me.

"This was almost full of jewelry," I continue. "Mostly just costume jewelry, but some expensive pieces that she inherited from her mother. Her old wedding ring was in here too. It's gone."

The officer shook his head, muttering, "Another one."

"Another what?" I ask.

"Burglary."

"What? Really? Around here?"

"Yep. This is the fourth breaking and entering we've seen in Thorncrest in the last month. A jewelry thief, breaks into houses, steals rings, watches, a few handbags, and then bam, he's gone."

"Why haven't I heard about this? Do they kill the homeowners?"

"No, this is the first one where someone was killed. It looks like our serial burglar has stepped up his—"

Stroud cuts off the officer. "Is that all you need from Miss Stone right now?"

The officer nods and looks down, realizing he overstepped his bounds by saying too much in front of me.

The detective motions me out of my mother's room.

My knees shake as I walk downstairs, and back to the sitting room, where I take my place on the couch. This time, Stroud remains standing.

"Do you think you'll be able to report exactly what jewelry

is missing?" he asks.

"I don't know. I'll try. I'll do my best to try to remember what she had in there."

"If you could get as detailed as possible that would help. Usually what happens in these scenarios is whoever steals it immediately turns around and tries to sell it and that's when we find it and track the person down. But we need to know what jewelry we're looking for."

"I understand. I'll take some time this afternoon and make a list of everything I remember being in there."

Our attention is pulled to the coroner carrying a black body bag into the house.

I scrub my hands over my face. "I just—I can't believe this... What do you think happened? What's your initial read of everything?"

"Well, only being thirty minutes into the case so far, best I can tell is that your mother heard the burglar break in and confronted him, likely with the aluminum bat lying next to her body. And the burglar attacked back with a knife."

"So you think this was just a burglary gone bad?"

"I don't want to close the door on anything else just yet."

"Why? What are you thinking?"

Stroud pauses, weighing how much he should say.

"Why, Detective?" I press. "Tell me." My voice suddenly pitches with desperation. "That's my mother in there. Tell me what you're thinking."

"It's a lot of wounds for someone who is just trying to steal some jewelry."

"What do you mean?"

"Well, if whoever did this only wanted jewelry, I'd say one stab would've unquestionably demobilized your elderly mother enough for him to get the jewelry and get out."

"So what do you think this means?"

"It suggests emotion. That the attack was emotional."

Just then another officer walks in. This one with the sheriff's department. I can tell because his uniform is different. His boots are dusty, his hair saturated with sweat. The scent of fresh air and pine sap follows a second later, still clinging to him from what appears to be a search in the nearby woods.

A plastic bag is clutched in his hand. Inside the bag is a kitchen knife, stained with blood. A few blades of grass are stuck to the tip. I immediately recognize the knife as my mother's favorite carving knife.

It's been nine days since the trial when Detective Stroud shows up at my doorstep.

Smoothing my tangled hair, I open the door, my stomach churning.

"Miss Stone, hi. May I come in?"

"Yes. Of course."

I lead the detective into the kitchen where a burned pot of oatmeal sits on the stove from earlier this morning. The room stinks. I stink. The whole situation stinks.

The detective removes his cowboy hat and clutches it in his hand in front of his stomach.

"I wanted to come here to tell you personally that we have verified that the kitchen knife we found outside was indeed the murder weapon, complete with your mother's DNA and a full set of Rhett Cohen's fingerprints along the hilt of the knife."

A knot forms in my throat, and I suddenly find myself unable to speak.

Just then, the name *Rhett Cohen* echoes from the living room television. Stroud and I stare at each other as we listen to the women discuss the case on a national daytime talk show.

"...Marjorie Stone's homicide has quickly become sensationalized, not only because of the brutality of the murder, but also because Rhett Cohen's tireless proclamation of innocence combined with his rugged, movie-star good-looks has made him a headline magnet. I mean, have you seen him? A tattooed Gerard Butler, someone called him."

Another host snorts. "Funny how something like cold-blooded murder becomes so easily overlooked through the lens of lust. Passion is more powerful than judgment, after all."

The main host continues, "From the moment he was arrested, Rhett Cohen swore he was innocent. He says he'd used the knife earlier in the day of Marjorie's murder, which is why his prints are on the hilt. But no one cares what he has to say. He's even questioning why his DNA wasn't on the bat that lay next to Marjorie's body, and why, assuming she'd used it to protect herself, wasn't he covered in bruises? . . ."

Detective Stroud frowns. "You understand that right?"

"Understand what?"

"Why the fact that Rhett wasn't covered in bruises, or the lack of DNA on the bat, was a big factor in his case?"

"No—why?"

"Because we have proof that the bat had been wiped down with bleach, and also, if Rhett had been bruised, his body would have had plenty of time to heal before his arrest."

I nod.

Detective Stroud rubs his chin. "Miss Stone, I just want you to rest easy knowing that this case was practically closed the moment it was opened because Rhett Cohen has no alibi and hits every point on the criminal trifecta. He had means, motive, and opportunity."

"What do you mean?"

"Well, for one, at six-foot-three and 230 pounds, Rhett Cohen had the means to break into your mother's home and overpower her.

"Two, we've learned that Rhett's carpentry business was underwater, and his home and car one month from being repossessed. Rhett was on the brink of bankruptcy. His motive was money.

"And three, Rhett had established a safe, comfortable relationship with your mother by being her hired help. He had access to her home, her valuables, this creating an optimal opportunity." The detective lifts his fingers one by one. "Means, check; motive, check; opportunity, check."

"So you're saying it's a slam-dunk case?"

"Yes, ma'am... not a doubt in my mind."

FOURTEEN

SYLVIA

It has been a week since I delivered the letters and necklace to the Thorncrest Police Station. I've received no calls, no emails, no follow-ups whatsoever. On a positive note, I have also received no more creepy letters. Everything has just kind of stopped.

I've busied myself in the garden, spending the days outside, under the crystal-clear autumn sunlight. I do love this time of year.

I've just sat on the couch, wondering if I will ever hear anything again on my mother's case, when a knock sounds at the door.

I mute the television and look at the clock—3:32 p.m.

I search for Shirley, finding her perched in the windowsill. The late afternoon sun streams through the glass, casting her long, black shadow across the floor and making her look triple her usual size. I swear she does this on purpose.

"Who is it?" I whisper to her, receiving a dismissive tail-flick in response.

I tear off the blanket from my lap and hide my half-empty wine glass under the end table.

Another knock.

Hurrying to the door, I feel my pulse increase with each step.

Officer Marino stands on the other side, eyes narrowed, lips pursed. Next to him stands Detective Johnny Stroud.

I clear my throat, open the door.

"Good afternoon, Miss Stone," Marino says.

Stroud nods in greeting.

There's an unmistakable air of tension emanating from the men, leaving no question that this is not just a casual check-in.

"Is everything okay?" I ask.

"Yes, I—Detective Stroud and I—would like to ask you a few questions if you don't mind."

"Is this about the letters and the necklace?"

"Yes."

"Okay..." I step back, open the door widely. "Come on in."

I hurry to the couch, straighten the pillows, toss the blanket on the armrest, and remove a stack of books from the recliner. "Sorry, I, uh..."

"It's fine," Detective Stroud says impatiently and I sense annoyance in his voice.

I set down the pillow I was fluffing and turn toward the two men. We stand awkwardly in the middle of the living room. I am painfully aware of the train wreck I must appear to be. I am wearing a pair of old Victoria's Secret sweatpants with the word PINK written across the butt, a long-sleeved T-shirt covered in dirt from the garden, and my hair is in a messy bun. No makeup. My mom would be so disappointed.

"I have a few follow-up questions about your visit last week," Officer Marino says. "About the necklace specifically: I want to confirm that the necklace was *inside* the envelope with the fourth letter, correct?"

"That's correct. It was tucked in the folded note that read, 'You are next.'"

"And you brought it directly to the station, the next morning, correct?"

"Yes."

"You didn't take it anywhere else?"

"No."

"Did anyone else touch it?"

"No." I shake my head. "No, definitely not. It was only in my possession for, literally, six hours before I brought it in."

Marino glances at Stroud.

"Why? What's going on?" I ask.

"Immediately following your visit last week, I sent the necklace and the letters to the state forensics department to test the blood drops on the pendant and scan for other traces of DNA."

I begin picking at a torn cuticle.

"We got the report this morning. The letters are clean of DNA, so nothing useful there. But the report does confirm the blood on the pendant belongs to your mother, so, we can confidently assume that the necklace was removed from her neck after she was killed, and was taken from the scene. Likely with the other jewelry that was stolen in the house."

The dead skin rips from my fingernail with a sharp sting.

Marino continues, "Your recent prints are on the side of the stone—from handling it, of course. But there is also someone else's."

My brows arch. "Whose?"

"It's only a half-print, and very old, but they were able to confirm that the print does *not* belong to Jesse Taylor—the missing boy who we think delivered the envelopes."

I blink, my brain taking a second to process this information. "So, if Jesse didn't touch the necklace that was in the envelope, then this means the envelopes must have been already sealed when he got them—and someone simply paid him to deliver it?"

"Yes, that's what we're thinking."

"Okay, so who do the prints belong to?"

Marino clears his throat. "We haven't been able to link an identity to it yet. You see, half-prints can be very tricky to authenticate, but the lab was able to determine that the prints on the pendant have been there for a very long time and also that—"

Detective Stroud cuts in. "The point, Miss Stone, isn't who the print belongs to, it is who the print *does not* belong to."

I slide my hand over my mouth, knowing what he is going to say before the words come out of his mouth.

"Rhett Cohen's prints are nowhere on that necklace, ma'am. The half-print does not match his."

"Oh, God," I whisper breathlessly, through my fingertips. "So he *was* innocent?"

"We are far from that conclusion, Miss Stone. That is an option, of course, but another option is that he could have had an accomplice that we were unaware of. Regardless, this definitely opens the door to take another look at the case."

I drop my hand from my mouth and nod feverishly. "Yes, good. Whatever you need from me, yes, whatever you need to do."

"Thank you. We'll be back in touch soon. Meanwhile, we are doubling our efforts to find Jesse Taylor, working under the assumption he delivered the letters, and therefore was in contact with whoever had your mother's necklace."

"You mean, the real person that killed my mother."

"Again, we are far from making that conclusion."

I nod. *Find Jesse.* He is the key to unlocking the first piece of this puzzle.

"What about the half-print? Will you be able to confirm who it belongs to?" I ask.

"We've sent the pendant to a fingerprint analyst up in DC. Will take some time, but it's the best we can do. Might come up with nothing, who knows."

"We also want to remind you to be vigilant, Miss Stone," Marino adds. "If it is true that Cohen is innocent and the real killer is still out there, or if he had an accomplice, you need to be careful."

The words of the final letter filter through my head—

You are next.

"Do you have friends you can stay with while we get this thing figured out? For security reasons?"

"I... Yes. I'll figure something out," I lie.

"Good. Sorry to bring up this very painful past all over again. I'm sure this is tough."

We stare at each other a moment, the "right" words eluding us.

"Have a good rest of your afternoon, Miss Stone," Detective Stroud says, ending the meeting. "Lock your doors and call us if you need anything."

"Thank you."

I watch the officers disappear down my driveway, then, on a deep exhale, fall back against the door. For a solid minute I stand there, motionless, staring at my mother's ashes on the fireplace mantle.

You are next...

FIFTEEN
SYLVIA

It is just after ten in the morning when I drive through the large, ornate gates of Deep Shadows, the only affluent neighborhood in Thorncrest. The heavily wooded subdivision is tucked away on the outskirts of town, and borders Crest Lake. It's a picturesque, beautiful area, especially in the fall.

I slow, peering at each property as I pass. They are all the same. Large Nantucket-style homes that scream old money. Either smoky gray or pale blue, each shingled exterior is outlined by bright white shutters and matching trim. Each lawn is meticulously manicured, trees trimmed, bushes shaped to perfection.

I roll to a stop next to a large stone mailbox with spotless brass numbers down the side. House number 423—otherwise known as the home of super-wife Janet Taylor, her doctor husband, Harris Taylor, and their son Jesse, before he went missing. It's the biggest house in the neighborhood.

I shove the Jeep into park, slide the key in my pocket, and get out. The neighborhood is eerily quiet, so still that I can hear the sound of the lake lazily lapping against the shore in the distance. I wonder if all the residents are on vacation.

After quietly shutting the door, I take a second to straighten my knee-length pencil skirt and adjust the matching suit jacket.

I spent an hour and a half getting ready this morning. Ninety whole minutes of scrubbing, shaving, brushing, drying, straightening, applying makeup. I dusted off my old work clothes and slipped into my favorite hard-hitting journalist power suit. The same suit I wore while running around town, following clues, chasing leads for whatever small-town mystery I was researching. I'm even wearing high heels. The only thing missing from the ensemble is a notebook and pen in my hand. I decide to leave those in the Jeep.

Chin up, shoulders back, I make my way down the narrow cobblestone walkway, my heels *tap, tap, tapping* against the silence. It feels like I'm working again. It feels good.

I step onto the porch, lined with overflowing pots of begonias. Reds, pinks, whites, there are thousands of them. I press the doorbell, frowning at the chipped nail-polish on my fingertips. I make a mental note to get a manicure soon, acrylics maybe.

Wait. I have no money. Never mind.

I ring again, hearing the polite chime echo inside the house.

No answer.

Frowning, I step back. The front windows are open. Long, sheer curtains blow in the breeze. The room behind the curtains appears to be dark.

I'm just about to peer through the crack in the curtains when I suddenly get that indescribable feeling like I am being watched.

A chill snakes up my spine.

No one knows I'm here. I didn't pass a single vehicle on the gravel road that leads to the gated community.

I clear my throat loudly and relax my stance, feigning a carefree confidence to whoever is watching me. A friendly, just-stopping-by-my-buddy's-house demeanor.

I casually look over my shoulder, spotting the neighbor's house through the trees. A blurred silhouette stands in a second-floor window, staring directly at me. Long fire-red hair flutters in the breeze.

Just then, the front door opens. Janet Taylor, the same woman I'd seen at the police station, stands before me. Today, however, her appearance is vastly different. What had been a disheveled, mismatched woman on the edge of a panic attack, is now a picture of poised perfection. Janet Taylor is wearing a pressed white sundress with lace trim and pointed flats. Her curly blonde hair is pulled back in a chignon, her makeup flawless.

She frowns when she sees me.

"Mrs. Taylor," I thrust out my hand in an overly professional manner. "My name is Sylvia Stone."

Her green eyes widen. She knows me. Of course she does. The entire town knows me as the daughter of the woman who was brutally murdered twenty years ago.

When she doesn't say anything, I continue with the speech I rehearsed on the drive over.

"I heard about your son, Jesse, and I want to say I'm sorry. I can't imagine what you're going through."

"Thank you." *Get to the point,* her expression says.

"I also saw you last week at the police station. I think you were waiting to speak with Detective Stroud."

Her frown deepens. "I'm sorry... how can I help you? Does this have something to do with my son?"

"Yes."

"Do you know where he is?" she asks quickly.

"No, but, if it's alright with you, I'd like to ask you a few questions about him."

"Why?"

"Well, considering the letters..."

"What letters?"

"The ones he delivered to my house last week."

"You saw my—*where?*"

I frown. Is Mrs. Taylor unaware of the letters? Surely the police would have told her, considering they know he was involved? If not, why? Doesn't she have a right to know? Don't they have an obligation to tell her?

"What are you talking about?" she presses.

I realize the woman is totally clueless—which confuses me.

I clear my throat, again. "I saw your son at my house last week. He delivered a letter to my doorstep, in the middle of the night."

Janet stares at me, baffled, then looks over her shoulder as if she's heard someone—or is checking for someone. When no one appears, she refocuses on me, takes a step back, and opens the door widely.

"Come in, come in."

I hesitate, surprised she's inviting me into her home.

I am nothing short of awestruck when I step over the threshold. Despite the weathered exterior, the inside of the house has been completely renovated.

The home opens to a large foyer with gleaming hardwood floors, a Persian rug that I guess costs more than my Jeep, and a gorgeous crystal chandelier hanging from the ceiling.

I'm glad I wore the suit.

Janet leads me past a wide, imperial staircase and through a large living space with lush leather furniture and windows lined with heavy drapes. At least a dozen family pictures adorn the walls, many of her missing son, Jesse.

"Can I get you something to drink?" This rhetorical question is followed immediately by, "What do you mean my son left you a letter?"

We step into the kitchen. She turns to face me. In the

corner of the room, the local news whispers from a flat-screen television mounted above a breakfast nook. A bowl of oatmeal and steaming cup of coffee are sitting on the table.

"The man who left me a letter was wearing a black sweatshirt with a white skull and crossbones on the back. I understand that's what your son was wearing when you last saw him, is that correct?"

Janet nods, an intense, yet very confused, gaze locked on mine. "What did the letter say?"

"Letters. There were four."

"You saw him *four* times?"

"No, only once. The delivery of the last letter. I found the rest sitting on my doorstep."

"What did the letters say?" she repeats, impatient now. Or, irritated? I can't tell.

I pull my cell phone from my suit pocket and click into the photos.

I hand her the phone. "Those are the letters. The police have them now."

Her hand trembles as she clicks through the pictures. Then, she thrusts the phone back at me as if it were a ticking time bomb. "I don't understand, this is the extent of the letters? Each letter just has three numbers on it?"

"The first three, yes. The fourth contained a necklace with a letter that appeared to be a threat of sorts."

"You think my son is *threatening* you?"

"Again, I'm not sure. I'm just trying to figure this out, like you are."

Janet looks at the phone in my hand. "Are—are they times? Like, a time of day or night?"

"That's the working assumption, yes."

She shakes her head. "I don't understand—what? Why? What do you think they mean?"

"Well…" I shift my weight. "I think they are related to my mother's death, twenty years ago."

"*How?*" she squeaks, obviously picking up on the implication that her son might have been involved in something very sinister. "Jesse would have just been a child back then."

"Do you know if he knew my mom back then?"

"But that guy did it," she snaps, defensively. "The carpenter. He was convicted and sent to jail."

"Right," I take a quick breath. "Ma'am, I'm not saying that your son is—"

"What was his name? The guy. Rex?"

"No. Rhett. Rhett Cohen."

"Yes, that's right…" She shakes her head again. "I'm sorry, hang on… do the cops know about this?"

"Yes, they're working on finding Jesse, while also trying to decipher what the numbers mean."

Janet looks out the window, begins rubbing the back of her neck.

"Did you see where he went?" she asks, still gazing outside. "After he left your house?"

"No. He ran into the woods. I yelled after him but he didn't turn around. I think it's safe to say he didn't want to be seen."

Janet nods as if this doesn't surprise her. She drags in a long shaky breath. I follow her gaze. Through the trees is a clear shot of the neighbor's house, where the silhouette stood in the window minutes earlier.

Janet clears her throat and refocuses on me. "Thank you for telling me this."

"You're welcome. Is your husband, Dr. Taylor home? I wonder if I can ask him—"

"No, he's at work."

"Okay… Do you have any idea why your son would be involved in this, Mrs. Taylor?"

"I don't know why Jesse has done many of the things that he has done over the last handful of years."

Our attention shifts to the television above the breakfast nook where the headline reads:

Local man accused of murder innocent?

My eyes widen. Janet's jaw drops.

Has the story of the letters, as well as my interpretation of them, already been leaked to the press?

"We have breaking news on a twenty-year-old case where a local women was brutally stabbed to death in her own home. In what appeared to be a burglary gone bad, local carpenter and owner of Cohen Carpentry, Rhett Cohen, was arrested and later charged with Marjorie Stone's murder. Cohen was convicted and sentenced to twenty-five years in state prison, despite his proclamation of innocence. The recent discovery of new evidence suggests that Mr. Cohen, who has spent the last two decades of his life behind bars, might be innocent. In light of this evidence, brought forth by an unnamed source, a new investigation has been opened into a case that rocked our small town so long ago. I spoke with the prison warden this afternoon and it appears Cohen is up for parole—the exact date of that hearing was not given to me—after having already served twenty years of his twenty-five-year sentence..."

Mrs. Taylor looks at me, her eyes the size of golf balls, mouth agape.

"I want you out of here," she snaps. "I don't want anything to do with this! Me, my son, my husband, we have nothing to do with this. Get out. Now." She pushes me toward the doorway.

I hurry down the hall with Janet on my heels. I have to fight from breaking into a jog. The woman is literally running me out of her house.

"Mrs. Taylor," I say over my shoulder, stumbling on the Persian rug. "I'm sorry, I didn't mean—"

"*Out.*" She yanks open the door.

I lunge outside.

The door slams in my face.

I exhale, my heart racing.

Once I gather my footing, I look at the neighbor's house through the trees.

The curtains in the second-floor window flutter in the wind. The silhouette is gone.

SIXTEEN

SYLVIA

Days later, I am bent over my vegetable garden, on hands and knees, sifting through dirt when, again, I get the feeling I'm being watched—a daily occurrence since visiting the Taylor home four days earlier. I look to the tree line, searching for my cat, Shirley, but she's nowhere to be seen.

I look over my shoulder and nearly jump out of my muck boots.

Not ten feet from me, a man looms over my garden, standing square center in the single sunbeam that has escaped the clouds above. His hands are stuffed in his pockets, his eyes black as coal. He is not smiling.

I recognize him instantly. My stomach flies to my feet, my heart stuttering in my chest.

Rhett Cohen was an imposing presence before he went to prison, but now, the man is nothing short of monstruous. Prison has hardened him, literally—by about twenty pounds of pure muscle. His body looks as if it has been sculpted from stone, the lines of his jaw razor-sharp, his arms swollen and corded with sinew.

The memory of when I first met him in my mother's kitchen

flash behind my eyes. He was staggeringly sexy then, and still is, but now in a dangerous kind of way.

The thin gray T-shirt he's wearing is stained and too snug, and his jeans are horribly wrinkled and also too tight around the thighs. I realize that these must be the clothes he was arrested in, twenty years earlier. Which means, he was *just* released from jail—and is now here at my house.

I slowly turn, stand, and face the man who was convicted of stabbing my mother to death.

A moment passes. We don't speak, just stare at each other. Him, a massive, ominous presence; me, the total opposite in a white tank top, pair of baggy boyfriend jeans, and hideous black gardening kneepads strapped around my knees. I remove the straw hat teetering on the top of my head and smooth the hair away from my face.

He speaks.

"I want to see the letters."

Like tires rolling over gravel, his voice carries the deep grit of someone who hasn't spoken much in years.

"What letters?" I say, feigning ignorance while I take a second to wrap my head around my current situation.

"I'm talking about the letters delivered to you from the person who killed your mother," he responds, cooly.

"How did you know where I live?"

"I looked you up."

He is so intense, from his gaze, to his stance, to his voice. It makes me self-conscious.

"They let you out? Of prison?"

He opens his arms: *Yes, obviously, because I'm standing here.*

"Where are the letters?" he repeats.

"I—I don't have them. I gave them to the police."

"Do you have copies?"

Of course I have copies. I have many copies hidden in various, inconspicuous places throughout my house in case I lose one—or something happens to me.

"Why don't you go ask the detective to see them?" I ask.

"I didn't kill your mother," he responds.

"The fingerprints on the knife found in the woods that night suggest otherwise."

"I was framed. This is why I want to see the letters."

"Why? What good does it do now?"

"Because, Miss Stone, I am going to find the man who framed me and I am going to kill him."

SEVENTEEN
SYLVIA

I stare at the former inmate for a solid ten seconds, gobsmacked.

I am going to find the man who framed me and I am going to kill him...

There was no hesitation in his voice, no waver in the intensity as he said it. In fact, the words were fueled with the confidence of an indisputable fact, like the sun rising in the east and setting in the west. After spending twenty years in prison and finally being released, Rhett Cohen's only desire is to kill. Not to drink himself into oblivion, not to find a beach to waste away on, or hike a mountain, or even to meet up with one of the many women who'd become obsessed with him over the years. Prison brides, they're called. Rhett Cohen only wants one thing: Revenge.

Officer Marino's words trickle into my head: *"If anything odd happens, call us immediately."*

Rhett Cohen showing up at my house definitely classifies as odd, right? His declaration of premeditated murder is also odd, yes?

Do I call the cops? Or do I ask one of the hundred questions running at breakneck speed through my head? Two ends of the spectrum, one governed by my head, the other by my heart.

He continues to stare at me, and I realize he is not going to go away on his own accord.

"How did you get here?" I ask, noticing there is no vehicle in the driveway.

"I hitchhiked."

My jaw drops. "You hitchhiked from jail?"

He tilts his head to the side. Not a man who responds to idiotic, obvious questions, I note.

I take a deep breath. "Come in. We'll talk."

I step past him, knowing he will follow. I have information he wants, after all.

I've become acutely aware of how terrible I look. How streaks of dirt cover my clothing, my arms, my neck. I can feel dots of dried mud on my face, too. I am aware of how these baggy jeans sag, making me look like I am wearing an adult diaper. How I am not wearing a bra and how it must be painfully obvious that underneath this thin tank top, my right boob is significantly smaller than my left. And lastly, how I am not wearing deodorant. This can only mean one thing. I am still as attracted to Rhett as I was the day I met him. Dammit all to hell.

Chin up, shoulders back, Sylvia.

We step through the back door, into the house. Rhett lingers on the dust mat just past the threshold. I feel mildly embarrassed by the ancient, two-story monstrosity I call home. I haven't done a thing to fix the cracked walls, leaky ceiling, or remove that musty old house smell.

I beeline to the coffee pot, feeling his eyes hot on my back.

"Would you like some coffee?" I ask over my shoulder.

"I want to see the letters." He doesn't move from the mat.

Frustrated now, I turn, sigh, and put my hands on my hips. "You got to give me a second here, Mr. Cohen. You show up at my house, unannounced—hell, I didn't even know you'd been released from jail—and the last time I saw you you were being escorted out of the courtroom after being convicted for killing my mother. *I need a cup of coffee, to busy my hands if nothing else. So I'm going to repeat the question: Would you like a cup of coffee?"

"No."

Fine.

My mind races as I go through the motions of making coffee. I pause, unsure if I have added two or three scoops. I add another—what the hell, feels like I'll need it.

Rhett remains silent, watching my every move.

I fill dead air while the coffee brews by retrieving two mugs from the cabinet and washing them, regardless that I removed them from the dishwasher only two hours earlier.

After what feels like an eternity, the coffee pot dings. I fill two mugs, add cream and sugar to one, and leave the other black. I will not drink this coffee alone.

Rhett is still standing by the door. I carry the mugs to the breakfast nook, a small, round table in the corner of the kitchen, set his down, then take my seat on the opposite end of the table. I gesture to the empty chair across from me.

He seems hesitant as he takes the seat, but does anyway, his movements tight and stiff. He sits rigidly in the chair. It's the demeanor of a prisoner, I realize. Someone who is always alert. Always vigilant. Always looking over their shoulder.

Despite the nerves churning in my stomach, I take a sip of coffee, watching him over the rim.

"Would you like cream or sugar?" I ask.

"I would like nothing other than the letters."

I lower the mug onto the table, wrap my hands around it.

"What do you know?" I ask.

"What do you mean?"

"About the letters. How did you find out?"

"I heard about it while I was still in. Someone saw it on the news. The news made its way to me pretty quickly."

"You're lying. The news story simply cited 'new evidence brought forth by an unnamed source' that would possibly reignite the case. Tell me the truth. How did you know that there were letters, specifically?"

"I'm not lying. I heard about the story through the news, but heard the details through gossip." He pauses. "Gossip also says there was a piece of your mother's jewelry included with one of the letters."

I narrow my eyes. "Why should I trust you, Mr. Cohen?"

"Rhett."

"Why should I trust you, Rhett?"

"Because I don't lie. And I did not kill your mother."

A moment of silence passes between us, two near-strangers trying to figure each other out.

"So then someone framed you? That's what you really think?"

"Yes."

I look down, begin circling the coffee cup between my fingertips.

"Do you believe me?" he asks.

I look up.

"Do you believe me?" he repeats. "Make the decision right now—right this second, at this table. If you believe me, I'd like to see the letters. If you don't believe me I will leave right now and you will never see me again."

"I believe you."

"Good, then can I please see the letters and the necklace?"

Please. The word seems out of place coming from someone convicted of murder.

"The necklace and letters are in police custody. But I have copies of the letters. I'll be right back. Stay here. Please."

I rise, step out of the kitchen, out of his view, and exhale.

My heart is racing.

I hurry to the bedroom, shut—and lock—the door, then grab a pair of clean jeans from the mountain of laundry on my bed, yet to be folded. After unhooking my kneepads and tossing them into the corner, I rip off my dirty jeans, slip into the clean pair and put on a bra under my tank. Then, I smear deodorant under my arms. After running a brush through my hair and adding a few dabs of concealer to the horrific dark circles under my eyes, I decide I look marginally more presentable. Feel more confident.

Manila envelope in hand, I hurry back to the kitchen, half of me expecting Rhett to be gone. Instead, he's still seated at the table, still in the exact same position as when I left. Back straight, hands on his thighs. He has not moved an inch, literally.

He glances at my jeans.

"I changed clothes—my pants were dirty," I blurt out. "I've been gardening all morning..."

He doesn't care. *Shut up, Sylvia.*

I set the envelope on the table.

"These are actual photocopies of the letters? Exact copies?"

"Yes."

Carefully, Rhett removes the four white pieces of paper and studies each.

"This is it?" he asks.

"Yes. Numbers and a threat with a necklace. That's it."

"I assumed letters meant... actual letters? Filled with actual words, paragraphs."

"Nope, except for the last one. The one with the necklace. The note reads, 'You are next.' As you can see."

He frowns at me. "You are next?"

"Yes."

"Your mother's killer sent you a note that reads, 'You are next'?"

"Correct. Assuming it is Mother's killer, yes."

Rhett blinks, surprised by this, then asks, "What did the cops do?"

"Took everything, told me to be vigilant, to buy some security cameras."

He shakes his head, displeased. "Who exactly took the necklace from you at the police station?"

"A kid named Officer Marino. Collected it as evidence."

"Kid?"

"Well, not exactly. Mid-twenties probably. He joined the station a few years ago."

Just then, Shirley saunters into the kitchen, pointedly ignoring our guest.

"What the—*is that?*" Rhett gawks, showing the most emotion I've seen in him thus far.

"It's a cat."

"Where's her hair?"

"She's a Sphynx cat."

Shirley shoots me a look before daintily jumping onto the counter, onto the top of the microwave, and curling herself into a ball.

I can't tell if Rhett is enthralled by my house pet, or totally, completely disgusted.

"Her name is Shirley. She's half-blind. I found her wandering around on my front porch one morning, and the rest is hairless history."

To my surprise, Rhett stand, walks over to her, and stretches out his hand. She sniffs, interested. Then, purrs loudly as he strokes her back.

So the man convicted of murder has a soft spot for animals. Interesting.

Finally, Rhett returns his focus to me. "Okay." He leans against the counter, crossing his arms over his chest. "Tell me everything."

I take a deep breath and recite the same story I told Officer Marino almost two weeks earlier. I tell Rhett about the black skull sweatshirt the person who delivered the letters was wearing, and the fact that Jesse Taylor, the missing Thorncrest man, was last seen wearing something similar. I tell him about the blood spatters on the necklace, the unidentified half-fingerprint on it, and that neither Jesse's prints, nor his, were on it. I tell Rhett that the necklace was not at the scene when police photographed it. I opt out of telling him that the cops' interpretation of all this is that it means either Rhett had an accomplice or paid someone to deliver the necklace to me—*not* that Rhett is innocent.

Rhett listens intently, hanging onto my every word.

When I finish speaking, he remains silent, unmoving, letting it all soak in. Then, he crosses the room, picks up his mug, and drains the entire thing in under five seconds.

I get up from the table, retrieve the pot, and top off his now empty mug. I wonder if it is the first time he's had good coffee in twenty years. I get a sudden rush of sadness and pity for him, and also guilt for playing such a huge part in his going to prison. I know that it was my testimony that sealed his conviction. It was my fault.

I top off my coffee and sit while he remains standing. "So. What do you think about it all?"

"I want to know more about Jesse Taylor," he says, "the guy who likely saw the man who framed me."

"The man who really killed my mother."

He nods and something flickers between us. Though we have different motivations, we both have a lot at stake in finding the man who wrote the letters.

"I want to know about Jesse's family," he continues. "Where they live, what they do..."

It occurs to me how long Rhett has been quarantined from society. How much has happened in Thorncrest in the last twenty years? Rhett's former schoolmates are middle-aged now, with families, jobs, mountains of debt, high cholesterol.

Jesse Taylor would have been eight when Rhett went to jail. Janet and her husband in their mid-thirties. I was nineteen when it happened.

Nineteen.

I wonder if Rhett remembers what I looked like back then.

Is he disappointed in what he sees now?

I tell him everything I know about Jesse and his family, describing his mother as the perfect housewife, his father as the trusted town doctor. I tell him about the gossip that Jesse had once been arrested for fighting and attempted theft.

"And how long has he been missing?" Rhett asks.

"I don't know... just over two weeks at this point."

"And no one has seen him other than you?"

"As far as I know, that's correct. He seems to have just vanished."

"Not if he came to your house four times."

"Yeah, I guess you're right."

"So he's probably still in the area."

I shrug.

"Who is in his circle of friends, do you know?"

"No, I haven't looked into it that much."

"What about his social media account? MySpace. Have you looked at that?"

I smirk. "MySpace isn't really a thing anymore."

"I mean social media in general," he says, a hint of embarrassment in his tone.

"No, I haven't looked."

Rhett's eyes shift to my cell phone sitting on the counter.

"Do you want to... now?" I ask.

"Yes. Now."

I retrieve my phone, click into Instagram and search for Jesse's name. Sure enough, like every other millennial in the world, Jesse Taylor is—was—extremely active on social media. I scroll through the images. Most feature Jesse with his friends, a motley crew of self-loathing youths with their middle fingers permanently stuck in the upward position. All dressed in black.

"Normal stuff." I slide the phone across the table. "Nothing that really stands out."

Rhett takes his time scrolling through the images in the feed. I find myself staring at him, noticing, again, how attractive he is. The mused brown hair, strong, angular jawline, aqua blue eyes. I remember the media circus and how many times Rhett's good looks were brought up, despite being totally irrelevant and inappropriate.

"Do you know if Jesse does drugs?" he asks.

"Not sure. I know that he's a troublemaker so it's really not that hard to imagine... Why? Do you think he does?"

"From the crew he hangs out with, yes."

"You know some of those kids?"

"No. I know their parents."

"How?"

He shows me the phone, points to one of the taller kids with a tattoo on his neck. "I recognize this one from pictures on his dad's prison cell wall. And this one?" He points to another. "Came to see his mom in the penitentiary a few times. Their folks are in prison." Rhett hands back the phone. "I think I know where to find him."

My brows shoot up. "Really?"

"I have a guess, yes."

"Where?"

"Inside Mount Mansfield State Forest."

"You think he's hiding somewhere in the woods?"

"Specifically, in a cave, yes. There's a maze of interlocking caves in the mountains north of Mount Mansfield. Off the beaten path. They call it The Hideout. It's a place where people go to buy and sell drugs."

"I've never heard of it. How do you know about this?"

"You learn a lot in prison—despite what you may think."

"Oh." I wonder what else Rhett knows that other normal, law-abiding citizens aren't privy to.

"Who is working Jesse's missing person case, do you know?"

"Detective Johnny Stroud," I say.

There is no mistaking the flash of hatred in Rhett's eyes. For a man as stoic as he is, this is an explosion of emotion. I'm not surprised there is bad blood between the two, considering Stroud was the lead investigator on Rhett's case, in which he was convicted of murder.

I clasp my hands together. "Do you... do you think we should call Stroud and tell him all of this? That you think you know where Jesse is? He's been looking for him for a while."

"No."

"Why?"

"I'll take care of it."

"What do you mean *you'll take care of it*?"

"I'll find Jesse."

"Aren't you on probation?"

"Probation doesn't mean that I can't look for someone."

"It feels reckless."

"You have absolutely no idea about recklessness, Miss Stone, and how it can completely destroy someone's life. *This* is not reckless."

I am speaking to a man driven by vengeance. Rhett doesn't care if he goes back to jail. His entire purpose in life is finding and killing the man who framed him. The man whose reckless actions destroyed his life. I am not dealing with a normal, sane person, I remind myself.

"How are you going to get to these caves?" I ask. "You don't have a car, right? Where is the vehicle you drove before you went to jail?"

"My truck was repossessed shortly after I went in."

"What about your house?"

"Same."

"What about friends or siblings or parents?" I ask.

"None, none, and dead."

I blink. The man has absolutely nothing. Literally, nothing. No means of transportation, no shelter, no home base, nothing. No wonder why he doesn't care about his future.

"You don't have any friends?" I press.

"Not since I went in."

"Surely—"

"No, Sylvia. Not many people want to be associated with a convicted murderer."

"When did your parents die?"

"Years ago." He drains the rest of his coffee. "Thank you for showing me the letters, and for the coffee."

I quickly push back from the table, almost knocking over my chair. Shirley leaps off the microwave and chases after me.

"Rhett, how are you going to...?" I am speaking to his back as he strolls out my front door. "Isn't there a halfway house you can go to? What about your probation officer? Can't they help?"

He says nothing, just strides down the driveway like he's late for some big appointment.

I catch up to him. "Where are you going?"

"I'm going to find Jesse Taylor and start there."

I plant my feet, my mind racing as I watch him walk down the driveway. My heart is roaring in my chest.

"Rhett!" I blurt before I can talk myself out of it, and lunge forward. "You need help—whether you admit it or not. And I can help you. I can take you to get some new clothes and we can figure out a car." As the words tumble out of my mouth, I doubt every single one of them. Yet I keep going, keep pressing, despite my swirling stomach. "You need food, rest, I'm sure..."

Shut up, Sylvia. Shut up, shut up, shut up.

"Rhett." I grab his arm.

Finally, he stops and turns to face me.

"*Listen*. My testimony is the entire reason you went to jail. It sealed the deal. And now—now I believe you didn't do it. And honestly? I think I always did. I feel guilty, Rhett. There. I admit it. Let me help you right now. It's the least I can do. Just let me freaking help you."

"I don't need help, Miss Stone."

"Stop calling me that. It reminds me of my mother."

At the mention of my mother, the emotions boil over. My cheeks pink and I feel like I am about to either cry or vomit. Ashamed, I turn my back to him and start back up to the house.

I am a train wreck. I am mad. I am sad, nervous, riddled with guilt. I am attracted, intrigued. Curious.

I am a mess.

A few seconds later, I hear his footsteps behind me.

EIGHTEEN
SYLVIA

The only way Rhett will accept food is if I tell him I am going to make lunch for myself. I know this. I also know that he probably doesn't consider wine an acceptable lunch, so, I throw together what I have. Two ham and cheese sandwiches—probably the Wednesday special in prison. I add a mountain of BBQ chips on the side, along with a fresh, sliced tomato from the garden sprinkled with salt and pepper. I'm proud of this addition. And finally, more coffee, because the man can't seem to get enough of it.

Rhett chooses to eat standing, leaning against the counter. I give him the space he seems to demand, choosing to sit at the table on the far side of the room.

I can't believe the bizarre twist my day has taken and I'd be lying if I said a part of me didn't feel invigorated. Excited even, in a messed-up kind of way. My life has been so boring for so long, then, *bam,* letters on my doorstep, *bam,* a mystery to investigate, *BAM,* Rhett Cohen.

We eat in silence. I've intentionally left the windows open, allowing the sound of the outdoors to fill the room. Birds chirping, squirrels skittering, the wind rustling the brittle leaves. I thought Rhett would appreciate the ambiance after living in concrete for decades.

While Rhett appears lost in thought, I'm anxiously awaiting his first taste of the tomato I'd harvested the day before. Surely the prison didn't offer fresh produce. When he finally tries it, I'm elated at the spark in his eyes.

Yes.

Satisfied with his response, I refocus on my food, but continue to sneak glances here and there.

I can't help but notice the way he eats. The way he stands a bit cockeyed, as if guarding his food. The haste in his bites, the way he barely chews before swallowing. A side effect from timed, group meals for twenty years, I assume.

I have to eat very fast to keep up with him, getting a stomachache in the process—though I think that's partly nerves.

Once Rhett finishes, I take his plate and stack it on top of mine in the sink.

"Thank you," he says, clearly uncomfortable with me taking care of him in this way.

I nod. "Okay, what's next? The clothes you're wearing need to be washed and I don't have any that will fit you in the meantime. So, I was thinking, let's run into town, get you a new set of clothes, and then we can go from there."

"It's not necessary."

"I have money," I lie, recalling the one credit card I have that isn't maxed out. "Don't worry about it."

Rhett's dark eyes narrow into a menacing glare. "Miss Stone —I mean Sylvia—I appreciate what you're doing. But you do not need to feel guilty about what happened. What's done is done and you don't need to take care of me. I am more than capable of taking care of myself."

He's about to walk out, on me, on this conversation. I can tell.

I step forward. "Well... you stink. Plain and simple." A

terribly rude lie, but it's the only thing I can think of to sway him. "So," I continue, "we will go to town, get you some clothes, then you can come back here and get yourself situated, and then we'll go find this Hideout place and see if Jesse's there."

This time I don't get an argument. No man wants to stink, especially one as prideful as Rhett Cohen.

We ride to town in silence. Rhett cracks his window open.

I keep looking over at him in the passenger seat, expecting to see an expression of awe and wonder on his face, like a child seeing Disney for the first time. However, he seems totally unfazed by the world around him, despite the fact that he's been confined in prison for twenty years.

Jesse Taylor's picture is everywhere. Tacked up on telephone poles, duct-taped on stop signs. Everywhere we look—*Missing.*

I click on my turn signal as we near the shopping center.

"No," he says. "Keep going."

"O—okay…" I turn off the signal and press the gas.

"Hang the third left up here."

"Into the pawn shop?"

"Yes."

"Wait." I stop in the middle of the road. "What—what are you looking for?"

"You think I'm going to buy a gun, don't you?" It's the first time I see a twinkle of amusement in his eye.

"No—I… well, yes, I guess I do think that."

"Don't worry, I'm not buying, I'm selling."

A car appears in my rearview mirror. I hesitantly turn into the lot.

"Selling what?" I ask, pulling into a parking spot.

Rhett pushes out the door the second I shove the Jeep into park. "Be right back."

I grab my purse and follow him into the pawn shop, my curiosity getting the best of me.

An old man sits behind the counter on a wooden stool, reading the newspaper. He is wearing an old, faded newsboy cap, and a pair of scratched round glasses on the tip of his nose. Best I can tell, the man doesn't recognize Rhett—or me. Thank God.

Rhett pulls a wristwatch from his pocket and sets it on the counter.

"How much can I get for this?"

The old man takes his time folding his paper, then limps over to the cash register. His bushy gray brows arch with interest. After a *humph*, he retrieves a magnifying glass from below the counter and examines the gold watch for a good minute.

"I'll give you $250 for it," the old man offers.

"Six hundred or no dice."

The old man narrows his eyes. "There're scratches on top."

"Six hundred," Rhett repeats.

The shop is quiet as the man mulls over the decision. Finally, he nods, then pulls six one-hundred-dollar bills from a bag under the counter and hands them to Rhett.

"Thank you, sir."

Leaving the watch behind, Rhett strides out the door. I'm both surprised and relieved when he doesn't use the money to buy a gun. Which begs the question—how does Rhett intend to kill the man who framed him once he finds him?

"Where did you get that watch?" I ask as we pull onto the road.

"It was my grandfather's, passed down to my dad, who passed it to me." His voice cracks. "I was wearing it the day I was arrested."

"I have a crazy feeling it was worth more than six hundred bucks."

"It was a vintage gold Rolex from 1971. Refurbished, it would probably be worth about six thousand today."

"*What?*" I gawk. "Are you serious? Geez, Rhett, we could have called around, gotten some quotes."

He shakes his head. It isn't the amount of money he is interested in; it's simply having enough to survive on until he can find who framed him. But it's clear by the way his voice cracked as he spoke about the watch that it had tremendous sentimental value to him.

I turn into the parking lot of the local big box store where I know they have men's clothes.

I find a parking spot away from the crowd.

"I'll stay here," I say, not prepared for the onslaught of questions and accusations if I, Sylvia Stone, am seen casually shopping with the man who was accused of killing my mother.

I watch Rhett stride across the parking lot like he owns the place. Such innate confidence he has. People look at him as he passes, but I don't think it's because they recognize him. Rhett's the kind of man who turns heads no matter where he is.

Six minutes later—*literally*—Rhett walks out of the store with a single bag clenched in his hand. He slips into the passenger seat, a waft of cologne following seconds later.

I wither in shame. Rhett must have either bought a bottle of cologne or sprayed a tester to remedy the stink I told him he had.

"That might've been the quickest trip anyone has ever taken in that store," I say. "I can't get in and out in under twenty minutes, ever."

"I know what size I am," he says as I pull back onto the road.

"You didn't try them on?"

The look he flashes me is a comical mixture of disgust and confusion.

I laugh. "Oh, that's right, men never try on clothes. I forgot."

NINETEEN
SYLVIA

Back at the house, I leave Rhett standing in the entryway while I dart to the master bathroom to make it as presentable as possible for a stranger to shower in.

The house has two full bathrooms and two half-sized. The full bathroom downstairs is cramped, has a very disconcerting rust-colored stain on the floor, and a shower the size of a postage stamp—definitely not comfortable for Rhett's size. So, my bathroom will be the one he showers in.

I find an old can of Comet buried under the sink, the top eroding with crusty powder. I quickly clean the sink, toilet and shower, then empty the trash. I hide my unusually large collection of female hygiene products under the sink, along with the vibrator I bought on impulse two years ago, still tucked in its explicit packaging.

As I'm doing this, I'm realizing how long it's been since I've had sex, or company in my house—other than Ginger the hairdresser.

When I return downstairs, Rhett is not where I left him. Instead, he's kneeling next to the front door, studying the baseboard.

Shirley is sniffing around his boots, showing a keen interest in the new man in our lives.

He glances over his shoulder as I approach. "You've got a leak."

"Yeah, I know. My house turns into a symphony of drips when it rains. I've got a closet full of buckets."

"No, I mean *inside* the wall."

I shift my weight. I should care, but I don't.

"See the separation here from the baseboard and the wall, and how the paint is bubbled around it?"

I bend at the waist, pretending to be interested.

"Could be a leak coming in from the roof, or a faulty pipe." He scratches his chin. "When was the last time you had your pipes checked?"

I bite my tongue. It's been *a long* time since a man has been anywhere close to my pipes.

I clear my throat. "I'm not sure I've ever had them checked."

This displeases him, and I remember that before Rhett went to prison, he was a handyman. A carpenter, a jack of all trades. Cohen Carpentry.

He stands.

I take a step back, rock back on my heels. "So... you can take a shower, if you want, before we leave for the caves."

Rhett follows me up the staircase. Per usual, the stairs creak as I climb them, but under his weight, the old wood slats sound like they're literally groaning.

"The layout of this house is kind of random," I say, embarrassed. "The master is upstairs, no clue why. The house has been added onto three separate times by three separate owners."

"Four."

I look over my shoulder. "Four?"

"It's had four owners. I've always liked this house. A long time ago, my buddies and I broke in while it was vacant, just to check it out. That was right before your mom moved here and took it over. It's got so much potential." He pauses. "You know, I knew Gerald."

I step onto the second-floor landing. "You knew my grandpa?"

"Yes."

"How?"

"My first job was at a mechanic shop downtown, sweeping floors. Remember he owned that mint-green '67 Chevy?"

No, I do not remember this. I know close to nothing about my mother's father. She rarely spoke of him. Scratch that—she *never* spoke of him.

Rhett continues. "I changed his oil once and we got into a conversation about the truck, and from that point on, he asked for me every time he needed his oil changed. We'd talk cars every time he came in."

I don't know why this surprises me so much. Thorncrest is a small town so it makes sense that everyone knew each other, but it's another random connection Rhett had to my mother that makes it even less likely that he would have murdered her.

I lead him into the master, otherwise known as my bedroom. My clothes are still on the bed, my dirty kneepads in the corner, but other than that, the room is clean. The late afternoon sun shines through the large windows, pooling on a glossy hardwood floor. Rhett is right, the home has character and potential, I've just never noticed it before.

The tour of my bathroom takes no more than four seconds. After leaving him with a clean towel, I shut the door.

Lingering in my room doesn't feel quite right, so I make my way downstairs to the kitchen, where I pace back and forth, uneasy at the fact that a man is naked, using my shower.

Actually... this is a lie. Uneasy isn't the only emotion I am feeling. I'm feeling excited—again—and energetic, and invigorated, and nervous, but all in a good way. The kind of way that makes you feel alive. I mean... *a naked man is using my shower.* For the first time in years, I am not alone in my house (aside from Ginger the hairdresser, of course). I have the interest of an insanely attractive man.... what kind of interest I'm not sure, but interest nonetheless.

My mind pivots as I find myself imagining him naked, and this is followed by a rush of insecurity. Has Rhett noticed the speck of mold in the corner of the shower, and if so, is he judging me for not cleaning well enough? Did I remember to use dryer sheets with this towel, or does it have that weird I'm-clean-but-smell-like-the-dryer smell? Did I look behind my toilet for any trash that might have fallen behind it?

The pipes groan as he turns off the water. I look at the clock —the man took a four-minute shower.

I jump to the sink and begin washing more dishes that don't need to be washed.

A minute later, Rhett steps into the kitchen.

My heart stutters.

His dark hair is wet and mussed to perfection. The pair of jeans he purchased at the store fits him perfectly, the long-sleeved T-shirt just tight enough to cling to his superhero chest. The shower has brought him back to life, I notice. His cheeks are a little pink, his eyes clearer. Alert. I wonder if this is the first time he has showered in a private space in a long time.

"Take a whiff," he deadpans.

"I'm sorry, what?"

"Take a whiff."

"Of what?"

"Of me."

"No, I'm sure—"

"Take a whiff. Smell me."

"Okay..." I dry my hands on a dish towel, walk over to him and make a show of sniffing him like a dog. The fresh scent of the soap lingers on his skin, mingling with the cologne he'd purchased at the store.

"Better?" he asks.

"I have a confession." I say, straightening. "You didn't really stink."

"Yes I did."

"No, really, you didn't."

A moment stretches between us.

"Listen..." he says.

My stomach drops. I know this tone. I've heard it many times before.

He continues, "I don't want you to feel like you need to get involved here. And honestly the caves... it's not the kind of place you want to be caught unprepared. It's best if I go alone."

"No." I plant my fists on my hips. "I'm going. Jesse Taylor started this whole mess by leaving letters, addressed to *me*, on *my* doorstep. Someone has threatened me, and whether the cops believe it's serious or not, I'm going to take it seriously. And Jesse knows who that person is. I'm as involved in this as you are, if not more. Besides, I've got the transportation you need to get there. And, for the record, I know how to handle myself in confrontations, if that happens."

I expect an argument. I don't get one. Instead, he stares at me for a minute, then finally dips his head, making a decision.

"Alright then, Ronda Rousey, let's go."

TWENTY
MARJORIE

Today there is a festival in town, the Cherry Tree Festival. This time every year the ache I feel for Anna seems to hit deeper than usual. I feel sicker. She loved this festival, the pony rides, the bounce houses, the petting zoo. I remember a goat threw up on her once and instead of crying, she laughed. And so, I laughed too.

Today I am thinking about the last time I took her to the Cherry Tree Festival. I can remember the day like it was yesterday.

Earlier that week, there was a doctor on Oprah (my favorite daytime show), a family therapist or something. The doctor talked about how important it is to spread equal amounts of attention between your children. That we, as parents, need to make an effort to do this. So, that day, I was making an effort. Extra effort, I should say. I even bought Sylvia a new dress. I'd pulled her aside in the kitchen that morning and told her I had a surprise. I unveiled it like it was the Hope diamond and then made a show of saying it was our little secret. I made a point to tell her that Anna didn't get a new dress. I was proud of myself afterward—of the effort I'd made.

But, by the time we'd loaded into the car to go to the festival, Sylvia's brand-new dress had a disgusting red juice stain down the middle. From the collar all the way down to the hem. Her short hair was sticking up on the side, even though I'd sprayed it with water and combed it for her an hour earlier. No matter what I did—no matter how much "effort" I put into it—Sylvia always looked a mess. Even her socks were chronically off-kilter, one pulled up, the other crumbled down. She was just so... she was a slob. I don't know how else to say it. All the time. Her appearance, her room, the way she ate, the way she talked.

People say identical twins are supposed to be the same. Not Anna and Sylvia. They couldn't have been more different. In every way, they were polar opposites. Anna was my straight-A student, my dreamer, my over-achiever, my beautiful little girl with perfect skin. Sylvia, on the other hand, has been behind her peers in every subject in every grade since she entered kindergarten. She is the most scattered human I have ever met in my life. For years, I followed her around, reminding her to do this, do that, pick-up this, replace that so she didn't lose it. She was like a toddler who never grew up—she still is in a way.

While Anna and I had this otherworldly bond, it seemed, Sylvia and I lacked every kind of emotional attachment a child and their mother could have.

God, I don't know why I can't just say it.

I don't feel love for Sylvia. There. That's the truth. From the moment she was born, it was like my heart was missing whatever maternal instinct I was supposed to have with her. Like God had messed up and only connected me and Anna in the womb and forgot about Sylvia. I don't know. I just look at her and feel nothing. Vacant. It's horrible.

About two hours after arriving at the festival, I ran into a mom I knew from school. While we were chatting, Anna asked if she and Sylvia could go get snow cones. I said yes and off they went. The mom and I ended up talking for a while, I think about twenty minutes.

When I turned around, Sylvia was walking toward me. She was alone. Anna was nowhere to be seen. I'll never forget the feeling I had in that moment. The moment you think your child has gone missing.

"Where's Anna?" I asked while frantically scanning the surroundings. "I don't know," Sylvia said.

I took off, my heart feeling like it was about to explode. I just knew someone pulled my beautiful Anna into their car and that she'd been kidnapped. I sprinted toward the snow cone stand, but saw an officer and ran to him instead.

It took us ten minutes to find my Anna. Ten. Minutes. She was trapped in a water embankment, sitting on a boulder, her knees hugged to her chest, soaking wet. She'd slipped off the foot bridge, and had fallen into the water, and was unable to climb the steep concrete walls to get out. She was hysterical because she couldn't swim.

She had a terrible fear of the water.

TWENTY-ONE
SYLVIA

It's late afternoon by the time we arrive at Fogmoore Trail, a lesser-known eleven-mile trail that cuts through the northern side of Mount Mansfield Forest. The rugged terrain is not for the faint of heart and has become infamous due to the number of incidents reported along its route. Dotted with steep drop-offs, dangerous cliffs, waterfalls, and caves, the trail ends in the middle of a thicket of pines. It just simply simply stops. No one knows why.

The small, pitted parking lot that marks the trailhead is crowded with a motley crew of hikers, some alarmingly novice with their flashy sandals and matching picnic baskets, others more adequately equipped with backpacks and trekking poles. All are seeking the beauty of the fall foliage. This time of year, it isn't uncommon for the crowds to linger on the trails well past dark, despite the multiple signs advising them otherwise.

Today, I can't blame them. The forest is postcard perfect, ablaze with dazzling golds, reds, and oranges, sparkling under the slanted autumn sun.

I calculate we have about two hours, max, until it's dark.

There is a sharp chill in the air. I'm grateful I grabbed a jacket before leaving, which I've tied around my waist. I'm also grateful I finally get to break in the hiking boots I purchased last year during a vodka-fueled night of self-loathing.

I pull over under a red maple, shove the Jeep into park, and look over at Rhett.

"Are you sure you know what you're doing?" I ask.

"No."

"Are you sure you know where you're going?"

"No."

"Alright then." I turn off the engine.

"I have a general idea," Rhett says as he unfolds himself from the Jeep.

Sounds like an adventure, I think, as I stuff my keys in my pocket and meet him at the hood of the Jeep.

"I used to hike these mountains as a kid," he assures me. "I know this land by heart. I know where the caves are, and I'm pretty sure I know the hidden ones the guys were talking about. They're off the beaten path, hidden under a bluff. Not many people know about them."

"Other than prison people."

"Exactly, *prison* people."

I grin at his *almost* eye-roll.

Rhett pulls a can of bug spray from his plastic bag of belongings and tosses it to me.

"You spent your money on bug spray?" I ask.

"You're from Dallas, right?"

"How did you know that?"

"Your mom and I actually spoke, you know, when I was working on her cabinets."

Right. "What's your point?"

"Figured Southerners, if anyone, would appreciate the offer of bug spray."

"This isn't the South."

"Are you really going to fight me on this?"

"No." I spray a few pitiful squirts on my ankles.

"Spray your entire body, trust me," he says.

Trust me.

I spray myself into a cloud of chemicals, then toss him the can. "So, how 'off the beaten path' are we talking about?"

"I told you you didn't have to come."

"I'm not griping, just asking a question."

"About a mile off the trail."

I watch as Rhett douses himself in bug spray. A mile hike in these woods, where there is not a manmade path, will be brutal. Even I know that.

After locking the Jeep, we set out side-by-side down the trail, immediately engulfed by wilderness. Sunlight spears through the thick canopy of trees, dappling the forest floor in swaying gold dots. The trees are so vivid that it reminds me of an enchanted forest. It's very romantic.

I take a deep breath, inhaling the spicy scent of fall.

"I didn't realize how beautiful it was out here."

I hear him take a slow, deep inhale next to me. I have to fight a smile. *This* is Rhett's version of a kid at Disney World. *This* is what he's missed. Not the town, not the people—the nature.

We walk a few minutes in silence, passing meandering hikers, dogs on leashes, and slowly leave them far behind.

"So you and my mom actually had legitimate conversations when you were working for her?" I ask.

"We did. She had a pot of coffee ready for me every morning when I arrived. Even made sure she had the kind of coffee I liked."

"What did you guys talk about?"

"Aside from the cabinet renovation?"

"Yeah."

"You. A bit. And other things."

Nerves bubbled in my stomach. "What did she say about me?"

"She told me about your newspaper gig, that you seemed to enjoy it, and this made her happy."

"What else?"

"She asked me if I knew Jesus as our Lord and Savior."

"What?"

Rhett chuckles. "I told her I did, and this also made her happy."

"You're not serious."

"I am."

I snort, shake my head.

"What?"

"It's just so funny... my mother didn't always believe in God, you know."

Rhett shrugs. "Takes some people a while. Some never."

"It's all so... ridiculous, isn't it? Come to Jesus and all of a sudden all your sins are just erased. Every one of them, boom, gone."

"It's called faith. You either have it or don't."

"Do you have faith, Rhett Cohen? After all you've been through? A man falsely accused of murder and sent to prison for twenty years?"

"I wouldn't have made it to the other side of all I've been through without it."

We walk a few beats in silence.

"Call me a cynic, but I believe some sins can't be erased." I kick a stone off the path.

"They'll be accounted for, one way or another."

"Is that so? By your hand, no? Isn't that what you're doing? Planning to kill the man who framed you? Vigilante justice, I think they call it. So tell me, man of faith, why not leave it to God?"

"You raise a solid question there."

"See? Not as black and white as you'd like it, is it? What else did you guys talk about?"

"We talked about your sister."

"*Anna?*" I squeak and immediately trip over myself. I am completely jarred.

Rhett notices the instant change in demeanor and frowns down at me.

"Are you joking?" I ask.

"No... why?"

"I... she... my mom never spoke of her. Not for years. When she left Dallas and moved here, it was like she made the conscious decision to never speak of my sister again. I don't even think people here know about Anna. I haven't heard that name... for *years*."

His frown deepens, indicating that my mother spoke plenty about Anna to him.

"What did she say?"

"She told me that Anna was your twin sister; that she passed at age twelve."

Rhett is obviously uncomfortable now, considering my over-the-top reaction. But I have to know more.

"What else did she say?"

"She mentioned you two were different, despite being twins."

I snort. "Comically so... Anna was the star child."

Rhett looks at me, interested, but says nothing.

"She was the beautiful one, got all the good grades, had all the friends. She had this... light about her. Do you know what I mean?"

He nods.

"People were just drawn to her. I actually joked that she should be an actress or something when she grew up." I inhale to continue, but stop. I don't want Rhett to know that I was the ugly one, that I always struggled in school, that I was shy and introverted and had zero friends.

My stomach is uneasy. I can't remember the last time I heard her name out loud. I can't remember the last time I spoke of her.

After my sister died, my mother created a world where Anna no longer existed. I know now that it was a coping mechanism. I remember one time, on what would have been Anna's sixteenth birthday, I said her name. Out loud. I'll never forget the look on my mother's face. Pure hatred—disgust—that I would utter a name so sacred.

"Sorry," I say, desperate to clear the air. "It's just weird to talk about her."

"I understand. And honestly, it wasn't much of a conversation."

"What else did you guys talk about?"

"You and Jesus were the depth of it. Everything else was small-talk. Weather, politics, she liked to talk baking. Pies. Rhubarb, specifically."

"You have a good memory. We used to have Sunday dinners and she would go all out on dessert."

He smiled fondly. "She was a nice lady."

I never once, in all these years, considered that Rhett had mourned the loss of my mother.

"Do you still work at the newspaper?" Rhett says, changing the subject.

"I was laid off."

"When?"

"About six months ago."

"I'm sorry to hear that."

"Thanks. I miss it, honestly. Mostly investigating stories."

"Wish you would've investigated mine a little harder," he deadpans.

I laugh, unsure if it was the appropriate response.

"You know I was offered a book deal?" I say for no other reason than to remind him that I am important. Interesting enough that someone wanted to tell my story.

"Me too," he says.

"*What?*"

"Yep. Several."

"In prison?"

"Yep."

"Why didn't you take them?"

He shrugs. "I had other things I was focusing on."

"Like plotting the death of the person who really did it?"

"That's one of them, yes. Why didn't you take yours?"

I take a deep inhale. "I don't know... everything was still so raw. I really don't know why I didn't take it."

We pass a man and woman, both mid-forties, holding hands as they stroll leisurely along the trail. Not a care in the world. The woman is wearing a yellow leaf in her hair, given to her by her lover, I assume.

"So what do you do now?" Rhett asks. "Since you've been laid off?"

"Nothing. I sit on the couch all day and watch reality TV with my hairless cat."

"That's something."

"It's nothing. Absolutely nothing."

"Why?"

"Why what?"

"Why do you sit at home all day?"

"I don't know," I say. And I mean it. I truly don't know why I let my life slip into such a dark, dreary place. I consider how pathetic I sound, but then remember the man I'm speaking to has been in prison for decades. Sitting on a couch all day probably sounds marvelous to him, right? Wrong. Because then he says:

"What's wrong with you?"

"Pardon me?"

"Why do you stay at home all day? By choice?"

"I don't know... small town... not a lot to do around here."

He makes a show of looking up at the trees, at the beautiful scenery around us.

"Yeah, I know." I shrug. "I guess I just don't really think about doing this kind of stuff. I will—I'd like to start getting out more, anyway."

"So six months without a job, huh? What's your plan?"

"I've been applying," I lie, officially embarrassed. "My skill set is centered around journalism, so I might have to move if I want to keep pursing that."

I stumble on a tree root. Rhett catches and steadies me before I face plant into a jagged rock. My cheeks heat as I look up at him, and that's the moment that I realize that I do, without question, have a ridiculous schoolgirl crush on this man. The man convicted of killing my mother. Because of course I wouldn't have a crush on a normal man. That would be way too *un*complicated.

We pass a family of hikers, a pair of twin toddlers giggling and stumbling their way down the trail. Memories flash behind my eyes.

Anna and me running through the woods trying to catch falling leaves. Anna and me climbing trees, and me teasing her because she was always too scared to climb as high as me.

Anna and me by the pool...

I shake that terrible memory away and look at Rhett. I wonder if he wants that kind of life now that he's out. Children, a family, a wife?

What a sensational story that would make: *Woman marries man convicted of her mother's murder.*

I contemplate this for the bulk of the remainder of the hike.

My quads are on fire when Rhett finally stops, looks around.

"I think..." he says. "Yes... This way..."

We swerve off the trail and into waist-high burr bushes that snag my clothes as I fight my way through. I am more grateful than ever for the bug spray.

Once out of the thicket, we walk single-file through the trees and after a few minutes I realize we are walking a barely visible footpath, one that appeared from out of nowhere—made by secret boots tiptoeing back and forth, back and forth.

I look up at the sky. The sun has dipped behind the mountains, the woods are beginning to grow darker.

It isn't long until the hikers' voices and barking dogs fade out behind us. I grow tired, weary, my body aching for a pair of fluffy couch cushions and a glass of red wine.

After what seems like an hour, the trees begin to thin and the terrain becomes more rugged. Boulders spear up from the ground, surrounded by rocky outcrops threatening to trip me with every step. Finally, we come to a small cliff crowded by treetops.

"Is this it?" I ask.

"I think so," he responds quietly, in a way that sends me on alert.

It's then that I realize we're about to walk into a potentially dangerous situation without any kind of weapon or way to defend ourselves. Aside from Rhett, I should say, whose body is a mountain of protection in its own right. But he isn't invincible. If someone has a knife or a gun...

I follow the fearless man down the side of the cliff, using tree branches for balance. Sure enough, about seven feet below the cliff is an underhang that leads to a narrow opening in the rock.

Grabbing onto the cliff with one hand, I bend over and peer at the dark crevice between the cliff and the underhang. It's a cave, its entry long and narrow like a mouth barely opening.

"That's it," he says.

My stomach tickles with nerves.

"You ready?"

Oh my God, are we really doing this?

I swallow the knot in my throat and nod.

Rhett pulls two small flashlights from his pocket, hands one to me and keeps the other for himself. I wonder how much of his $600 he's already spent.

We have to squat and waddle through the opening of the cave. It's a rock sandwich, with us in the middle. However, once inside, the cave opens up into a large room, about eight feet tall. The air is cold, moist, and smells like mold and dirt. The walls are covered in spray paint. Gang symbols, anarchy signs, and some explicit paintings that remind me of the story I once reported on about kids spray-painting penises on school property. At the end of the room is a tunnel, pitch black.

I can hear a distant echo of voices.

My pulse begins to thrum.

Rhett steps into the tunnel, no hesitation, no fear of the unknown. I wonder what it's like to have that much confidence.

The cave begins to close in around us as we slowly walk through the tunnel, eventually becoming so narrow that we have to turn our bodies sideways to make it through.

All of a sudden:

"Hey."

The voice is close and whoever it is must have seen our lights bouncing off the walls ahead of us.

Rhett doesn't answer, nor stop.

My legs suddenly feel like rubber underneath me.

The tunnel opens up to another room where at least a half dozen teenagers sit in a circle around a campfire of flashlights. My mouth drops. The large room looks like someone's backyard, except in a cave. There are folding chairs, even a few lounge-style lawn chairs, a plastic table packed with canned food, coolers, cases of cheap beer, backpacks. A blow-up mattress in the corner. Magazines are stacked everywhere, as well as bags of trash.

The pungent scent of pot clings to the wet air.

And then I see it—a black sweatshirt with a skull and crossbones.

TWENTY-TWO
SYLVIA

"I'm here to talk to Jesse Taylor."

No one answers Rhett. Instead, the group slowly stands, one after the other, a slow wave of intimidation.

Six pairs of bloodshot beady eyes glower at Rhett and me, leaving no question that we are unwelcome here.

The group consists of all boys, ranging from sixteen to twenty, I guess—aside from Jesse, who, standing in the shadows, looks even older than his twenty-eight years. The runaway looks pale, significantly skinnier than in the photos splashed all over the news.

Two of the boys are unquestionably brothers, possibly even twins, with sandy blonde hair and tall, lean bodies. Both wear tie-dye T-shirts and harem pants. Their skin is pale and sallow, lips dry and cracked. It isn't a stretch to imagine that these two indulge in more than just the occasional joint. Come to think of it, everyone in the group is skinny, suggesting food has not been as easy to come by as drugs.

What a life.

The others share the same disgruntled expressions on their

skeletal faces. One is shirtless, proudly displaying a chest full of tattoos, one of which is a swastika.

I wonder if they are all missing teens like Jesse, or runaways, or perhaps simply have parents who don't care.

Which is worse?

I pity them, in that moment, every single one of them. On a very deep level, I understand their plights.

All eyes are fixed on Rhett, except for Jesse's. Unlike the others, Jesse appears to be alert, not high. He's staring at me, his expression a mixture of surprise and confusion. He recognizes me. There is no question now that Jesse is the one who delivered the letters to my doorstep.

"You a cop?" one of the twins ask Rhett.

"That's Jesse," I whisper, pointing at the man in the shadows, aptly fulfilling the role of scrawny little sidekick. "The one in the black sweatshirt. That's him."

"Answer the question. Are you a cop?" Jesse steps forward, repeating his buddy's question.

"We aren't cops and we're not here to cause trouble." Rhett shifts his weight toward me. A protective stance. "I just want to have a quick chat with you."

"Go fuck yourself," Jesse responds, indignant.

Rhett doesn't flinch. "Jesse, one of two things can happen here. You can take a walk with me outside and we can have a nice, calm chat, and then you can go about your business. Or I will drag you out by your hair and hold you down until you speak to me. It's your decision. I'm fine either way."

"Hang on..." The tattooed kid's eyes widen. "You're Rhett Cohen, aren't you?"

Someone gasps.

The twins take a step back.

The cave falls deathly silent.

There is an instant power shift in the room.

No matter the path Rhett chooses for his life he will always be remembered as the man who stabbed an innocent woman to death. There will be no man—or group—whom he can't intimidate. A blessing and a curse, I muse.

"What do you say, Jesse?" Rhett asks.

Tattoo-kid grabs Jesse's arm and whispers in his ear. He must be number two in charge.

My eyes sweep the room.

I notice a mound of empty bottles in the corner, beer, liquor, wine. One catches my eye immediately—a cheap, knockoff brand of rosé. My mother is the only person I have ever seen drink that brand and flavor of wine.

Fragmented memories begin flashing behind my eyes.

Broken glasses. Broken bottles. The rotten, sour scent of alcohol.

I squeeze my eyes shut, trying to chase away the visions. But instead I see her—her round, ruddy face, her broken body. Blood covers her torso, a bat next to her body, a bottle of rosé on the counter. She cries out for me:

Help, Sylvia, help.

My breath catches and I take a step backward. When I open my eyes, Rhett's looking intensely at me.

He dips his chin—*You okay?*

I nod—*Yes.*

Yes. *Yes, yes, yes. Get it together, Sylvia.*

"I'll come with you under one condition," Jesse says, pulling me back to reality.

"What's that?"

"That you won't tell my parents or anyone where I'm at. And same for these guys, too," he gestures around the room. "Never say you saw them."

"Done."

Jesse nods in victory, then flashes his friends an *I-got-this* look before stepping forward. His eyes lock on Rhett's as he passes, a glare of intimidation—as if the scrawny rat would stand a chance against him in a physical altercation.

Jesse leads the way through the cave.

I keep glancing over my shoulder, expecting the rest of his crew to stab us in the back on the way out.

Finally, the waning sunlight glows at the end of the tunnel. Jesse dips outside, Rhett follows, and then I emerge, inhaling the fresh mountain air. I decide promptly that I never want to return to that cave again.

Jesse crosses his arms over his chest.

"I want to know about the letters," Rhett says, cutting to the chase.

"What letters?"

"I'm not playing this game with you, boy."

Jesse rolls his eyes. "I was paid to deliver them, that's it."

"Someone *paid* you to do it?" I ask and feel validated because this is exactly what I suggested had happened to the cops.

"Who paid you?" Rhett asks.

"I don't know."

Rhett lunges forward, grabs the kid by the collar, and lifts him off his feet. I stumble backward, my pulse skyrocketing.

Jesse's legs kick ineffectively as he gasps for air, eyes wild with fear.

"Who paid you to deliver the letters?" Rhett asks in a cool, calm tone that is absolutely terrifying.

"Someone..." Jesse chokes out. "I never saw his face. I promise. They were wearing one of those ski mask things. I swear, man, I didn't see their face. I'd tell you—I don't give a shit."

Rhett releases Jesse and he crumbles to the ground, clawing at his neck. He stumbles upright, gasping and spitting. This time, instead of puffing his chest, Jesse distances himself from us, eyeing the ex-con like a venomous snake.

"Keep going," Rhett says.

Jesse rubs his neck where red streaks are already beginning to form. "I was approached in the alley behind the pool hall."

"What pool hall?"

"Benji's. You know, downtown. By the courthouse."

I know Benji's. Everyone does. It's a place frequented by a certain crowd that you don't want to be seen with after dark. I'm not surprised Jesse hangs out there.

"It was nighttime—I don't know, maybe ten or eleven," Jesse continues. "I was outside smoking a cigarette and somebody just came out of the shadows. Thought it was the cops, but they already came by looking for me an hour earlier. Devon—you don't know him probably—hid me in the bathroom. Anyway, the person scared the shit out of me."

"And you didn't see their face?"

"No, to be honest, I almost jumped him. I thought I was getting mugged."

"What were they wearing?"

"A black ski mask and black clothes."

"How tall and heavy—was it a kid or an adult?"

"Honestly, dude, I don't know. I was high. It wasn't a cigarette; it was a joint I was smoking. I just know they were wearing a mask."

"What did they say?"

"Nothing. Just handed me an envelope."

"And you took it without asking anything?"

"Yeah, man, when somebody hands something to you, you take it."

Rhett glances at me.

"What was in the envelope?" I ask.

"The four envelopes that I delivered to your doorstep along with a note for me with instructions, and five $100 bills in payment to do it."

"And you didn't even think to take this to the police?"

"Hell, no. Five hundred bucks? No way. I'd just run away from home, five hundred bucks felt like hitting the lottery."

"Where is the note with the instructions?" Rhett asks.

"I burned it, dude."

Rhett shakes his head, clearly pissed.

"Why did you run away?" I ask.

Jesse shrugs, looks down, a hint of shame in his eyes.

"Answer the question," Rhett says.

"I don't know... I just hate my life. I hate my parents."

I think of Janet, his mother, the perfect wife, and his father, the successful doctor, and their perfect house in the perfect gated community.

"Why? What's to hate?" I ask.

"My parents... they're just... I don't know... I don't really want to get into all that bullshit. You're not my therapist."

Jesse kicks a rock, sending it tumbling over the edge of the cliff.

"Tell me about your dad," Rhett says.

"I don't really know my dad. He's never home."

"Working?"

Jesse scoffs. "That and other things."

"What other things?"

"He's a cheating asshole. I'm pretty sure he's got at least a few girlfriends on the side."

"Who?"

"Don't know." Jesse shifts his weight. "Don't care."

A moment of silence stretches between us, Rhett and I studying Jesse, Jesse staring at the trees.

"What are you not telling us?" Rhett asks.

"Nothing, man."

"There is more to this story, with your dad."

Jesse shrugs.

"Do you have an idea of who gave you the letters?" I ask, returning to the point.

Jesse shifts his weight again, avoiding eye contact.

"Who do you think it was?" Rhett presses.

"I don't know—honestly, I don't know."

"Then tell us whatever it is you're holding back."

Jesse takes a deep breath and suddenly seems much younger than his twenty-eight years. The guy is a lost soul, floating aimlessly in a life that he hates. I feel sorry for him.

"There's this abandoned house..." he says with a touch of reluctance. "At the end of the cul-de-sac in my neighborhood, Deep Shadows. I've seen my dad go into it a few times."

"Into the abandoned house?"

"Right. After dark, like, in the middle of the night."

"Did you go with him?"

"No. I followed him—this was before I ran away. Saw him sneaking out one night and wondered what the hell he was doing. The next few nights I stayed awake, hoping to catch him again and I did. He went in through the back door of the house, came out an hour later, and went back to bed like it was no big deal. Anyway, the next morning I broke into the house. I wasn't two steps inside when I heard someone shuffling around inside. I called out just as someone ran out the back door."

"Did you see who it was?"

"No."

"Did they see you?"

"I don't think so. It was dark as shit. But they definitely heard my voice."

Rhett looks at me.

What is the town doctor up to?

"Anyway," Jesse continues, "it was the *next* night that somebody in a black mask was waiting for me outside the pool hall with the letters. Coincidence? I don't know—doesn't feel like it."

"Could it have been your dad?"

"No way, dude, I would know him. I would recognize the shape of his body, the way he moved—no way."

I step forward. "So you think whoever was in that abandoned house is the same person who approached you at Benji's?"

"I don't know—I'm just telling you it was a weird coincidence. I saw somebody in that abandoned house and the next night, I get a handful of letters to deliver to Sylvia Stone."

Our attention turns to two squirrels racing up the treetop next to us, fighting viciously over a nut. Loud squeaks and screams like nails on a chalkboard.

Rhett pulls a hundred-dollar bill from his pocket and hands it to Jesse.

Jesse's eyes round, as do mine.

"Stay safe," Rhett says. "And don't be stupid."

Jesse takes the hundred-dollar bill, staring at Rhett in disbelief.

"...Thank you."

TWENTY-THREE
SYLVIA

We're in a race against dusk as we speed to Deep Shadows, the neighborhood that seems to tie into everything. The cool night air whips through the Jeep, invigorating our energy. I'm glad I'd left the doors off as Rhett seems to enjoy the open space.

An excited anticipation bounces between us. We talk nonstop the entire way. I'm a chatterbox of theories, like a Chatty Cathy doll wound much too tightly.

"So, do *you* have any ideas of who was this mysterious masked person who approached Jesse behind the pool hall?"

Rhett shakes his head. "Not yet."

"Why him, I wonder? Why did the person choose Jesse, specially? And why the pool house? And why now, all these years later?"

"I don't know but I intend to find out."

"Do you think this masked man is the real person who killed my mother and framed you twenty years ago?"

"Who else would know the details of the clocks? Who else would be in possession of the necklace Marjorie was wearing when she was murdered?"

I nod. He's right. The facts are too glaring to ignore.

I begin chewing on a cuticle. "When I gave Officer Marino the letters and necklace at the station, he asked if I'd told anyone else the details of the murder. I haven't, have you?"

"No, of course not."

"I didn't think so. We also briefly listed who else had access to the case, who might have known the intimate details."

"That list would be long with many holes. Your mom was killed twenty years ago—*twenty* years ago. How many times has the Thorncrest police department's personnel turned over since then? How many forgotten names and faces? The case was available for anyone to view. But..."

"What?"

"There is only one person who was involved in Marjorie's case and is still employed with the department now: Detective Johnny Stroud."

My brows shoot up. I picture the bald tattooed detective speaking to Officer Marino as I was leaving the station. "Do you think he's the masked man? The man who framed you?" I laugh. "There is no way the small-town detective is a cold-blooded killer."

Rhett shoots me a hot look. "Not all cops are good, Sylvia."

We ponder this along with a dozen other jumbled ideas that make no sense.

As we approach the large iron gates of Deep Shadows, I can't help but think how quickly my life has changed, in an instant it seems. Days ago, I couldn't get off the couch, comatose with boredom. Now, I am racing through the night, chasing down leads with an ex-con.

"Is this it?" Rhett asks, peering at the large, ornate entry to the neighborhood.

"Yes. This is where Jesse's parents live... You've never been here?"

"No."

I frown. "But this neighborhood has been around forever. You were born and raised here, you said?"

"Not on this side of town."

I recall the angle Detective Stroud used twenty years earlier at his trial. Rhett was born poor and grew up poor. His carpentry business was underwater and his home and car were a week from being repossessed. He needed money—fast—and *this* is why he broke into Marjorie Stone's house to steal her jewelry.

The neighborhood is lit in the blue glow of dusk. Long black shadows stretch along the manicured lawns. A chorus of bugs roar through the air. The atmosphere is starkly different than when I visited the day before. Then, it had been eerily still; now, however, the neighborhood is a bustle of activity.

The driveways are no longer vacant, instead filled with cars, some even parked along the street. We pass a white Tesla with loud bass booming through the windows, a stray dog darting through a row of bushes, and an elderly woman powerwalking with weights in her hands and a steely look in her eye—one on us, one on the wayward dog.

Rhett and I turn our cheeks as we pass the woman.

"That's the Taylors' house right up there," I say quietly, as if anyone could hear us.

Rhett slows, studying the property as we pass.

Unlike before, the house is alive with energy. The windows glow with light, the porch swing sways in the breeze, squirrels skitter about the lawn. But there is no one in sight.

I twist in my seat, peering back at the neighboring house where I had seen the woman with red hair watching me from the window. She's there, again, standing on a terrace of vines, a tall, statuesque silhouette.

"Who are you looking at?"

"The house next to the Taylors'—their neighbors. When I

visited the other day, I saw a silhouette watching through the windows. Who owns the house, do you know?"

"I didn't even know this neighborhood existed, remember?"

I turn back around with a *humph*. "We need to figure it out."

"Add it to the list."

At the end of the cul-de-sac, two houses sit closely together. Both are similar in style, sharing the neighborhood aesthetic of two-story Nantuckets. One is blue, like the Taylors', the other a stained, weathered yellow that was probably considered "buttercup" many years ago. The first-floor windows are boarded up, the second floor's are cracked, some streaked with duct tape. The sides of the home are overgrown with gangly brown vines. The yard is covered in a blanket of moldy dead leaves. This abandoned home has been vacant for some time.

Next door, an elderly man in overalls and a brown straw hat is tending to his landscaping. He straightens when he sees us, and immediately frowns in suspicion.

"No," Rhett says, as I brake to turn into the abandoned home's driveway, "keep going."

"Really?"

"Yes, really."

I accelerate, turn the wheel and circle the end of the cul-de-sac.

The old man's craggy, pale face fills my rearview mirror and I am certain he is taking note of my license plate.

"We'll have to check out the house sometime later, when curious eyes aren't watching." Rhett says. "Do you know who that man was?"

"No clue. I don't recognize him."

"Well he sure didn't like us pulling into his end of the neighborhood."

"I imagine he doesn't get much traffic unless it's for him."

We peer at the Taylors' home again as we pass, and I notice

the silhouette who was standing on the terrace next door is gone.

What a peculiar place this is.

"Where to now?" I ask, exiting the neighborhood and turning onto the gravel road that leads back to town.

"That's it for today," Rhett says.

Disappointment grips me. That's it? No more sleuthing? No more adventure?

An awkward moment passes... So what am I going to do with him now? This ex-con of mine?

"What would you—"

"Just drop me off downtown."

"Where?" I ask. "What are you going to do?"

"I have to meet with my parole officer, call him before midnight."

"Do you want to use my cell phone?"

"No."

I want to ask more, but bite my tongue. My mother's voice echoes in my head. *A woman should never be too eager.*

At the first stop sign in town, Rhett suddenly releases his seatbelt.

"Here?" I frown.

"Yes. Thank you, Sylvia. I've got it from here."

"Wait, what...?"

The question fades on the cold air as Rhett grabs his plastic bag of belongings and slips out of the Jeep.

Streetlights flicker on above us.

"Where are you going?"

Rhett doesn't answer. Instead, he steps onto the sidewalk, dips his head and descends into the shadows.

I watch his monstruous frame in my review mirror until it fades under the blinking lights of Benji's Pool Hall.

TWENTY-FOUR
MARJORIE

The day Anna died was like any other. I suppose that's how all deaths start. You never know when someone is going to die. There is no announcement, no preparation, no warning. It just happens and then you're left to pick up the pieces and figure out your new place in the world. The new you, minus the one who died.

It was summer. July 14th, to be exact. I'd taken both girls to the city pool to escape the brutal heatwave. Despite her fear of water, Anna loved going to the pool because she had a crush on the lifeguard, though she would never admit to this. Anna, age twelve at the time, had just begun to look at boys with interest and curiosity. Sylvia, on the other hand, still thought they had cooties.

Both girls had new swimsuits. A spur-of-the-moment purchase when I saw they were fifty percent off. Anna's was red, Sylvia's was blue. Sylvia complained about hers.

The pool was incredibly crowded that day. The heat, I guess. So much so, I remember thinking I was surprised it wasn't closed due to maximum capacity. Regardless, I'd lucked out and found two lounge chairs in the back corner, in the shade.

I remember thinking how blue the sky was that day. Electric blue. Not a single cloud anywhere in sight. I planned to use this time to work on the cookbook I was putting together. Nothing formal, just something to record my recipes so that the girls would have something to remember me when they were raising their own families. A good memory to replace the bad ones.

Sylvia took to the water immediately, diving straight into the deep end. Anna asked if she could dangle her feet in the shallow end. I grinned and winked and said yes. I knew the only reason she wanted to do this was because she wanted to show off her new suit to the handsome lifeguard. Nick, his name was. Funny I remember that. While she walked away, I reminded her, "Chin up, shoulders back." It's something I would say to Anna every day. I wanted her to have the confidence I never did.

She turned and smiled the biggest, prettiest smile at me.

I remember watching her walk away and wondering how I got so lucky. I took in her tall, skinny silhouette. Her beautiful blonde hair, flawless skin. In a few years she'd become a woman, find interests beyond our home. I felt a pang in my chest. I wanted her to stay young. To stay mine.

If I could only go back to that exact moment. If only I could. I would've said no, that she couldn't go near the water. I would've said no when Sylvia asked if we could go to the pool. Or I would've gone into the water with Anna, held her hand, and inhaled at the exact moment she did, so that we could have died together.

I remember looking up from the notebook I was scribbling recipes in—how stupid of me; how not important— and not seeing Anna sitting by the shallow end. I sat up and frantically looked around. *Anna can't swim*, the words pummeled through my brain.

And then I saw Sylvia, in her bright blue swimsuit, peering into the water, a weird, almost confused expression on her face.

I knew in that moment that something was wrong.

I screamed Anna's name as I sprinted to Sylvia.

I remember looking into the water, at Anna's body, hovering just above the bottom of the pool, the shape of it contorted by the waves. Her arms were drifting lazily by her side, her hair like snakes slithering around her face, her legs lifeless.

The next memory I have is staring down at her body as the lifeguard administered CPR.

I remember thinking that the last monumental memory Anna would ever have of me was my hand connecting with her cheek the night before.

TWENTY-FIVE
SYLVIA

Two days have passed since I watched Rhett disappear under the blinking lights of Benji's Pool Hall. I have received no calls or information from Detective Stroud or Officer Marino regarding the mysterious half-print found on my mother's pendant. It's like everything just stopped.

It makes me crazy.

I haven't seen or heard from Rhett. Not that I expected to. There was a certain finality in the last words he'd spoken to me, in the tone of his voice as he'd stepped out of the Jeep. It wasn't just "thank you for the ride," it was, "thank you for everything."

Thank you, Sylvia... I've got it from here.

The message was clear: He was done with me—but I am far from done with him. The last forty-eight hours, Rhett Cohen has dominated my thoughts.

I've spent the days in a mental game of time-warp ping pong, bouncing between memories of the trial, so long ago, and to now, to his re-entry into my life. I've replayed every word spoken between us, every look, every touch. I've analyzed it all.

Two days ago I dusted off the folder kept hidden in my

bedroom bookshelf which contains every article published on my mother's murder. *Marjorie's Death Folder,* I call it.

I studied everything, again. Reread every word, revisited the timeline of events, the points of evidence. Then, I spent hours studying old photos of myself, contemplating how much younger—*better*—I looked back then. The old me, the one Rhett remembered.

I dug out the outfits I was wearing in each picture taken at the trial. Thin, poly-blend suits (what I could afford), a few cute, conservative dresses. I washed and pressed them all, then hung them on my bedroom walls like a fashion show dressing room. Using a pair of kitchen scissors, I recut the layers around my face, exactly as I'd worn my hair twenty years ago. The last time Rhett saw me.

I rearranged my room. Scooted the bed to the corner, replaced the rug, rearranged my dresser and armoire. I taped up a picture of my mother on my closet door, like a preteen would a NKOTB poster in the '90s.

I transformed my room and myself, to match exactly as everything had been in the weeks surrounding the trial.

For two days, I have done this and nothing else.

Dirty dishes sit piled in the kitchen sink, mounds of laundry are strewn over the floors, spoiled milk in the fridge. I've even forgotten to feed Shirley, to clean her litter box, refill her water. She responded by ignoring my existence. I don't care. My thoughts are elsewhere, unable to focus on anything that didn't involve Rhett, or murder.

I've wondered many things over the last few days, like where is Rhett staying? What are his means of transportation? Is he out of money? I even wondered if he was already back in jail, caught doing something he shouldn't have been. So, I'd called the jail, said my name was Patty Plates—the best name I could come up at the spur of a moment—and I asked if they were holding a man named Rhett Cohen.

The dispatcher's response? "Not yet." She is obviously not a fan of Rhett. Most Thorncrest women aren't. Something about the brutality of the murder he was convicted of.

But the question above all else, the one that I couldn't shake from my thoughts: Is he with another woman?

In the evenings, I immersed myself in literature and articles highlighting life after incarceration and how difficult it is for an inmate to form meaningful relationships and reintegrate into society. Whether it be reconnecting with family and friends, finding a place to live, a job, learning how to cope with the stigma, or finding love, everything is a challenge for them.

I learned that Thorncrest does not offer any kind of halfway house for prisoners once released. No matter their circumstance, how long they've been in jail, or their mental state, ex-cons have zero options once their sentence is completed. They are simply given back whatever belongings were collected at the time they went in and kicked out the door.

To someone like me, post-prison assistance sounds somewhat trivial. You've just been released from a cage (literally) and handed your freedom. You should be happy, right? You get your life back. Get to start over. That's great, right?

Wrong.

Most ex-cons can't get jobs. Most lose their friends and family—either to death or to shame. And despite hating prison, they have gotten used to the structure and routine that incarceration offers. Every second of every day is planned by someone else. Even their food, when they eat and what they eat. They don't have to think about the day-to-day stuff because it is taken care of for them. Then, when their sentence is served, they are just tossed out, back into the real world. It's jarring. Much like a soldier coming home after war. You are forever changed and everyone just expects you to be grateful and step back into the role of productive citizen once again. But you can't. It's like you can't reset to the way you used to be. You are something entirely new, you *have become* something entirely new.

I understand this far too well.

I remembered the rigid way Rhett held his body, the way he guarded his food, the cold, callous way he spoke. He's been forever changed. In ways he's yet to notice, I'm sure.

I downloaded multiple resources for family members, each offering advice on how to reconnect to someone who has just been released from prison. Use humanizing language, one suggests. Don't refer to the former inmate as, well, exactly that, or, ex-offender, ex-con, parolee, delinquent, or offender. Instead, use words like "person previously involved in the justice system."

I learned that ex-cons (because "person previously involved in the justice system" is just too much of a mouthful) are at an increased risk of suicide compared to the rest of the population. It is a sliding scale of severity. If the person has been incarcerated once, he or she is forty-two percent more likely to kill themselves once out. If the person is incarcerated twice, he or she is 67 percent more likely, and three times, a whopping 113 percent more likely. Also, the longer the inmate is incarcerated, the higher the risk.

Rhett served twenty years.

The thought of him taking his own life, after being wrongly accused, makes me sick to my stomach.

It was my fault. My testimony is the reason he was locked up.

I owe him.

I owe him.

And with those three words tattooed on my brain, on day three, I pull myself together. I wash, dry, and straighten my hair. Put on a full face of makeup, perfume, a brown cashmere sweater that once belonged to my mother. Skinny jeans and sneakers. With renewed energy and an ill-considered plan in my head, I set off for town.

Because I owe him.

TWENTY-SIX

SYLVIA

It's another cold, cloudy autumn afternoon. The days are growing shorter, the nights colder. Winter appears hellbent on arriving early with no regard to the tourists who are desperately seeking one last glimpse of fall foliage.

Downtown is a bustle of activity, a mismatched crowd of coats and scarves, shorts and shirtsleeves. No one knows how to dress in this weather. Tourists weave in and out of the locally owned shops that are struggling to stay open, the restaurants, the only bar in town.

I slow as I pass the courthouse, peering in the windows, looking for Rhett. Just seems like the place an ex-con would need to go to for something, right? Where does one go to meet his probation officer?

I hang a right and pull into the small gravel parking lot of Benji's Pool Hall, the last place I saw Rhett three days earlier. Four trucks are parked haphazardly by the front door. I slide into a spot off to the side and turn off the engine.

My plan was to go inside and ask the bartender if he had seen Rhett. Instead, I find myself staring at the dilapidated brick building, wondering what Rhett was up to the night I dropped him off. The obvious guess is that he was following up on the details Jesse supplied to us, about how the masked person with the letters had approached him there. But Rhett had made a promise to Jesse that he wouldn't tell anyone they spoke. Who had he talked to?

Two drunk cowboys stumble out the front door, leaning on each other's beefy arms for support.

They spot me immediately, a woman alone, sitting in her doorless Jeep. Like a moth to a flame, they pivot, beelining it to me.

Shit.

I quickly start the engine and back out, my tires spitting rocks in my wake. I'll come back later, or tomorrow, the second they open, before the drunks file in.

I look at the clock as I pull onto the road—6:07 p.m. Well, plan number one of the evening is a fail.

Feeling discouraged, I pull into the line at the liquor store, three cars deep.

Ahead of me, sits a vintage yellow Volkswagen. The back window is covered in stickers. I wonder how the driver can see through the rearview mirror. The license plate reads LIV HPY.

Live happy.

I think of my mother and wonder if she was ever—*ever*—happy.

A group of construction workers loiter in the accompanying lot. Recently excavated, mounds of dirt surround a group of men standing in a circle, covered in grime, wiping their sweaty foreheads. A few are smoking cigarettes, the others chugging bottles of water. Winding down for the day.

Twin backhoes sit parked in the corner of the lot. A line of little pink flags run down the middle, marking some sort of underground piping.

I see one man in the shadows, working alone, completely isolated from the rest of the crew. He's digging a hole while the others seem to ignore his presence. Almost mechanically, the shovel rises and falls, each stab into the earth, each scoop, identical to the last.

I squint and lean forward over the steering wheel. I recognize the brown hair, the wide shoulders, thick arms.

Rhett.

I yank the steering wheel, hit the gas, swerve out of the line and into a parking spot behind the liquor store.

I climb out of the Jeep, the cashmere sweater I'd chosen snagging on the door frame, showing a flash of midriff before settling back down.

The conversation halts between the group of construction workers.

Chin up, shoulders back, I stride across the dirt.

Rhett looks up.

Our eyes meet.

He straightens, jabs the tip of the shovel into the ground and rests his hands on top, sending me a curious, albeit tired, look.

"Well hey there," I say as I approach, feeling the gaze of the other men on my back.

"Hey," he responds, his eyes flicking to the crew.

"What you doing?"

"Digging a hole."

"I can see that. Why?"

"Work."

"You got a job?"

"Temporarily. I offered to help in any way I can for some cash."

"You just walked up to these guys and asked for a job?"

"Yep."

I glance back at the crew, at the glowering faces pointed in our direction. I can't tell if they are angry that I am interrupting their hard-working coworker or concerned for my safety—considering who it is that I am speaking to.

I refocus on Rhett.

"Good for you," I say, admiring his grit.

He doesn't respond, just stares at me. It drives me crazy when he does this.

"Have you…" I step closer, lowering my voice, "found out anything new about who paid Jesse to deliver the letters?"

He begins pushing the dirt around with the tip of his shovel. "No."

"Well, I have and I wanted to spitball something with you…"

"Yeah?" His brow cocks.

"Yeah. Yesterday I found out who Dr. Harris Taylor's redheaded spying neighbor is. Her name is Gloria Lopez. Rumor is she's an illegal immigrant, been here for about three years. No one really seems to know her. Doesn't go out much."

"How do you know this?"

"I called my hairdresser—otherwise known as the town gossip."

He nods. "So Gloria owns the house?"

"No. The police chief's brother, Allen Reed, owns it. I know him."

"The *chief's* brother?"

"Yep. I know him."

"How?"

"Well, I don't *know him* know him, but he was interviewed for the paper once. He owns a small stocks and bonds company and gave an interview about the economy, I think. I don't know, I didn't read it. Anyway, he's got an apartment in New York where he stays most of the time. I guess she stays here, alone."

"Are they married?"

"Engaged—she's his fiancée. He's divorced. His ex-wife and kids live in New York."

"So she's a bored, nosy neighbor."

"Maybe, maybe something more. Okay, so I also found out who owns the abandoned house at the end of the street. It's a real estate company based in Burlington. They bought some homes in the area when prices were low. Couldn't sell that particular home, and it's just sitting there now."

"How did you get this information?"

"Called in a favor from my old source from the newspaper."

"Hitting the streets again, huh?"

"I told you I missed it."

"Well nice work. What did you want to spitball with me?"

"I was thinking... The Hideout seems to be a pretty obvious place to look for a missing person, right? You said it yourself that locals know about it."

"Yeah..."

"Well then, why haven't the cops checked it? How has Jesse not been found in this teeny-tiny town?"

Rhett tosses a mound of dirt onto a pile. "Where are you going with this?"

"Detective Stroud is a local—he was born and raised here. He is lead investigator on Jesse's missing person case... why wouldn't *he* think to check the caves? Have you ever thought about that? Or, at the very least, talk to someone who would have suggested he look there. *Or* did he already and isn't telling anyone? Could he be in some sort of alliance with Jesse? Think about it... Stroud is tied to everything. He worked my mom's case, was there at the scene—so he would know about the clocks and necklace—and he was the one who put you in jail. And now he's working the case of the missing teen who delivered my dead mother's necklace to my front door. What are those odds?"

"I've thought about all this, too. But if you're right, that Stroud is the killer and the guy who framed me, this is one thing

I can't wrap my head around: what does he have to gain by all this now? The letters, the necklace. He got away with it—twenty years ago at that. Why bring it all up again? Think about that."

I exhale, frustrated. I should have known Rhett would find the hole in my theory, the same one that kept me up last night. No matter how I twist it, I cannot think of a single reason Stroud would reignite a twenty-year-old case that he got away with.

I notice then that Rhett is wearing the same clothes he'd purchased from the big box store days earlier.

"Have you got a place to stay?" I ask.

He nods to the sky. "Under the stars."

"You're sleeping on the street?"

"That's dramatic."

"So is being homeless."

"Could be worse. Trust me."

I wonder if this is the mentality Rhett will carry for the rest of his life now. Accepting life on the streets and living in poverty, yet grateful, because, hey, it could always be worse.

What a way to live.

I fist my hands on my hips. "What time do you get off here?"

"I work until they make me leave."

I glance over my shoulder. "Looks like they're packing up."

"Likely so."

"Have you been back to Deep Shadows? To the abandoned house?"

"Not yet."

"Let's go back tonight. Figure out who Dr. Harris Taylor is meeting in the middle of the night. Let's see if it's Detective Stroud," I say. "Finish your hole digging and I'll come back after the sun sets. And afterward, we'll swing by the store and you can get another outfit with all this money you're making now."

He doesn't laugh at the joke—but he also doesn't argue.

"I'll be back in an hour."

Rhett stabs his shovel into the ground. "Sylvia..."

I bite my tongue, keep walking away before he can protest—because I have already decided I am going back to that damn house. And Rhett is going with me, whether he likes it or not.

TWENTY-SEVEN
MARJORIE

Travis came back again today. This is the sixth time he's visited in the last month. The sixth time in fourteen years. He heard about Anna's death through the news. I'm sorry, he'd said, unable to look me in the eye. I wanted to slap him across the face. Travis doesn't care about the loss of one of his daughters. Not like I do, anyway. He'd never even met her.

He brought me a gift today. A pair of gold earrings. Stolen, I'm sure. Or fake. He handed them to me in a brown paper sack. He didn't say a word, just gave them to me. It was awkward and weird. I don't know why he did this other than that he's very desperate for my help. My financial help, to be clear. Which, now that I think about it, confirms that the earrings were stolen and also are fake. Otherwise, he would have sold them.

I still have the jewelry he gave me when were dating. Cheap and inexpensive, but I loved them. Now, I hate them.

He's different now, a totally different person than we were together so many years ago. Hardened. I know he's spent time in prison, but I don't think he knows I know that. He doesn't know that I've kept up on him, even after he left town—left me.

His latest arrest was for possession with intent to sell. I think it was his fourth arrest.

Every visit is the same. He tells me he's matured and that he's learned from his mistake—if you call abandoning a pregnant woman a "mistake." But then he asks for money. Every damn time. He thinks Gerald is giving me money. I don't know why. He couldn't be more wrong.

My father hasn't even called since Anna died. Scratch that, he hasn't called since before that. Since Mom died in the house fire. Do you want to know what's crazy about that? I don't care. I don't care that he hasn't called, just like I didn't care when I found out my mother burned to death. There was nothing. No emotion. None whatsoever. In fact, I don't care so much, that I don't even care to write about it.

I don't care about anything now that Anna is gone.

Today, I gave Travis all the cash I had on me—about seventy dollars—and told him that was the last time I was going to give him anything. I've given him about three hundred dollars since he started coming around again. Today he asked for more. Said he knew I had more money hidden somewhere. I asked him what he needed it for, and what he was spending it on. He beat around the bush and didn't give me a straight answer. Luckily, the school bus pulled up to the curb before it got too heated, and he ran out the back door before he was forced to interact with his one remaining daughter.

On the outside, Travis and I are very different. But on the inside we are very similar. Perhaps this is why I was drawn to him in the first place.

Travis doesn't know. He knows the stuff my dad did to me, but he doesn't know that I have my own similar struggles. Sometimes I think it's for the best that he doesn't know. Sometimes I wonder if the girls would have been better off with him. Sometimes, I wonder if I would have been better off without the girls.

After he left, I got drunk.

I am drinking more than I ever have before—way too much. I know this. But it is another thing that I can't bring myself to care enough about to do something about it.

I have lost a child. I have held a dead child's body in my arms. I have purchased one of those tiny caskets. I have had a funeral for a child. I have buried a child. Drinking is how I cope. It's the only thing that numbs the feeling of sick inside my body.

I hate Sylvia. I hate that Anna died and she lived. I can't hide it anymore. I know she knows. She's always known that Anna was my favorite.

Something isn't right with her since Anna died. She's withdrawn, which I'd be lying if I said bothered me. She stays in her room all the time. Hardly ever comes out. When she does, we don't speak.

Sometimes, late at night, I sneak in to check on her. Often, I find her standing next to the window just staring out of it. Staring at nothing. It's weird.

Last week, she got into a fight at school. I guess the kids are starting to pick on her.

I can't handle all this.

I'm considering moving. Leaving Texas and moving far away. Somewhere Travis can't follow and take my money. Somewhere Sylvia could start over. Somewhere I could start over. I think about this a lot—starting over. Sometimes I think about becoming someone else. Pretending I am someone else entirely. Pretending that I never even had Anna.

TWENTY-EIGHT
SYLVIA

Rhett is still digging in dirt when I return at dusk. The lot is vacant now, aside from two backhoes backlit by the setting sun. The other construction workers are gone, either at the bar or home with their families.

Not Rhett. He is all alone, same shovel in hand, same sweat-stained T-shirt, same grit in his eyes, except now, he's twenty feet further down the tunnel. The man has not stopped digging since I left him hours earlier.

My respect and admiration for the man triples with each new meeting.

He looks up as I park.

"Time for a break," I call, climbing out.

He squints, looks around as if realizing, for the first time, that he is all alone. I wonder if he has actually been enjoying the work. Being outside, by himself. Being a productive member of society again.

He stabs the shovel in the dirt and dusts off his hands as I stride across the dirt.

"Ready to go sleuthing?" I ask, jovially.

"You changed."

I glance down at the black leather jacket I'd put over an old Fleetwood Mac tee, my skinny jeans, and boots.

"Just dressing the part," I wink, pleased he noticed.

We fall into step together, my legs working double-time to keep up with his long strides.

I am acutely aware of the line of trucks at the liquor store and how, although their windows are darkened by shadows, the people inside the vehicles are staring at us. Rhett is aware of this too, and has tilted his chin downward, as if this would do anything to mask his identity. His height and weight alone are enough to make him stand out in a crowd.

Chin up, shoulders back, Sylvia.

I slide behind the steering wheel as Rhett ducks into the passenger seat, plucking the grease-stained paper bag from the floorboard.

"What's this?"

"Food," I say, "eat."

"Sylvia," he releases an exasperated breath. "I'm not a stray dog. I'm getting along just fine."

"I know—I have no doubt about it. But I got you food regardless, so instead of making a big deal out of it, why don't you just eat it." I shove the Jeep into reverse and send the line of liquor-store trucks a glare before pulling onto the road.

Rhett has devoured his bacon cheeseburger and is polishing off the last fry when we pull into Deep Shadows.

It's dark enough outside for the streetlights to click on. The homes are illuminated, both inside and out. It is dinnertime, and I imagine the residents tucked behind long dining tables, pretending to enjoy each other's company while avoiding eye contact and sipping red wine—aside from the redheaded neighbor, Gloria, of course, who is probably staring out her window.

This time, I zip along the narrow, windy road. I don't want to be seen. Two visits in one week would raise suspicion.

I am grateful that the old man who lives next to the abandoned house isn't outside tending to his garden, like last time. In fact, the home is dark, not a single light on.

I click off my headlights and pull into the cracked driveway.

Rhett and I see it at the exact same time—a shadow darting past the front windows. Before I can turn off the engine, Rhett is out of the truck and sprinting to the back of the house.

"Dammit!" I shove the keys into my pocket and jump out. After checking over my shoulder, I jog to the front door. It's locked.

I look in the windows, expecting to see Rhett confronting someone, but there is nothing—no movement, no sound.

I jog around the side of the house, my skin tingling with adrenaline, my senses working in overdrive as I strain to hear any noise or see any movement in my peripheral vision. I leap onto the back porch, careful to avoid the rotted planks of wood. The back door is standing wide open. But, still, it is silent. I squint into the surrounding trees, thinking maybe Rhett has chased whoever was inside into the woods.

My heart starts to pound. The lack of noise is unnerving.

I tentatively step over the threshold, and pause to allow my eyes to adjust to the darkness. What remains of daylight pitifully seeps through smeared, cracked windows, allowing just enough illumination to discern shapes and objects in the rooms.

I step deeper into what appears to be a laundry room. A washer, dryer, a sink, and countertop, all covered in a thin layer of dust. Cobwebs hang from the ceiling; brown leaves cover a stained tiled floor. Dead insects are everywhere.

My pulse is roaring as I step into the kitchen.

Like a wolf hovering over its prey, Rhett is towering over a small, boney woman, balled into a corner. Streaks of blood run down his cheek—four long marks as if he has been clawed by a tiger. His fists are clenched, his chest heaving. The woman's eyes are wild with fear, a deep rasp rattling her lungs as she inhales and exhales.

She clawed him, and based on the amount of blood, the wounds are deep and will likely scar.

The woman appears to be middle-aged, late forties or early fifties, and is as skinny as a toothpick. Her knees, bent and pulled up to her chest, look like two broken candle sticks. Tattoos cover almost every inch of her skin. Long, frizzed dreadlocks fall around her shoulders. A dozen necklaces hang around her neck and about the same number of bracelets teeter on her bird-like wrists. She is wearing multiple layers of clothing: a cardigan, a vest over a long patch-style dress. No shoes. A backpack, drink, and food wrapper are on the floor not far from her.

She is attractive, I realize, despite the sunken-in sharp angles of her face. Feline-like blue eyes and a round sultry mouth, against fair skin, give her an ethereal look. No makeup, no frills, just a natural beauty. Like a fairy, or some exotic alien on the cover of a paranormal monster romance.

"Okay," I lift my palms in a show of surrender, a feeble attempt to ease the tension. "Everybody calm down."

The woman doesn't take her eyes off Rhett. I understand how she feels. I remember the feeling I got when I first saw him looming over my garden. He can be a terrifying presence, especially with blood dripping down his neck.

I slowly step forward, place my hand on Rhett's arm. "Everything's okay. Let's just all calm down." After a warning squeeze to Rhett's bicep, I step in front of him, between him and the woman. "My name is Sylvia Stone."

The woman finally takes her eyes off Rhett.

"Crystal," she snaps out, "Crystal Cheri."

It's a painfully obvious fake name, but I don't press.

"Crystal. Nice to meet you. I apologize for my friend here. He needs to work on his manners."

I shoot Rhett a look, but he isn't paying me any attention. Instead, he's studying the woman with such intensity that I wonder if he knows her.

"We'd like to ask you some questions, if that's okay."

"I'm sorry," she barks over my shoulder, referring to clawing Rhett's face. "You scared me—I'm sorry. A—are you guys cops?"

"No. Is this your house?" I ask, knowing that it isn't, but not quite sure how to begin the questioning.

"No," Crystal responds, relaxing a bit. She picks up a flashlight laying haphazardly on the floor next to her, and clicks it on. A dim orange light reflects off the yellow-stained wall and illuminates the room. Dark shadows slash across her face giving her a ghostly appearance.

"I'm just..." She shifts into a cross-legged position and another tattoo reveals itself, this of a wolf howling on her inner thigh. "Staying here for a little while."

She's homeless, like Rhett.

"Are you from here?" I ask.

"No. From Tennessee. Just traveling through." She nods to the camera on the floor, next to her bag. It is an expensive-looking camera and I wonder if she stole it. "I'm a photographer. Landscapes, mostly. I travel through here every year taking pictures of the fall foliage. And then sell them online."

Her attention has shifted onto Rhett again, but this time, her consideration is different. Curious rather than fearful. I remember this feeling also. After the surprise of the man wears off, there is the sudden acknowledgement of: *OMG, this man is sexy.*

I don't like the way she's looking at him.

"How long have you been here?" Rhett speaks.

"A while."

"I heard that someone saw you in here and you ran, is that right?"

"The *missing* guy, you mean?" She snorts.

"Yes. His name is Jesse Taylor."

She nods. "His pictures are tacked up all over the telephone poles. He's come in here a few times. Only saw me once, though. And yes, I ran. We never spoke."

"Have you seen anyone else?"

Crystal shifts, looks away.

"His dad, maybe?" I press. "Older man, brown hair."

She refuses eye contact. I glance at Rhett, who has also picked up on the instant demeanor shift as well.

"Jesse Taylor's dad. You've seen him, haven't you?" Rhett asks.

"Listen," she says, grabbing the flashlight from the floor and turning the room into a discotheque of light as she repositions it next to her. "I don't want to be involved in this. I'll pack my bag and be on my way. Please don't call the police. I'm just passing through. I'll be gone in an hour if you guys will just let me be. I don't mean any harm..." Looking at Rhett's bleeding cheek with remorse, she repeats, "I'm sorry. I thought you were going to attack me. I didn't mean—"

"I know you didn't." There is empathy in Rhett's tone. I notice he is looking at her differently now, too, like he understands her.

Jealousy twists in my gut. He's attracted to her. Of course he is. She is prettier than me. She is skinnier, smaller than I am. She's eccentric and interesting. Yes, I assume that's the kind of woman Rhett likes. Not a boring tabby cat like myself.

"When was the last time you saw Jesse?" he asks.

"It's been a while."

Could it have been Crystal who approached him? For some reason, I can't see it. And if so, she is so short and skinny that no matter how high Jesse was when he was approached, he would have remembered that the person was small in stature.

"And what about his dad?" Rhett asks. "When was the last time you saw him?"

A scowl squeezes her face. She looks over her shoulder, out the window, as if looking for someone.

"Please," I say. "Anything you could tell us would help."

Crystal refocuses on me, hesitates. "Let's just say around one o'clock in the morning... things get real interesting around here."

"What do you mean?" I ask.

She shifts onto her knees and begins gathering her things. She's done with this conservation, and with us.

"What do you mean?" I ask again. "What happens—"

"One a.m.," Rhett interrupts, "thank you."

Crystal nods, continues packing.

I frown at Rhett's dismissal of me.

He jerks his chin to the door—*let's go*—and exits the room.

I flicker another glance at Crystal. I don't like her, and I don't like this situation. I feel like she's keeping something from us.

Rhett calls my name from the front door, his deep voice echoing through the vacant house.

I don't move.

"What aren't you telling us?" I ask.

"Nothing." Crystal zips up her pack and hurries past me. "I have nothing more to say to you."

"Wait."

"Sylvia, let's go!" Rhett calls again.

I chase Crystal out the back door. Rhett chases after me, grabs my arm.

"Let me go!" I swat him away and step out the back door.

But like a ghost, she's gone.

TWENTY-NINE

SYLVIA

"What was that about?" Rhett snaps, pulling me around the side of the house. The streaks of blood have dried down his cheek and neck, but the skin is now disgustingly swollen and puffy. My response catches in my throat as we step directly into the blinding glare of two headlights. We freeze like deer—literally—caught in headlights.

Rhett's grip tightens around my bicep.

I shield my eyes from the light. The truck door squeaks open. A man steps out, his dark silhouette stretching across the driveway. Tall and lanky, his hand is resting on the gun on his hip.

I recognize the large spotlights on the top of the truck and the gait of the man as he strides toward us.

Detective Stroud.

What is *he* doing here? Did someone report us lurking outside the abandoned house? If so, surely a beat-cop would have responded. Not a detective.

I frown, look up at Rhett and then cringe at the angry red claw marks running down his cheek.

Oh God, this does not look good.

Stroud is advancing quickly, as if he considers us a flight risk. There's no mistaking the vile hatred etched on both men's faces. They look like they are about to pummel each other. And then it hits me: This is the first time Rhett has come face to face with the lead detective who accused him of killing my mother twenty years ago.

Shit.

My adrenaline spikes, my body preparing for the inevitable fist fight, one that would undoubtedly end in puddles of blood and multiple broken bones. But Rhett can't get in a fight, I remind myself. He'll go back to jail for life—both he and Stroud know this.

"Don't say a word," I whisper-hiss to Rhett. "Let me handle this."

I jerk my arm out of Rhett's hold and take a step forward, ready to launch myself into the altercation if needed. The spark of protectiveness surprises me. I'm protective of Rhett, of my partner in this crazy story of mine.

"Detective Stroud," I say, like a suspect in a cheesy cop movie.

Stroud doesn't look at me. He's studying the scratches on Rhett's cheek. They are very obviously nail marks from a woman, and I can only assume that the detective thinks they are from me, trying to defend myself from something Rhett did—or was trying to do—to me.

"What's going on here?" Stroud barks.

"He fell," I say, before Rhett can respond.

"Fell, huh? Into a barbed-wired fence? What are you two doing out here?"

I shrug. "Just out for a drive."

"Visiting Mrs. Taylor again, are you?"

I blink. "How do you know about that?"

"Doesn't matter."

I stutter. "I, ah, just had a few questions for her. I felt it was important that she knew that I saw her son at my house, that we think he delivered the letters."

"Why did you feel like that was your job to do that?"

I realize then that Stroud's beef is with me, not Rhett. My stomach dips with nerves. Perhaps he's been patrolling the neighborhood since my visit to the Taylors'.

He continues, "She was extremely upset by your visit, by your implication that her son could have, or is, somehow involved in your mother's case from twenty years ago."

Rhett is no longer staring at the detective, instead, he is scanning the woods. For what? Who? Crystal?

"Miss Stone, I'm going to have to ask you to leave Janet Taylor alone and I strongly suggest you stay out of this case. We're working on it."

I fist my hands on my hips feeling a blow of impatience. "Are you? Really? Have you even found Jesse yet? Have you found who delivered those creepy letters to my house? The person who *threatened* me? What about the half-fingerprint on the pendant? Come on, Detective, shouldn't you be—"

"What can we do for you, Stroud?" Rhett cuts in, his voice cold as ice.

"This house is private property," the detective says. "You're trespassing."

"We were just leaving."

"Why did you come here in the first place?" he asks.

"We were just leaving."

"Leave *now*, then."

"My pleasure," I mumble, grabbing Rhett's arm and pulling him past Stroud as they glower at each other like two boxers in a ring.

"Don't you dare turn around," I hiss to Rhett, dragging him down the driveway. "Get in." I shove Rhett into the Jeep, then quickly jump in, start the engine and reverse out of the lot.

"What the hell was that?" I snap, watching Stroud's silhouette fade in my rearview mirror. "You know you can't get in a fight with him. If I hadn't been there, you two would have bashed each other's faces in and you'd be back in jail. I could see it in your eyes."

Instead of answering my question, he asks his own. "What were you asking Crystal about when she ran out? Why did you chase her?"

"Answer my question first. There's more between you and Stroud than just the obvious connection to the trial." I scowl as we pass the Taylors' home. Bitch.

"Stroud's a piece of shit."

"We've established that. Why?"

I blow past the gate and turn onto the gravel road that leads into town. Night has fallen. A few stars are beginning to twinkle around the top of the moon peeking out from the tree-tops. Cold air whips through the cab of the Jeep.

"Stroud and I went to high school together," Rhett says.

"Are you guys the same age?" Keeping one hand on the wheel, I open the console with the other and pull out a pack of baby wipes.

Rhett frowns.

"Clean yourself up, you look like Freddy Krueger."

He yanks a wipe from the pack, passively taps his cheek—nowhere close to the wound—then tosses it out the window.

I shake my head. "Keep going about you and Stroud."

"I'm one year younger than he is," he says. "He was a bully in high school. The cliché jock who fed his ego by bullying kids who couldn't fend for themselves." He glances over his shoulder, checking to see if the detective is following us. "One day, I was leaving school and I saw him and his buddies picking on this nerdy kid that everyone made fun of. They were taking his lunch, dumping everything out of his backpack. Just being idiots."

I shake my head. I despise bullies.

"The kid's name was Andy. He was notoriously poor, the smelly kid in class. He wore shoes covered in duct tape, relied on the summer lunch program to eat. I think I only saw him wear three outfits the entire time he went to high school. He was a kid to a single mother who I think was addicted to drugs."

"And what happened?"

"I snapped. Ran up and kicked their asses. Broke Stroud's nose and gave him a black eye in front of all his buddies."

"No kidding?"

"That's not all. His dad showed up at my house later that night, drunk, wearing one of those old Bud Lite *I Love You, Man,* T-shirts. You know, from the '90s commercials?"

"Yeah, I remember."

"Yeah, one of those. I don't know why I remember that. Anyway, he confronts my dad. They get into a fistfight, right there on our front porch. Two grown men going at it like idiotic teenagers."

"You're *joking.*"

"Nope. One of the neighbors called the cops. It was a whole ordeal. I was so embarrassed—even though I'd started it all."

"No, you didn't. You defended an innocent child—don't blame yourself."

"There's the pot calling the kettle black."

I roll my eyes. "My testimony is what got you locked up, so yes, I blame myself and always will. Anyway, then what happened?"

"The cops showed up, as did everyone in the neighborhood. Nobody pressed charges because it was equally everyone's fault at that point. The entire town knew about it within hours. It was the gossip for weeks. People took sides. The jock versus the bad boy. Jock won. After that, I became the outcast, which was fine, and Stroud went on to join the police force and eventually become a detective."

"And you've carried bad blood for each other ever since."

Rhett nods. "And then when everything with your mom went down a decade later, the asshole jumped at the chance to convince everyone that it was me who killed your mother."

I frown, chew my lower lip. "Okay, so I can see why he was probably biased during the investigation, but do you think he framed you? Do you really think he did it?"

Rhett doesn't respond.

"If so," I continue, "you can't kill a *detective*, Rhett. My God, there is no way you'd get out of that one."

"I know that, Sylvia. And I don't know if it was him who framed me. Yes, we hate each other, but our fight was in tenth grade. Why wait for revenge until I was twenty-two? We've been through this; it doesn't add up. He has nothing to gain by doing all this now."

"Maybe he was jealous that you grew up and made something of yourself? Started your own business. Cohen Carpentry."

Rhett snorts. "I was on the brink of bankruptcy, Sylvia. I was nothing to be jealous of. He was the big, bad cop who was just promoted to detective. Hell, he made more money than I did."

"Okay, then maybe he felt like the opportunity was finally there... he was a detective and you were a sitting duck. I've thought about this a lot, Rhett—Stroud seems to link to everything, but I couldn't find a motive. But now, this, revenge: he wants to get back at you."

Rhett ponders this a moment, then shakes his head. "I really don't think the guy would hold a grudge for that long. I mean we'd seen each other in town over the years, in bars. There were plenty of opportunities for him to bring it back up —he didn't. And by the way, why the hell would he kill your mother? There is *no way* he was that desperate to get back at me."

My brow cocks. "Maybe he knew who actually did it, and

was protecting whoever that was. Maybe he and this person were in it together, and framed you."

"That's a thought. A crazy longshot, but a thought."

I nod, feeling like I was onto something. "We need to figure out who Stroud's close friends are. His girlfriends, past and present. I'm pretty sure he's divorced. I'll see what I can dig up."

"Watch yourself, Sylvia. The deeper you dig the more eyes are going to be on you."

"I don't care, Rhett. Stroud is the one constant through all this. We have to exhaust that angle."

"This isn't *Crest County Newspaper*, Sylvia. You aren't interviewing the winner of the annual hotdog eating contest."

"It's apple around here."

"Right. Now tell me why you freaked out on Crystal."

"She's a liar. I can tell. She's not telling us something."

"Of course she's a liar, but she gave us information."

"I'm going to research her."

"It's a fake name."

"I know, but maybe..." I drag in a deep inhale. "I need to go through my file again."

"What file?"

"I have a folder of everything about my mother's case, past and present. I've been going through everything again, feeling like there's something that will help us figure out what's going on now."

"You have everything from the trial?"

"Yeah, copies."

I hang a left onto Main Street and I realize I'm not sure where I'm going. Rhett is homeless, and therefore has nowhere to go.

I slow below the speed limit, buying time while I try to decide what to do.

Rhett makes the decision for me.

"We've got five hours to kill..." he says.

"Five hours until what?"

"One o'clock." He nods to the clock. "Crystal told us things get, quote, real interesting here around one o'clock in the morning."

In the aftermath of Stroud's surprise appearance, I'd forgotten she'd said that. I look at the clock—7:47 p.m.

"Well..." I glance at Rhett, my mind racing with all the things we can do. "You hungry?"

"Yeah. Pull in here real quick."

I flick on the turn signal and pull into a small convenience store.

Rhett jumps out, while I stay behind the wheel.

Through finger-smudged windows fogged with condensation, I watch as Rhett moves quickly through the store, piling items into his arms. Bread, lunch meat, a few bottles of water. Four packs of beef jerky—*four*. What is it with men and beef jerky? The man has little to no money to his name, yet will splurge on an eight-dollar bag of dehydrated animal flesh.

He pays, and I am acutely aware of the sneaked glances from under the cashier's false eyelashes.

Rhett slides back into the Jeep and I reverse out of the parking lot.

"Well, looks like you're all set, but I'm still hungry, so we'll camp out at my house until one. Okay?"

He nods, ripping into his loot.

Rhett munches on jerky the remainder of the ride, devouring two packs by the time we get to my house. Once inside, I remind him where the spare bedroom is if he should want to take a nap before we go. He declines.

Rhett lingers in the living room, watching the news that I clicked on as we passed by, as I put away his convenience-store food in the kitchen. It is all strangely not awkward. That's the thing about Rhett. Once you get to know him, the awkwardness quickly vanishes because you realize that he will simply say what's on his mind, about whatever situation you are in with him. The guy will literally ask you to leave the room if he doesn't want you in it. I find it very refreshing.

"Want some wine?" I call out, pulling down a bottle from the cabinet.

"No, thanks."

I startle at the deep voice behind me and spin around, nearly dropping the bottle in my hand. "Jesus. You scared me." I frown. "What?"

"I'd like to see this evidence folder you talked about in the car."

"The what?"

"You said you have a folder on your mom's case."

Ah...

I slide the bottle onto the counter.

Rhett Cohen didn't come to my house to spend time with me before our next adventure. Rhett Cohen didn't come to my house because he is mildly interested in me.

He just wanted to see Marjorie's Death Folder.

And I am so, *so* stupid.

THIRTY
SYLVIA

"Wake up."

My eyes flutter open at the sound of Rhett's voice.

"It's time to go, Sylvia."

Like a startled puppy, I frantically right myself on the couch, my wine-muddled brain taking its sweet time to regain consciousness.

I fell asleep. Despite promising myself I wouldn't, I freaking fell asleep.

Rhett is hovering over me, his face in blurred focus. He is a vision, bright, alert, fresh as a daisy—aside from the jagged claw marks on his cheek.

"I'm—I fell asleep." I stutter, stating the obvious.

I'm embarrassed. How much wine did I drink? The last thing I remember is topping off my third glass, pretending to watch the news while secretly watching Rhett pore over my mother's death folder.

"What time is it?" I turn my cheek in fear of rancid morning breath.

"It's midnight. I figure we could go to the house now and find a spot to just sit and watch for a while."

"Okay. That sounds good." I push myself off the couch, a woozy wave sweeping through my body. My head feels like it's caught in a blender. I chide myself for drinking. "Give me just one second."

I hurry to the bathroom, check my reflection. I look like a heroin addict. My eyes are red, swollen, and rimmed black from the mascara I'd applied hours earlier. My hair is limp and stringy. One strand is stuck to the side of my mouth where I must have drooled while I slept.

I grab a box of wipes from under the counter and remove the mascara streaks from my face. I quickly brush my teeth, my hair, and pull myself together. After a few squirts of body spray, I grab a sweatshirt from the hamper and yank it over my T-shirt. I don't need to walk outside to confirm that the temperature has dropped with the night. The chill in the house is enough.

Rhett is pacing by the bathroom door when I step out.

"Ready?"

"Yes."

We drive to Deep Shadows in silence, me swearing off a headache, Rhett tense as an iron rod. The cab is thick with anticipation as we chase down our first real clue.

Rhett reaches over and clicks off my headlights as I drive past the iron gates, punctuating the secrecy of this clandestine op.

Just me and my ex-con... Nothing to see here.

I slow while my vision adjusts to the darkness. Wisps of clouds have moved in while I slept, long and thin, stretching across the moon.

The Taylor home is completely black—not a single light on.

"Where do you want me to park?" I ask.

"There's a shed behind the abandoned house. Park behind it."

"How do you know that?"

"I saw it earlier."

Slowly, I inch into the driveway at the end of the cul-de-sac, careful not to wake the old man next door.

"I can't see the shed."

"Keep going." Rhett grabs the wheel, guiding the Jeep as we round the back of the house.

Sure enough, an outline of a small structure sits a few feet from the edge of the backyard. Luckily, my compact Jeep hides easily behind it.

I turn off the ignition. The night is still and silent. Not even a whisper of a breeze through the copse of oaks around us.

Rhett climbs out. "We need to get a clear view of the house while we wait."

I follow suit, pocketing the keys and climbing out of the Jeep.

My eyes sweep the surrounding woods, one black mass in the dark night. I glance up at the moon, then at the old, decrepit house ahead of us. Despite the affluence of the neighborhood, this lot is creepy, like a scene in a horror film. I can *feel* something in the air, an energy that sends a chill up my spine.

Staying low, we skirt the tree line on the edge of the property. Rhett crouches behind two thick trees, fused together at the base, parallel to the side of the house. The spot provides a clear view of the front and back porch.

We settle in and wait.

And wait.

And wait.

My knees ache, my quads burn, my back hurts. My nose is ice cold and has started running, demanding my full focus to keep from sniffing every three seconds. I hate people who sniff all the time.

We have been squatting for almost an hour, me shifting my weight every few seconds, heaving annoyed, impatient breaths, while Rhett hasn't moved a muscle. He's bigger than I am and must be in pain, but he doesn't show it.

I'm on the brink of announcing that I need to stand and stretch my legs when a twig pops somewhere in the distance.

My pulse kickstarts with a heavy *thump*.

Rhett puts his hand on my knee, a nonverbal reminder to stay still and quiet.

Seconds later, a dark silhouette emerges from the woods opposite of our hiding spot. Long, lean legs lumber quickly across the yard. The figure disappears through the back door and into the abandoned house.

"Definitely not Crystal, right?" I whisper.

"Right, too tall."

"Okay... What now? Do we go in?" I start to stand.

"Wait," he hisses, grabbing the hem of my shirt and pulling me back to the ground. He's squinting into the woods where the person emerged moments earlier.

"What do you see?" I ask.

Before he can answer, another silhouette steps out of the shadows, this one smaller, with quick, nimble steps. A woman.

She disappears into the same door as the man before her.

Rhett and I watch the house, frozen in place, ears perked, eyes scanning the windows for any movement.

Five minutes pass.

Ten.

I have no idea what Rhett is waiting for.

Finally—

"I'm going to go in," he says.

"Okay—"

"You're staying here."

"What? No, I—"

"You're staying here, Sylvia. It's not safe. If you hear anything or get scared for any reason, run to the Jeep and get out of here, okay? Leave me; just get out."

"No way. I'm going with you."

"No, you're *not*—and I'm not doing this with you right now."

"This is just as much my business as it is yours," I hiss as Rhett stands and steps around the tree trunk.

"Rhett!"

But he is gone, jogging silently across the yard to the house.

I am furious. How dare he cast me aside like this? We wouldn't even be here if not for *my* Jeep. Who is he to tell me to "stay"?

I surge to a standing position and peer around the trunk.

A minute passes, two.

"Screw this."

Staying in a crouch, I jog across the yard, leap into the shadows and press my back against the slatted side of the house. I exhale, listen.

Nothing.

Slowly, I creep along the shadows until I reach the back door. Heart pounding, I push it open and step over the threshold.

Only hours earlier I stood in this exact spot, while Rhett pinned Crystal Cheri to the corner of the kitchen.

The house appears to be silent and I wonder if whoever snuck in has already left and somehow we'd missed it. Maybe it was nothing more than a quick drug deal?

My pulse thrums as I step through the kitchen, using the moonlight to illuminate my way.

I pause under the arched entry to the hall.

Just then, a faint *thud* sounds from upstairs. Another, then another.

My knees are shaking as I reach the staircase. One step, two, my eyes bulge from their sockets trying to see through the darkness.

Once I reach the second-floor landing I stop, listen, and hear it again. Shuffles, thuds from a room at the end of the hall.

I take a step but am halted by a hand clasping my arm. Before I can scream, another hand covers my mouth.

"I told you to stay outside," Rhett hisses in my ear.

I'm too startled to speak.

"*Dammit*, Sylvia. I told you to stay outside."

He releases me. I spin around. Though his face is concealed by shadows there is no mistaking the anger in his eyes.

"I *told* you—"

"I'm sorry," I whisper.

He shakes his head. "Just stay behind me."

I nod, feeling like a child after being scolded..

We descend the hallway, littered with leaves, empty beer cans, wads of newspaper—a shoe, a shirt, a belt... A trail of clothes.

The noises grow louder from the last room on the left. More thuds, shuffling, heavy breathing.

My heartbeat is a drum in my chest. *Boom, boom, boom.*

I am wholly unprepared for what I see when we approach the room.

Moonlight streams through open windows, pooling onto a dirty, splintered hardwood floor.

A woman is naked, on hands and knees in the middle of the floor. Grunting and groaning like an ape, a man holding her long, red hair, taking her from behind.

The room is rank with the sweet, sticky smell of sweat and pheromones.

Rhett grabs me, says something, but I don't move. I can't. I faintly hear his footsteps fade, but I am frozen in place, gaping at the sex scene ahead of me.

Just then, the woman gasps and begins jerking as I realize she is having an orgasm. The man groans as he comes with her.

My knees weaken. My pulse hammers between my legs. My privates are wet, swollen and throbbing. I stumble backward, slamming into the door frame. The woman's face turns toward me.

"Harris," she hisses.

Holy shit. The masked man is Dr. Harris Taylor, Jesse's father.

And then it hits me—the long, red hair. The woman, Harris's mistress, is their neighbor, Gloria. The same woman who watches from the windows. Dr. Harris and his neighbor are having an affair.

I am suddenly yanked backward with such force that my teeth chatter.

"Run!" Rhett hisses in my ear.

We sprint down the hallway, down the stairs, through the kitchen and laundry room, and burst out the back door. I trip down the steps, into Rhett's arms. He steadies me back into place, and we stumble through the darkness to the Jeep.

My heart feels like it is about to burst out of my chest as I start the engine.

"Go, go, go, go."

I slam the gas, fishtailing on loose dirt before straightening again. Dr. Taylor bursts out the front door, clothes haphazardly strewn over his body.

"What the *hell* were you doing?" Rhett yells at me—actually *yells* at me—as I watch Harris's silhouette fade in the rearview mirror. "I told you to stay right behind me! I thought you followed me out!"

"I'm sorry!" I yell back, tears stinging my eyes. He is so mad at me.

"Dammit, Sylvia." Rhett scrubs his hands over his face. "I told you to stay outside. There's no question they saw you."

Rage mixes with the embarrassment. "Listen, I'm sorry, alright? You can't just leave me out in the damn woods in the middle of the night."

"I should have never..." he sneers between grinding teeth.

"You should have never what?"

"I should have never allowed you to be a part of this."

"*Allowed* me? Are you serious?" The Jeep squeals around a corner. "I'm already part of it. Someone *threatened* me—"

"Exactly! And now, the town's beloved doctor just saw you see him banging his neighbor. If Harris is involved with the letters and what happened with your mom, he now has even more reason to—"

"To what?"

Rhett roars with frustration. "Ah, fuck it."

I click on the turn signal to take the road that leads to my house.

"No," he snaps. "Keep going."

I swerve back onto the road. "Where?"

"Take me back to the construction site."

"What?" My stomach drops to my feet.

"Take me to the damn construction site."

The sting of rejection feels like I have been gutted.

I feel sick as I drive to the construction site, reminded of how I felt in high school—and also in my own home. Wanting so badly for someone—anyone—to like me. For my mother to tell me she loved me, for my schoolmates to simply notice me. But no one cared about me. Hell, I wasn't even good enough to be formally rejected.

Just dismissed.

By the time I pull up to the curb in front of the construction site I am fighting tears.

"I'm sorry," I say again, my voice quivering.

"It's fine, Sylvia," Rhett mutters as he climbs out of the Jeep.

He turns, braces himself on the top of the Jeep, peers into the cab. "This is it, okay?" He gestures between us. "No more. Thank you for everything, really, but this is done. I don't want to see you anymore. You need to lie low until this whole thing is over."

With that, he turns and disappears into the night.

Tears spill down my cheeks.

THIRTY-ONE
RHETT

Three days later, I look up from the hole I'm digging as a gray dually with roof-top floodlights pulls up to the curb. Its comically large tires glint in the single beam of sunlight that has escaped this cold, cloudy day. The truck is nothing short of absurd, especially considering Detective Stroud hasn't been off-roading since he offered Sammie Richards a joint in exchange for a hand job at the end of Turtleneck Road his senior year. I've been away for a bit, yes, but some things don't change. Pussies like Johnny Stroud are one of them.

I glance around, gauging the reaction of the other men on site, though no one seems to give the truck that has just pulled up to the curb much attention. They are cliquey, these construction workers, and this suits me just fine. When I first started, a few would acknowledge me, but that stopped when I showed up with claw marks down the side of my face.

The truck door opens, the window dramatically reflecting the sunlight like a beam of fire from Zeus's staff. The only thing missing is the cheering crowd.

Detective Stroud steps out in a navy-blue suit and tie, loosened around the neck, suggesting a hell of day. Sitting behind a computer, in an ergonomic chair, in a heated office, I muse.

My teeth grind as I return to digging. I can actually *feel* him walking toward me. I can *feel* his eyes on me. And *dammit* if a rush of nerves doesn't get me. As much as I hate to admit it, the man has power over me. Stroud was the driving force behind my guilty verdict, my removal from society, my loss of life, the stain on my name, the twenty-year sentence. And today, he is the one man who could get me locked away again if I make one, single misstep.

"Mr. Cohen."

Mister Cohen. What a dick.

I continue to dig.

"Mr. Cohen," he repeats.

The detective's footfalls stop at my back and I get a whiff of cologne. Something obnoxious and artificial. Suits him.

"Rhett," he barks, not one to be ignored.

Still not turning around, I glance up, under my lashes. The crew has now taken notice of the detective on the scene. They frown, squinty, judgmental eyes in my direction. *What has he done now, that introverted ex-con?*

"Rhett, Jesus Christ—*hello?*" Stroud steps around to face me, kicking a mound of dirt into the hole I've spent the morning digging.

I continue to dig.

But then, he says—

"Sylvia Stone is missing."

The tip of the shovel spears into the dirt. I freeze. My entire body tenses.

There is no way I heard him correctly.

A long moment stretches between us, him staring at me, me at the shovel while my mind races.

There is no way this is correct.

"Mr. Cohen, I strongly suggest you give me your attention

now because the last person Sylvia Stone was seen with was you. Literally, by my own eyes, three days ago in Deep Shadows."

Heart racing, I straighten and give Detective Stroud my full, undivided attention.

"What do you mean she's missing?"

Stroud's dry, cracked lip quirks up. He thinks I'm being evasive—and therefore I've just made this a game to him.

"Sylvia Stone is missing," he repeats. "When was the last time you saw her?"

"Three days ago. In Deep Shadows, when you saw us."

"Really?"

"Really."

"Well, Mr. Cohen, she's been missing since then. Since that night."

"For three days?"

"Yes, sir."

Sir.

"How do you know this?" I ask.

"An acquaintance stopped by her house this morning after Miss Stone failed to answer several of her calls."

"Who?"

"Her hairdresser, Ginger Dubois. Says she went by her house to drop something off—a conditioning kit or something."

"And?"

"And Sylvia wasn't there. A few UPS boxes were piled at her doorstep, one with the delivery date of October 17th, the day after I saw you and her—technically, the morning of. Ginger got worried, and called us for a welfare check."

He makes a show of examining the scabby scratches on my cheek.

"I didn't hurt her if that's what you're thinking."

"I know, she told me you fell, remember? She said that's where you got those ugly claw marks down your face that look just like the mark of a woman's fingernails." He grins, baiting me. "Can you walk me through that day, Mr. Cohen? How about you start here: Why were you two at an abandoned house in the middle of the night?"

"House-hunting."

He snorts. "You always were a smartass. Fine. For who? You?"

"Yep."

"Ah that's right," he snorts. "Your house, truck, and your business, all got repossessed right after you went to prison for murdering her mom."

"I didn't murder Marjorie Stone."

"Give it up, Cohen. No one believed you then, no one believes you now, and you served your sentence, just give it up."

"It would be easier to give it up if you'd leave me alone."

"We can do this here or at the station, your choice."

Anger spreads like fire up my neck. I feel sweat beading on my back. I hate that he can do this to me.

"Now," Stroud continues, enjoying this far too much, "tell me what you two were really doing."

"House-hunting, I said."

He rolls his eyes. "And after?"

"She dropped me off here."

"For what?"

"Sleep."

"You're sleeping here? At the construction site?"

"That's why I'm house-hunting."

Another roll. "And after that?"

I gesture to the ditch. "This. Work and sleep. I haven't seen her since that night."

"I don't believe you."

"Shocker. What about her phone, purse, personal things?" I ask, trying to remember what she had with her that night. "Did you see those things in her house?"

"Yep—all sitting on the coffee table. A frozen dinner had gone cold in the microwave, a half-drunk glass of wine sat on the counter. The television was on, the heater on blast."

"So she went home after she dropped me off. Is her Jeep there?"

"Yep."

"Is there any sign of forced entry?"

"Nope."

The implication hits me like a wrecking ball. If Sylvia was taken from her house, with no signs of struggle or forced entry, then whoever took her was likely someone she knew.

Me.

My stomach roils. Flashbacks race behind my eyes. This is eerily similar to how it started all those years ago, right before my life was taken from me.

My heart roars in my chest. I grip onto the end of the shovel to steady myself.

"Listen." I force eye contact, though it feels like my insides have turned to liquid. "I don't know where she is."

"Well how about you come to the station to answer a few more questions, you know, considering you were the last person seen with her."

"I'm not going to the station, you son of a bitch. You have no reason to arrest me."

"Where did you get those scratches on your face, Cohen?"

"None of your business."

"They look like a woman's fingernails... *exactly* like that."

He steps closer, so close I can smell his rancid coffee breath. "I won't tell... Being in prison changes a man, I get it. You need really hard stuff to get your rocks off now, I get it."

I grit my teeth so hard that my jaw throbs in pain.

He laughs, takes a step back. "So. What were you guys doing out at that house? The truth, this time." He glances at his watch. "I've got an appointment to get to."

"None of your damn business."

"Listen, Cohen." He steps forward, again, inches from my nose. "You little piece of shit, I could get you—"

Just then, a figure appears next to us, a familiar face from the construction crew. Juan Cortez, an illegal immigrant who works his ass off and gets paid in cash, just like I do.

"Is there something I can help with?" Juan asks in broken English.

Stroud scans him like a gnat on the bottom of his shoe.

"No," I say, "the detective was just leaving."

Stroud weighs his options. Juan and I are a combined four-fifty, easily, and coupling that with the fact that his visit has now drawn attention from not only the crew, but bystanders as well, he decides to keep his professional reputation intact.

It's all about reputation, after all.

"I'm watching you, Cohen." He points his finger at my chest. "If I were you, I would do everything I could to find Sylvia Stone. Because the second the town hears she's gone missing, you are going to become the number one suspect. You killed her mother and now killed her. Revenge for her testimony against you. Maybe roughed her up a little first and—"

I lunge forward.

Chaos erupts around me, distorted shouts and pounding footsteps as Juan yanks me off my feet and drags me down to the dirt, restraining me like a rabid dog.

It takes four men to hold me down.

Detective Stroud looms over me, a crooked, taunting grin on his face. "Welcome back, Cohen."

I jerk out of Juan's hold, surge upward, and watch as the detective saunters back to his truck.

The crowd disperses, disappointed at the lack of phys-icality.

"You gotta get your shit together," Juan says, low and threatening.

I growl, jab my fingers through my sweaty hair.

"I know who you are," he continues, "and I don't think you did it. You need to focus on not going back where you just came from."

I begin pacing.

"Listen," he continues, "I've got an old truck I ain't using. Might break down, won't get you very far, but you can use it until you figure something out."

I stop, gape at him, speechless. The man knows nothing about me, other than my reputation for stabbing an elderly woman to death.

"You'll have to pay for gas," he continues. "Ain't got money for that, but you can have the truck as long as you need it. Better than sleeping in the dirt."

I am dumbfounded by this man's kindness and as much as I despise handouts, I accept his. Because Detective Stroud is right. If I want to ensure my freedom, I need to do everything I can to find Sylvia Stone before they find a reason to arrest me.

THIRTY-TWO

RHETT

I put in a full day, working nonstop to counterbalance the thoughts racing through my head.

The seriousness of the news hit me quickly.

There is no question everyone will think I am involved in Sylvia's disappearance. Stroud was right, and he'd already worked an angle—revenge.

Just like with Marjorie, I had means, motive, and opportunity.

Means: I am at least one hundred pounds heavier than Sylvia. The short, skinny brunette wouldn't stand a chance against me in a physical altercation.

Motive: Revenge. She testified against me in court.

Opportunity: Since being released from prison, I've spent multiple hours with Sylvia, in her home, in town, building her trust. She would go with me anywhere.

And as if all that weren't enough, I am sporting a series of nasty scratches down my face that are unmistakingly from a woman's fingernails. Stroud is no idiot. He knows I didn't fall.

In other words, I am royally fucked if Sylvia isn't found,

unharmed, immediately. (Unharmed enough to *verbally* confirm that I had no part in her disappearance).

Truth? I did want revenge, but not on her. I wanted it on the man who framed me. Marjorie Stone's real killer.

Truth number two? I don't want to go back to prison, therefore, I know I can't murder Marjorie's killer once I find him. I mean I could, but I can't risk the chance of being convicted. To be clear, the day I was released I fully intended to kill the man who framed me. I'd spent twenty years of my life plotting it out. But, to my surprise, a few days of breathing fresh air, feeling the sun on my face, watching it rise and set, did something to me. Cleansed my soul, if you will. In fact, it was while watching my second sunrise that I made the decision that I would not take another man's life. Besides, if I did, I would immediately be the number one suspect.

Much like I am now.

I decided that instead of killing someone, I would find honest work, save up, and buy myself a plot of wooded land somewhere. I have this absurd aspiration to build my own home. A simple one-room cabin with a wraparound porch. Then, I'll get a dog, a few perhaps, adopted from the animal shelter. Save them from behind bars because I understand that kind of misery. I still think of Nacho, my little jail rat and wonder how he's fared without me. That rat served a profound purpose in my time behind bars. I know now that animals can save someone's soul. Now it's my turn to save a few of theirs.

Lastly, I made a promise to myself to never miss a sunrise, my dogs at my side.

I don't need a halfway house, friends or family, I need a goal. One that does not allow for murdering another human being.

. . .

Just after five o'clock, a woman pulls up to the site. Juan's sister, delivering the truck he'd promised to loan me.

Juan wasn't kidding. The 1987 single cab Ford Ranger is one pothole away from falling apart—like the Fred Flintstone mobile, a stick there, a stone there, flap of animal flesh there, until eventually the driver is just sitting in the middle of the road on a stone seat.

A thick layer of rust covers the hood, streaking down the side like dried blood. Obviously having been painted several times, a faded blue has merged with hunter green like a melting candle. A few spots of red peek along the fender. It is anyone's guess what the original color was. The tailgate is spray-painted camo and I can just make out the word *perra* hidden in the swirls. I'll have to look that one up.

Despite all this, it's the most beautiful thing I've ever seen. *My* truck (if only temporarily). My freedom. The opportunities personal transportation offer are endless.

I thank Juan profusely and promise I will make it up to him, though he is having none of it. I get the vibe he's also spent a stint in prison at some point in his life. Perhaps along the way, someone had given him a handout, like he is giving me. The power of paying it forward. I will never forget it and I will pay him back, I vow. In one way or another. This being another motive to not kill a human being. Pay Juan back.

Five minutes later, I am on my way to Sylvia's house to begin my own investigation into her disappearance.

The most obvious suspect is Dr. Harris Taylor—the man who saw her watching him have sex with a woman who was not his wife. The trusted town doctor, delivers your babies during the day, fucks your wife during the night.

His motive to kidnap Sylvia makes sense: Harris Taylor gets busted having sex with his neighbor and needs to silence the person who saw him, therefore he kidnaps her. He has much to lose, after all. His hot wife would divorce him and take half his money quicker than he could say "you're going to feel some pressure." He would likely lose his practice, driven away by the unrelenting small-town gossip.

God knows I understand that.

Dr. Harris has means and motive, but what about opportunity?

Did Harris Taylor drive to Sylvia's house after his late-night tryst? How did he know where she lived? And why would she answer her door to him, having just seen him in a compromising position with another woman?

No, no, no, this doesn't make sense. If Stroud is right, and there was no forced entry, then Harris Taylor didn't have clear opportunity to abduct Sylvia Stone. He was obviously mad, chasing after us, after having been caught. She wouldn't have opened the door.

Regardless, I need to trace Harris's steps since that night. But how? My trust level within the community is only marginally better than an adulterer.

Three days.

Silvia Stone has been missing for *three* days, according to Stroud. This means she disappeared after she dropped me off, after 1 a.m., Wednesday night. She'd gone home, put a frozen dinner in the microwave, poured a glass of wine, turned up the heater.

Then what?

Had someone visited her then? Or early the next morning? I don't recall her saying she was expecting company.

I replay our conversations from that day, her demeanor, our argument before she dropped me at the curb. The way she looked at me after I told her it was over between us.

I shift in my seat, feeling a tingle at the base of the neck.

That *look*.

There is something about Sylvia Stone that intrigued me from the start, drew me in. Not in the way you may think. She is an attractive woman, yes, but there is something more to Miss Stone, deeper, that emanates from her. Weird vibes, my mom would call it.

I remember the way she looked at me, watched me like a hawk, during the trial. There was an eerie calmness, a detached iciness in her eyes that sent a chill up my spine. At times, her gaze on me was so intense that I swore I could feel it. An invisible beam, an alternative way of communicating that only she could manifest. Like she was speaking to me with those deep brown mysterious eyes.

What? What had she been trying to tell me? If anything at all?

I remember a story she'd told on the witness stand, of her and her mother. When asked by the prosecutor what she and her mother enjoyed doing together (conjuring sympathy from the jurors), she'd said "baking." This spun into a painfully long narration of their baking teamwork, their favorite recipes, the secret ingredient in their famous "Stone Cookies." Midway through a story about fruit cake, she just stopped. Stopped talking, like a doll whose battery just fell out.

The entire courtroom went silent. The type of silence where you can hear white noise in your ears.

Her body began to tremble, her chin, shoulders. Tears started streaming down her stoic, expressionless face. Then, she doubled over and vomited on the floor, a splash of chunky bloody goo.

Court was adjourned for the day and Sylvia was rushed to the hospital where she was treated overnight for a panic attack and ulcers.

I'd felt the same weird vibes from her after showing up at her house after being released from prison. Red flags ignited—keep your distance. But I needed information on the letters she'd received. And yes, I will admit, when I realized Sylvia's interest in me went beyond surface level, I used this to my advantage.

I'm not proud of this.

The more time we spent together, the more I was able to observe her behavior. I made note of her constant need to apologize. Her social isolation, her low self-esteem. The guilt that seemed to plague her about the trial, about locking up an innocent man.

Were the letters really the turning point? Was this when she realized I didn't do it?

As I pull into Sylvia's driveway I can't help but wonder...

Has Sylvia known all along that I didn't do it? Or, at the very least, did she have doubts?

I search my memory, replaying the day she testified on the witness stand.

The day Sylvia Stone put the final nail in my coffin.

THIRTY-THREE

State versus Rhett Cohen
Courtroom Transcript

Clerk: Please stand. Raise your right hand. Do you promise the testimony you are about to tell before this court shall be the truth, the whole truth, and nothing but the truth, so help you God?

Miss Stone: I do.

Clerk: Please state your first and last name for the record.

Miss Stone: Sylvia Stone.

Clerk: Thank you. You may be seated.

Deputy DA: Miss Stone, I have a few follow-up questions from the statement you gave yesterday. Is that okay?

Miss Stone: Yes.

Deputy DA: In your transcript you stated that you saw the defendant, Rhett Cohen, at your mother's house on June 17th, 2004. Is this correct?

Miss Stone: Yes.

Deputy DA: Can you describe what he was doing when you saw him? Set the scene, if you will.

Miss Stone: Yes. He was in the kitchen, working on the cabinets—my mother hired him to help renovate the kitchen. She was upstairs, folding laundry.

Deputy DA: Where exactly upstairs?

Miss Stone: In her room.

Deputy DA: What room?

Miss Stone: Her bedroom.

Deputy DA: Did you talk to Mr. Cohen when you entered the house?

Miss Stone: Not initially, no. He was outside, in the backyard.

Deputy DA: Doing what?

Miss Stone: Cutting wood on his sawhorse.

Deputy DA: Then what?

Miss Stone: I went upstairs to find my mom.

Deputy DA: What was the nature of your visit to her?

Miss Stone: I wanted to talk to her about a few things with my house.

Deputy DA: What specifically?

Miss Stone: I'd recently discovered termites, so I wanted to talk to her about getting that fixed.

Deputy DA: Does your mother know how to exterminate termites?

Miss Stone: No, I needed—was requesting—her help with paying for it.

Deputy DA: Ah, I see. Termite treatment can be very expensive, I understand. Did your mother seem different in any way, during this visit?

Miss Stone: No.

Deputy DA: She didn't seem particularly nervous, or scared, or uneasy?

Miss Stone: No.

Deputy DA: Distracted, maybe? Like something was on her mind?

Miss Stone: No.

Deputy DA: Miss Stone, how many times had you been in your mother's bedroom at that point?

Miss Stone: Oh… I don't know. A lot.

Deputy DA: Ten, twenty, thirty times?

Miss Stone: I'm not sure. I visit every Sunday.

Deputy DA: On your last visit, did you happen to notice the jewelry box she kept on her armoire?

Miss Stone: Not particularly. I mean, I know it was there, but didn't look at it.

Deputy DA: I see. So, it's safe to say that if something in that room had been rearranged, like the jewelry box, you would have noticed?

Miss Stone: I think so, yes.

Deputy DA: Did she mention Mr. Cohen during this visit?

Miss Stone: Yes. She said the cabinets were coming along well.

Deputy DA: What else?

Miss Stone: That's it.

Deputy DA: Nothing else about him?

Miss Stone: I think she might've said something about him being done soon.

Deputy DA: And then what?

Miss Stone: She told me to go ahead and call about getting the termite service completed, and that we would figure out the bill later. And not to worry about it.

Deputy DA: After that?

Miss Stone: We talked a bit about the day, what I had been up to, how my garden was coming along, then she asked me to take her coffee cup downstairs to the kitchen on my way out. Then I said goodbye and went downstairs.

Deputy DA: And did you see Rhett then?

Miss Stone: Yes. He was in the kitchen.

Deputy DA: Doing what?

Miss Stone: Working on the cabinets. Opening boxes, specifically.

Deputy DA: Boxes of what?

Miss Stone: I don't know—like cabinet liner or something.

Deputy DA: How close did you get to him?

Miss Stone: Well, I put the cup in the sink, which was right next to where he was standing.

Deputy DA: Exactly how close would you say?

Miss Stone: Probably two feet away.

Deputy DA: Miss Stone can you describe, in detail, what Rhett Cohen was doing at this exact moment? You said he was opening boxes, can you elaborate?

Miss Stone: Yes, he was using a knife to open the top of the boxes. I recognized it. It was one of my mother's knives, from a set she has.

Deputy DA: Can you describe the knife?

Miss Stone: Yes, it was a large blue kitchen knife with a checkered handle. She got it with a set she ordered online. Rhett was using this knife to open the box.

Deputy DA: You saw it in his hand?

Miss Stone: Yes.

Deputy DA: And can you tell me the next time you saw that exact knife?

Miss Stone: Yes. Right after I found my mother's body. An officer brought it in from the woods. It was covered in blood.

Deputy DA: And later, forensic testing confirmed that it was Rhett's fingerprints on the knife, and your mother's blood on the blade.

Miss Stone: Yes, that's correct.

THIRTY-FOUR

RHETT

I expect Detective Stroud to be at Sylvia's home when I arrive, lying in wait, armed with handcuffs and snide remarks while I walk headfirst into whatever booby trap he's conceived to ensure my re-entry into the prison system. Even as I park in her driveway behind her Jeep, even as I slowly circle her house on foot, I look for him.

He's in my head. If not physically here, the man has taken up residence in my brain.

Whose fault is that, I wonder, as I glance up at the sky.

Thick, billowing clouds move swiftly overhead, in time with the rapidly dropping temperature. It is a gray and bleak dusk, as if autumn has simply given up, yielding to the impending winter.

Once sure I am alone, I return to the top of Sylvia's driveway and begin my investigation. I search for any sign of suspicious activity, fresh tire tracks, boot tracks, footprints, drag marks. Blood. Anything to help me understand why Sylvia has suddenly gone missing. Because right now, my future depends on finding this woman so that she can tell Stroud that I had nothing to do with her disappearance.

The front door is locked so I go around back. Nothing seems out of place or out of the ordinary. Everything is exactly as it had been the last time I was with her.

The back door is locked. Stroud—or whoever responded— must've locked it back after their welfare visit.

I fist my hands on my hips and look around, studying the dozen dirt-filled planters scattered along the back porch. Sylvia's half-assed effort to spruce up the space abandoned for a glass of wine, a reality show, and a self-loathing bubble bath.

What is it about Sylvia that bothers me so much?

I begin tipping each pot until—*bingo*—I find a shiny gold key.

And just like that, I am breaking and entering into Sylvia Stone's home.

A wall of stale, humid air hits me like a brick wall. The heater is still running on blast. Why didn't Stroud turn it down when he left? I register an odd scent in the house, one that I can't quite put my finger on. Chemicals mixed with stale coffee, is it? Not like Pine-Sol or bleach, just a strong chemical scent.

I look around the kitchen.

The frozen dinner Stroud mentioned is still in the microwave, slowly rotting away. Dishes sit piled in the sink, a shimmering layer of goo beginning to congeal them all together. Three dead flies float in the stagnant water. The trash, overflowing, smells like wilted broccoli. On the floor next to that sits two bowls full of cat food, and a mixing bowl filled with water.

Nothing appears to be askew, more than usual any way. Nothing to suggest an altercation had taken place.

Foregoing the lights, I search the living room—I'm losing light quickly—then make my way upstairs to Sylvia's bedroom.

The soft scent of her vanilla perfume lingers in the air. I feel a twinge of guilt. I played her, manipulated this woman to get what I needed and nothing else. Hadn't she been through enough already?

A soft meow startles me.

Shirley tiptoes into the room, curious.

"Hey, you."

I watch as she slowly crosses the room, her tail high, flicking in interest. She stops two inches from my feet.

I squat down, scratch behind her ears. Shirley leans into me, rubbing her head against my jeans.

"Where's your mama?" I ask.

She meows, looks at me with her one good eye.

"Tell me what happened."

I give her a few more scratches behind the ear, then stand and resume the task at hand.

I search Sylvia's bedroom, her closet, her bathroom.

Like the rest of the house, nothing seems abnormal or out of place. Naturally, I look for missing jewelry, but everything appears to be intact.

I study the items on her nightstand. A half-drunk glass of water, tube of lotion, a flashlight, handful of used tissues, an old PayDay wrapper that has hardened around the edges, a bottle of pain pills, and sleeping pills.

I retrieve the pocket flashlight I picked up at the gas station and click it on, quickly lowering the torchlight at the floor, expecting Stroud to jump through the window with a dramatic *ah-ha!*

He doesn't, so I continue.

Securing the light between my teeth, I slide open the top drawer of the nightstand. Stacks of magazines, a few paperback books, more used tissues. Eye drops.

I slide open the second drawer.

I blink, freeze.

For a full ten seconds I stare down at the pile of pictures that fill the drawer. Pictures of *me*. My own face stares back at me in a collage of images carefully cut from newspapers, magazines, online articles.

My heart starts to race as I pilfer through the pile, pausing on a jagged, torn page of a yearbook—a yearbook from *my* senior year. A red lipstick heart encircles my acne-riddled face.

"Holy. Shit."

The light falls out of my mouth, popping intermittent flashes of light against the wall as it hits the floor.

Shirley darts out of the room.

I retrieve the flashlight, and after blowing off the dust motes, I replace it between my teeth and squat in front of the open drawer.

I pull out the contents one by one. Images of me in the courtroom during the trial—actual pictures. More, printed from the countless internet articles about the case. A newspaper clipping of the announcement of my new business, Cohen Carpentry, from twenty-five years ago.

At the bottom of the pile are snapshots of me on the television. As if someone had taken a picture from their couch and then printed it from their phone.

I repeat—*holy shit*.

THIRTY-FIVE
RHETT

I cannot believe what I'm staring at. This goes far beyond Sylvia collecting stories of her mother's death—Marjorie's Death Folder, as she'd called it. This is *all* about me. And it appears to be an extremely unnerving obsession.

My stomach rolls and suddenly I want nothing more than to get the hell out of this house.

I replace everything just as I'd found it, then make a final run through each room to ensure I've left no trace of myself.

I keep the spare key.

I jump into my (Juan's) truck and make my way to Deep Shadows.

If Sylvia is this obsessed with me, why didn't she make a move, given the amount of time we've spent together over the last week? Try to seduce the man she's pined after for so long, now within her grasp. But she didn't. In fact, she made no indication of exactly how interested she was in me—and this makes me wonder what else she's hiding from me.

Unfortunately, I am far too familiar with hybristophilia. A mental disorder characterized by intense sexual interest in people who commit crimes. The more heinous, the greater the obsession.

While in prison I was the focus of multiple female-driven groups who wrote to me daily and visited weekly. There was Cohen's Cupcakes, (a clever play on my now-nonexistent company, Cohen Carpentry), The Cohen Commitment Crew, (women who were—you guessed it—committed to breaking me out of prison) and, finally, the Free Rhetts (the least creative of the groups).

One commonality between these women and Sylvia? An extreme obsession. One major difference, however, is their communication of this obsession. The groups were very vocal about their feelings. Sylvia kept hers hidden.

Why?

I scoot lower in my seat as I drive past the iron gates of Deep Shadows and make a mental note to buy a baseball cap next time I fill up on gas.

The streetlights stutter on as I pass the Taylor home, which appears locked up. No lights, no movement inside. I slow as I round the cul-de-sac. The abandoned house sits darkened under the shadows of the bushy, unmanicured trees that surround it. The house has an entirely different feel now that I know what happens under its roof after midnight.

Exiting the neighborhood, I turn onto a secondary road—not so much of a road, really, as a parallel path of rutted dirt—that snakes around the back of the properties. For maintenance trucks, I assume.

I park behind a thicket of trees, then make my way through the brush until I reach the back of the Taylors' home.

I settle in and watch.

For hours I watch, eyes peeled for Sylvia.

· · ·

Harris and his wife arrive home shortly after nightfall. I'm becoming more and more certain that there is nothing more to this family than a very dysfunctional marriage. Dr. Taylor was cheating on his wife with his neighbor. Their troublemaking child became sick of the drama and ran away, accepting five hundred bucks from a stranger to deliver letters to a woman's house.

That's it. I'm sure of it. But this doesn't tell me where Sylvia is.

I'm just about to call it a night when I hear a twig break somewhere to my right. Silence, followed by another *snick*, then another and another. I'm no tracking expert but based on the equally spaced repetition of each breaking twig, it appears to be a human walking through the woods.

Looking from window to window, I confirm Harris and his wife are still inside.

The steps grow closer and I'm sure whoever it is has no idea I'm here.

So what to do now?

The decision is made for me when I am literally almost run over by this mystery person.

I lunge backward, tripping over a scrub brush and almost falling on my ass. The woman screams, a terrible, ear-piercing shrill of noise.

"No, no, no," I rush toward her, palms up. "*Shhh*, it's okay, it's okay."

The woman freezes. It's so dark between us that although we are facing each other, we are nothing more than silhouettes. Black cardboard cutouts of two people.

I catch the scent of her perfume, and considering how still the night is, that's saying something. It's a strong, pungent scent, the kind that preludes your arrival. The kind that women who want to be taken notice of wear.

My eyes rake over the outline of the woman's body. She's tall, with long red hair that hangs down to her waist.

The neighbor.

We recognize each other at the same time.

"It was *you.* I saw you running away with that girl who was watching us." Gloria Lopez hisses. "You—" She jabs a finger into my chest.

I blink, my brain taking a moment to catch up with this emotional swing from crippling fear to apparent anger.

"It was *you* in the house that night." She's slurring badly, her breath laced with alcohol. I have to fight from taking a step back. The woman is completely inebriated. And then it hits me —she's likely on her way to the abandoned house to meet Dr. Harris for a round on the floor.

"I'm sorry..." I say. Typically, I would assume that a woman would be embarrassed to run into a man who saw her naked, on all fours. However, I don't get this vibe from her. Gloria is nothing more than pissed. "I didn't mean—"

"You didn't mean to watch me like a sick pervert?" I inhale to respond, but she cuts me off. "Did you tell anyone?"

"Ah—"

"Oh God, did you tell anyone?" Her tone switches from anger to panic and I realize then that the woman is more than just drunk. She's also high on pills, maybe even cocaine.

"Oh my God," she says to my lack of response, then collapses into sobs.

I look around, not that I can see anything, but if this woman doesn't pull it together, we are both going to get busted.

Her sobbing increases, loud spurts and sputters of incontrollable emotion.

I'm staring at her like an idiot, the stereotypical man who doesn't know how to console a crying woman. Guilty, I admit.

Gloria grabs onto a tree branch as she doubles over in hysteria, the combination of standing and crying proving to be too complicated for her wine-fueled system.

Awkwardly, I tap her shoulder and say, "There, there."

She grabs my arm, collapses into my chest.

I want out of here. *Now.*

"Please don't tell anyone," she sobs. "He'll kill me. He'll kill me."

I frown, gently grab her shoulders and pull her off my chest. This close, I can make out her features. Black eyeliner circles puffy, bloodshot eyes. Her lips are red and glossy.

"Who will kill you?" I ask.

"*He* will."

"Harris? Dr. Taylor will kill you?"

"No, no, no..."

"His wife? Janet?"

"No!" she snaps, frustrated.

God, I *hate* drunk women.

"You can't—I can't ... he can't find out," she attempts to collapse into my chest again, but I hold her in place.

"*Who?*"

"Johnny," she wails.

"Johnny... as in, Detective Stroud?"

Gloria nods feverishly.

"Why? Why would he be mad?"

"He's—we're together..."

No *fucking* way.

"No one knows," she continues.

My jaw drops. Gloria and Detective Stroud are dating, behind her fiancé's back. Meanwhile, Gloria is secretly meeting up with her neighbor, Dr. Harris Taylor. What kind of fucked up love triangle is this? (And *wow* this woman gets around. I don't know if I should chide her or give her a high five.)

And then another thought hits me: Gloria's fiancé is the

police chief's brother. The police chief is Stroud's boss. Stroud would get fired in an instant if this affair came to life.

I ask, "How long have you and Stroud been—"

"None of your damn business," she says. "Just keep your mouth shut."

"Okay." I release her, step back.

It registers that Gloria hasn't even asked my name or what I'm doing in the woods behind the Taylors' home. But I have no doubt she will tell Dr. Harris about our encounter. Not Detective Stroud, because she obviously doesn't want him to know she's having sex with her neighbor. No wonder she's so freaked out he'll find out. Stroud's fragile ego would not take this well.

I need to get out of here.

I take another step back, and another. Gloria is wiping the tears from her face. She's realized her makeup has smeared and this has become her number one priority.

I slowly retreat, keeping my eye on her, until I am finally able to make a break for it, not looking back as I jog back to the truck.

My head is throbbing as I exit the woods and pull onto the dirt road that leads into town.

A pair of headlights emerge from the corner ahead.

I glance at the clock—12:17 a.m.

In the handful of times I've been to Deep Shadows, I've never once passed a vehicle.

I shift lower in my seat.

As the truck closes in, I noticed the flood lights on top.

Detective Johnny Stroud.

I turn my cheek as we pass. He doesn't know the vehicle, but I can't be too careful. Is he looking for me? Or is he looking for his girlfriend, Gloria?

In the rearview mirror, I watch his taillights enter Deep Shadows.

"You're going to get busted," I whisper, subconsciously willing Gloria to get back into her house.

Not my problem, I remind myself. Although as I drive back to the construction site I can't shake the feeling that something isn't right.

I park under a tree next to the site, lean back in my seat, and close my eyes.

I am not prepared for what I wake up to.

THIRTY-SIX
SYLVIA

A bloated maggot slithers up my big toe, white, fat, and greasy. Twisting and turning like a hairless, eyeless rodent having just fallen out of its mother's womb.

I'm not dead yet, I telepathically inform the disgusting little insect.

Not yet.

I can smell the rotting corpse a few feet away, decomposing on a pile of moldy hay. A cat or small dog, I can't really tell. I think it's a cat. A surprising amount of flies, considering the cold temperature, spiral around the carcass, zipping in and out of the wounds.

It's a girl. I don't know how I know this, but I do.

Probably mauled by a fox, or maybe even a mountain lion, the feral cat had come into the barn to die, half its face torn away, one eye and one ear missing, her stomach shredded to pieces as she'd clawed to get away.

I imagine she came into the barn right before I did. Died not long after I was tied up. I wonder if she was still alive when he chained me to the wall.

I picture her, entrails dragging, leaving a bloody trail in her wake as she drags herself to the only pile of hay, seeking any comfort she can find.

Comfort that never came.

My nightgown is the same color as her fur. A steel gray, and just like hers, it is speckled with dirt, hay, and dried blood.

It's funny, I asked for shoes and a coat when my kidnapper dragged me out of my house. With a black pillow case wrapped around my head and a knife at my throat, I Sylvia Stone, asked my abductor if I could get shoes and a coat.

I close my eyes and turn my head away from the cat, wincing at the pain in my neck. A sharp, searing pain that is only getting worse with each passing hour of my arms tied above my head. Bound at wrists, hooked to something hanging from the wall or ceiling.

I never saw his face. Never heard a word from his mouth. I was blinded, hog tied, driven to a barn out in the middle of nowhere, then tied to the wall and left for dead.

I let my neck hang, as if it were loose and broken, attempting to stretch the muscles.

My mouth feels like sand. My throat is raw from screaming.

I am beginning to get delirious. I've lost count of the hours. The sun has disappeared and come back up twice now. Or is it three times?

Squeezing shut my eyes, I wiggle my fingers, and attempt to move my hands in a circle. I can no longer feel them. I'm not even numb anymore. The zip-ties are too tight, cutting off my circulation. I wonder if I am going to lose my fingers, or even my hands.

I picture my mother's hands, strong, callused.

Broken visions of her have appeared before my eyes several times since being left for dead in this godforsaken barn. Each time, she is walking through the barn, toward me. She is wearing the same white and yellow house dress as the day she died, stained and splattered with blood. Her skin is white, lumi-nescent under a bright aura that circles her.

Each time I begin crying, despite myself. Begging for her to help me, to set me loose.

To save me.

To love me.

But in this vision, she never speaks, just advances close enough where I can almost—just *almost*—touch her with my toe.

Mom. Come here, Mom. Mommy, come here.

Help me.

She stares down at me, watching me beg with minimal interest. An apathetic expression of *I told you so.*

It's your fault.

I sob, continue to beg, growing more and more desperate, my insides feeling like they are about to come out of me. Then, she smiles. But her teeth aren't human, they are animal, sharp, pointy, and covered in blood.

"*Chin up, shoulders back,*" she mocks before fading away, into the cloud of gnats hovering overhead.

Chin up, shoulders back. Do you know what's funny about that? My mother said those words often, but never to me. Never. Not once. It was always Anna.

I viciously kick at a mosquito buzzing low in the air. The maggot goes flying from my toe, lands somewhere in the dirt.

There is nowhere else to suck blood from me, I think as I scowl at the mosquito. My arms and legs are riddled with angry, red insect bites. A hot, bright red rash has formed on my inner thigh.

I bend my knee, bring my foot to the inside of my opposite leg, and begin scratching away at one of the bites with my toenail. Harder, harder until sweat beads on my brow and the pain feels like electricity shooting through my veins.

Tears run down my face.

Where is Rhett?

Jesus Christ, *where is Rhett?*

THIRTY-SEVEN
MARJORIE

I'm scared of my daughter. There, I said it. I've realized that I've been scared of Sylvia ever since that day at the Cherry Tree Festival when I found Anna at the bottom of the water embankment. Anna would have never gone close to a water embankment because of her fear of water.

Last night I woke to Sylvia standing over my bed. I asked what she was doing. She said nothing and turned and walked out of the room.

It scared me.

I didn't go to sleep again after that. I don't think I will tonight either.

I need to get this out. I need to say it. I need to tell someone. I need to tell someone that I don't think that Anna slipped and fell into the water embankment that day. I think that Sylvia lured her there and pushed her without Anna realizing it. Call it a mother's instinct. But who would believe me? After all, I have secrets, too. I'm certainly no angel of a mother. If they begin poking into Sylvia's life, they'll also poke into mine.

No. No. The church would be so disappointed in me.

How do I handle what I know in my heart is true?

The day Anna died, the day she drowned in the city pool, I think Sylvia pushed her into the pool. I truly do. She's always been so jealous of Anna. And the pool was so crowded and loud that day, no one would have heard, or acknowledged, if Anna had screamed. Everyone was screaming.

I think she did it.

I think she killed Anna.

There is something wrong with Sylvia, really wrong. I know it. I know it in my gut.

I am scared of her.

THIRTY-EIGHT
RHETT

My eyes pop open. I sit up, grasping for the steering wheel. I'd laid down the driver's seat—as far as it would go anyway—hoping to get a solid night's sleep.

No dice.

At least a half-dozen faces, each twisted and contorted with anger, are peering into my windshield, screaming, jabbing stubby little fingers into the air.

Screaming and pointing *at me*.

Dawn, barely broken through a thick blanket of clouds, washes the crowd's faces in a creepy, bluish tint.

A string of brown spittle splats across the window, this from a man yelling angrily through a wad of chewing tobacco. My pulse kickstarts, my sleep-hazed brain trying to figure out what *the hell* is going on.

"Where is she?" an overweight woman screams, her wrinkled skin mottled with hives.

"You *monster*," adds another, this one wearing a baggy *Thorncrest Cheer Mom* sweatshirt and a knitted scarf pulled tightly around her neck like a noose. Her nose is as red from the cold morning air.

"Where did you get those scratches on your face? Go back to jail where you belong!" a man yells behind her, baring rotted yellow teeth.

"Yeah, we don't want you here!" the crowd jeers, their thick coats bouncing off each other like a human game of bumper cars.

Sylvia.

The news of her disappearance has been leaked to the gossips—and, as expected, they think *I* am responsible.

Shit. *Shit, shit, shit.*

I jab the key into the ignition—yes, the medieval Ford I'm driving still uses an actual key—and glance at the clock as the engine coughs to life. It's only six forty-five in the morning. News of Sylvia's disappearance must have hit the local diner not long after its 5 a.m. opening.

"Move! Get out of the way," I mouth, swinging my arm from side to side as I shove the gear into reverse. *"I said move!"*

"He hit me! He hit me!" a woman melodramatically screams before my truck has even moved an inch.

Fists pound the side of the truck as I reverse away from the tree I'd parked under.

Once away from the crowd, I peel out, onto the street and watch the silhouettes fade in my rearview mirror.

My body spins into a borderline panic attack, the visceral response immediate, embedded deep inside my psyche from my experience twenty years ago. The *exact same* experience—angry screams, spit, threats—hurled at me while I walked into the courtroom.

I roll down the window and gulp the cold, crisp morning air.

You have done nothing wrong, you have done nothing wrong, you have done nothing wrong, I repeat, over and over in my head. This does nothing to calm me, however, because I remember that I did nothing wrong twenty years ago, either. And look where that got me.

Once I'm sure no one is following me, I pull into a gas station, and park around back. I dip into the small convenience store, turning my face away from the old man sitting behind the counter. He's engrossed in the paper, paying me no attention.

Soon my face will be on the front page, next to Sylvia's, the missing daughter of the woman I was convicted of murdering.

I can already see the headline: *Has he done it again?* Or maybe: *Killer Part Deux?*

I duck into the bathroom and splash cold water on my face until the icy tingle begins to calm my pulse.

Gripping onto the sides of the sink I stare at myself in the mirror. Bloodshot, puffy eyes, tangled hair, greasy forehead. I *have* to shower soon.

A knot catches in my throat, followed by a surprising rush of emotion.

This is not who I want to be.

"*Dammit,*" I shove away from the sink, my hands balled into fists. It takes every deep breath I have to not slam them into the mirror.

"Okay, Rhett. Stop. Think." I mumble. "Think. Think. Think."

One word materializes in my head—

Act.

Do something. Anything. Take the next step.

So I wash my face, my armpits, brush my teeth with my finger, and flatten my hair with a sprinkle of water. After buying a cup of coffee and loaf of expired bread, I climb back into the truck and assess my current situation.

I come up with nothing. Not a single plan. There are only two things that I know to be true: I need to work because I need money. And I need to find Sylvia so that she can tell the world I am innocent. And both of these truths demand that I don't skip town. Also, I wouldn't do that to Juan. I wouldn't steal his truck like that.

After the buzz from the coffee kicks in and the bread fills the empty hole in my stomach, I begin to feel human again. Stronger.

I've dealt with this shit before. Ignorant, half-baked asshats who believe everything and will say anything. I dealt with it during the trial, and I dealt with it in prison.

I can deal with it again.

After a manly thump on the chest, I retrace my path to the construction site. I have a job to do and that's that.

Do the job, find the crazy girl, then, get the hell out of this godforsaken town.

Luckily, the crowd is gone.

I pick up my shovel, position myself to be face to face with the rising sun. I close my eyes and take a deep breath.

The sun is always there for you.

With that assurance, I begin to work.

By noon, I'm fired. Well, formally asked to leave, I should say. Even Juan couldn't save me.

The morning had been an absolute circus.

Cars, trucks, and even a few four-wheelers had gathered around the construction site, spilling into the liquor store parking lot.

Hordes of people came and went, marching in drunken circles, chanting, holding signs that read *Where Is She*, and *Let Her Go*. Some filmed me—actually *filmed* me—with their cell phones. A group of teens took pictures of me, taunting me to take my shirt off, because naked pictures of me would sell for a higher price.

The workers became increasingly annoyed, casting me sidelong glances of disapproval as if this were all my fault.

A local news crew showed up around ten. A young, pixie-haired blonde jogged up to me, her heels sinking into the over-turned red dirt, giving her a lubberly masculine gait that didn't fit the suit. She shoved a microphone in my face. A freckle-faced redhead hovered close behind with a camera perched on his shoulder.

"Mr. Cohen, I understand you were the last person to see Sylvia Stone alive, is this true?" "Mr. Cohen, did you two have a love affair? I heard she was pregnant with your child—can you confirm this?" "Where did those scratches on your face come from? Did you hurt her?"

I remained deliberately silent, mechanically swinging the shovel up, down, up, down, imagining her bright red mouth under each stab into the earth.

Eventually the owner of the liquor store got fed up with the crowds, who were now blocking his drive-thru, and the cops were called.

Two black and whites pulled up to the curb just as the Cohen's Cupcakes burst onto the scene, proclaiming my inno-cence, declaring their love for the wrongly accused. One partic-ularly burly woman with a tattoo that read, simply, BEANS, written across her left breast, punched a naysayer in the mouth.

All hell broke loose.

And this, I decided, was the perfect diversion.

THIRTY-NINE
RHETT

I drop my shovel and sprint into the woods that line the construction site. I can hear BEANS screaming at someone to "Come at her again, bruh" as the war rages behind me.

I don't stop until I'm out of sight from prying eyes, and sneaking down an alleyway behind a row of brick buildings on the town square.

After a quick look over my shoulder, I slide into the back door of Hammer Time, a tiny hardware shop squeezed in between the courthouse and the diner.

A bell rings as I open the door and the owner sees me immediately. He jerks his chin to the office, giving me the okay.

He's not surprised to see me, I note, and I find a bit of comfort in that.

William Sandler and I were old classmates. Billy, as he's called, was my partner in shop class and the two of us bonded over woodwork. He spotted me at the construction site a few days ago while in line at the liquor store. The six-foot-four former lineman—now the size of a refrigerator—parked his dually, got out, and strode over to me with a crooked grin. He looked almost the same, add fifty pounds and a thick black beard that covers almost his entire face.

Billy spoke to me like a human, treated me like an old friend, not like a dangerous ex-convict, like everyone else did. After a brief catch-up, Billy patted me on the back and told me if I ever got into trouble, I could come to his shop.

Well, Billy, this qualifies as trouble, my old friend.

I look around the small office which is cluttered with boxes of tools, some stacked dangerously tall, others opened, half their contents spilled onto a stained concrete floor. A simple metal desk sits in the corner. It's tiny and I imagine my old friend looks comical sitting behind it. The walls are barren. There isn't a single picture hung anywhere, a passive aggressive announcement of the man's lack of family, I muse. This doesn't surprise me. Billy was a troublemaker back then, and much like Stroud, wasn't the type to change his ways.

I pace the tiny room, back and forth, back and forth, not knowing what to do but grateful I'm no longer out in public getting screamed at.

I listen to my old friend engage a customer, crack a joke, sell a wrench.

About twenty-five minutes later, Billy comes into the office, a cup of coffee in each hand.

He offers one to me.

"Thanks." I take the styrofoam cup from his monstrous hand and move to the corner of the room so not to crowd his space.

"I take it you saw the news," he says, weaving around the boxes to his desk. His flannel shirt catches on the tip of a hammer poking out of a box, momentarily revealing a holster clipped to his belt.

"No," I say, "I haven't caught the news in a few days."

Billy frowns. "No? What brings you here, then?" He sinks into the small, plastic chair that bows under his weight.

"The crowds. I had to get away. They came to the construction site…" I shake my head, realizing how embarrassed I am. Humiliated to be the center of attention—*again*. I want to scream from the mountaintops for everyone to just leave me alone.

"It's because of the news…" he says over the rim of his coffee cup.

"Fill me in, Bill."

"Sylvia Stone's disappearance is the top story."

"I figured that much."

He continues, "The fact that she's missing is immediately followed by the fact that you were just released from prison and that *you* were the last person to be seen with her—you know, the daughter of the woman you supposedly killed."

"Do you really think I did it, Billy?"

"Naw, man. Never did. And just so you know, there are a handful of locals who agree with me—never thought you did it. But everyone else did, and does, and now everyone thinks you're involved in her daughter's disappearance."

I jab my fingers through my hair. "What station aired it? KNWV?"

Billy works a deep swallow. "Naw… national news."

"*What?*" I stumble backward, slamming into a file cabinet. Papers spill onto the ground.

"Jesus, dude, *move*." Billy surges off the chair, steps around the desk.

I stumble to the side, words catching in my throat. Billy kneels, begins gathering the papers.

I stare down at him, gaping like an idiot.

The story has gone *national*.

Just then, the front door chimes. Billy replaces the papers to their rightful place on top of the file cabinet, then grabs his coffee from the desk. "Duty calls. Just stay in here until I close, wait for things to cool down a bit. Help yourself to anything you need. There's some leftover pizza in the mini fridge under the desk. Oh, and I got a cell phone I don't use, a burner I used while they were working on my other one. Got some minutes on it and can even connect to the internet. It's in the bottom drawer. Take it, I don't need it."

"Thanks."

"I'd offer you to stay in my house—I heard you ain't got a place yet—but I just got these Doberman puppies and shit, man, they shit everywhere."

"Didn't figure you as a puppy kind of guy."

"Where I live, out in the sticks, you need dogs, man. Guns and dogs to guard my property."

"Whereabouts?"

"I own twenty acres out on Black Bear Mountain," he says, a hint of pride sparkling in his eyes. "Out in the middle of nowhere."

"Good for you."

"Thanks." He starts for the door, pauses, and turns back. "Hey... I'm sorry. I can't imagine... I'm just sorry, dude."

"Thanks."

The moment the door closes, I beeline it to the mini fridge. Sure enough, a grease-stained box of pizza sits crookedly between the slats. My mouth waters.

I am starving.

Since being released from prison, my appetite has come back tenfold. The moment I realized I had the freedom to choose my own food, suddenly that's all I want. Food. Doesn't even matter if it's good. I just want to eat and eat and eat. I am absolutely ravenous, constantly, this insatiable appetite reminding me of who I was before prison, like that man is slowly coming back.

I have mixed emotions about this.

Before I went away, I was a mess. A naive country boy with little direction in life and zero ability to balance a checkbook.

But this is no excuse for the financial pitfall I found myself in. I look back on that kid, the ungrateful little punk who thought he was invincible, and I want to punch him in the face.

In prison, I read this quote: Unhappiness is being in a constant state of wanting. It's so true. I watched too many men shrivel and die to this kind of victim mentality while behind bars. They hated everything about their life, blamed others, the system, the country. Wanted anything and everything that was just out of their reach. This never-ending cycle of discontentment slowly poisoned their brains.

I vowed, very early on, that I would not be like those men.

Some days I don't know who I am anymore. I know who I was before I went into prison, and I know who I was inside prison, but it is an entirely new man that has come out. It's unnerving but also liberating, because I can make this man whatever I want him to be.

I shut the fridge door, deciding at that moment, that the man I want to be will not live off other people's charity.

I'll get my own food.

My own truck.

I just have to get this current situation behind me first.

FORTY

RHETT

I wait until Billy is deep in conversation with a customer before slipping out the back door. While I'm grateful for his offer to hideout in his shop all day, I have no time to waste. The gossip around the latest headline is only going to increase, the accusations will get more brutal, and the only way I can shut it down is by finding Sylvia.

Before leaving the shop, I pocket the cell phone and slip a fifty-dollar bill in its place.

I sneak back to the construction site and Juan's truck, where Detective Stroud is waiting on me. Like an extra in *CHiPs*, he's leaning against the hood, arms crossed with a cocky expression on his face that makes me want to slam my fist into his nose.

My heart rate increases. My entire body shifts to defense mode. I *hate* that he can do this to me.

The silver lining is that the mob is gone. That's the funny thing about mobs. They are ruthless and unyielding, until they become hungry, or tired, or bored, or find something else to hate. The motivation to leave this time, I guessed, were the gray storm clouds swirling overhead.

"Get off my truck."

"Your truck?" He spins a toothpick between his lips.

"Yep. Look familiar?"

His eyes narrow. "Can't say that it does."

"Think harder."

"I don't have time for games, Cohen."

"You did last night, didn't you?"

Stroud pushes off the truck. "Where you going with this, Cohen?"

"I saw you late last night at Deep Shadows."

Stroud's jaw twitches.

Yeah asshole, you're busted.

"You're mistaken." He spits the toothpick into the bed of the truck.

I shake my head, savoring the fact that I'm getting under his skin. *I'm* getting to *him* for a change.

"No, I'm not mistaken. I was visiting an old friend of mine. Gloria. The police chief's brother's woman. Hey..." I tilt my head to the side. "Isn't that your boss, the police chief?"

His cheeks flush.

He takes a step forward, fists balled. I've hit a nerve. Good.

I push harder, taking a shot in the dark. "I also ran into a woman named Crystal Cheri... I think you might know her, too."

His eyes flash, round with shock.

Bingo.

I step forward, closing the inches between us. "Imagine what everyone would think if they heard the detective in town was having an affair with the chief's brother's woman, and bribed a homeless woman, Crystal, to look the other way while letting her squat in an abandoned house." When I realize by his expression I'm right, I keep digging. "And she's willing to tell everyone about the bribe and the affair, FYI."

"You're a little punk, you know that."

"Sucks to have someone all up in your business, doesn't it?"

"I'm going to fucking bury you, Cohen."

"I didn't kidnap Sylvia, Johnny. I don't know where she is. I'm telling you the truth. So back the fuck off me and let me live my life."

"Doesn't matter if you took her or not. You of all people should know that. I sent you away once, I'll do it again. I'll find an angle."

"Not if everyone in town knows your fucking your boss's brother's fiancé in your spare time."

He lunges forward, shoving me backward.

Rage consumes me.

"Do it," he hisses, fists up. "Punch me, you fucking pussy."

My heart drums against my ribcage. My fingertips tingle.

"*Do it*." He shoves me again.

This time I trip over a rock and fall to the ground.

I see red.

I surge to my feet, lunging forward, and grab his shirt collar just as he takes a step back. I twist the thin fabric, yank him to me.

He gasps for air.

"You're not worth it." I shake him like a rag doll. "You're not worth it, you little shit."

FORTY-ONE
RHETT

I take a different route to Sylvia's house, looping around town twice, and dipping in and out of side streets along the way. Neither Stroud, nor anyone for that matter, is following me, but I must be sure.

A new sense of urgency grips me. Stroud realizes now that I can't be baited, that I'm not stupid, and that I will stand up to him. More than that, he knows I know his little secret. Therefore, sending me back to prison has now become his number one priority. His ego is bruised, and I will bear the consequences.

Beads of rain begin to dot the windshield as I turn into Sylvia's driveway. A fresh layer of leaves covers the yard. The morning has grown darker, an ominous gray mist swirling through the woods.

The sprinkles turn into a steady downfall the moment I step out of the truck.

Ducking my head, I circle the house, checking for new tracks or signs that anyone has been by since my last visit—including Sylvia herself. A part of me is simply waiting for her to return. Shopping bags in hands, a grin on her face, a fresh suntan from her mini-vacay she forgot to tell anyone about.

Using the spare key I'd pocketed earlier, I unlock the back door and step inside. I can tell instantly that no one is here. The same stale scent sits on air, so thick it's like wading through mud.

Shirley greets me instantly.

I kneel down, stroke her head, feeling a pang of sadness that she's alone. I can't take her, of course, so I empty the litter box, then check her food and water, both still overflowing.

"Looks like you're good to go," I scratch behind her ears. "I'll keep checking on you until we get this whole thing sorted out."

I take a quick run through the house—just to be sure I'm alone—then make my way through the curtain of rain to the mailbox. It's the only thing I didn't check yesterday, and I've been beating myself up about it.

The rain pours off my nose as I yank open the box. There is a surprisingly large amount of mail considering Sylvia is the only resident at the home.

I stuff the stack under my drenched T-shirt, jog back into the house and dump the envelopes onto the kitchen table.

A puddle of rainwater gathers underfoot as I sift through the mail. Bills, solicitations, and one long white envelope that sticks out like a sore thumb. It is addressed to Sylvia in typed font—not handwritten—and is stamped, but there is no return address.

Another letter—just like the ones she'd received that started this whole mess.

Carefully, I open the letter while mentally refreshing myself on the contents of the previous four letters.

3:02

3:04

3:11

You are next

Inside is a single white sheet of paper, just like the others.
Typed across the middle is a single line containing a combi-
nation of letters and numbers. Fifteen characters total.
I frown, reading each character out loud.
Is it a password?
A code?
A passcode for a lock?
I glance out the window toward the mountains.
I know exactly who to ask.

FORTY-TWO

RHETT

The deluge is relentless as I roll to a stop in the small gravel parking lot that marks the head of Fogmoore Trail. Unsurprisingly, the lot is vacant.

I tuck the Ziplock bag holding the envelope into my waistband, then slide the keys in my pocket and get out. Despite being almost eleven in the morning, the woods are a muted, gloomy blue, due to the weather. It's a miserable, rainy day.

I dip my head against the rain and descend into the trees, following the same trail Sylvia and I walked days earlier, until I reach the secret footpath that leads to the caves.

The Hideout lives up to its name in this weather, barely visible behind the sheets of rain and leaves swirling in the wind.

I click on my pocket flashlight. The bottom of my boots are caked with mud, and the combination of mud and slime makes for a dangerous descent into the cave.

Drips echo around me.

After squeezing through the narrowest of openings, I see a dim light glowing from deeper in the cave.

My pace quickens.

Today, there is only one person sitting in the large room at the end of the tunnel.

Jesse startles when he sees me, nearly falling backward in the folding chair he is sitting in. He appears to be doing nothing. Literally, staring at the wall. Only two flashlights illuminate the room, one a few flickers away from dying. Scattered around him are the same sleeping bags and empty bottles that I noticed during my first visit.

He quickly stands, but this time, it's less of a defensive posture, and more one of embarrassment. Of shame. He's changed clothes, I notice. The black skull sweatshirt has been replaced by a long sleeve T-shirt riddled with holes. Jeans, and scuffed combat boots. No coat.

"You here alone?" I ask.

"Since about two hours ago, yeah."

"You high?"

"No."

"Drunk?"

"Soon."

"Well hold off for a bit. We need to talk."

Jesse frowns. "What's going on?"

I pull the letter from my waistband, hold it up. "Did you deliver this to Sylvia's house? Like you did the others?"

Jesse frowns. "No." He walks over, studying the envelope. "No, man. Never seen it."

I tilt my head to the side, cock a brow.

He peers closer. "Dude, I promise. Look," he points to the stamp. "It went through the mail system." Jesse looks up. "What does it say? Can I open it?"

I nod.

His hands are steady as he opens the envelope. He definitely isn't high or drunk, and I wonder if he indulges in those vices only to fit in with his buddies.

Jesse studies the letter, then looks at me. "When did you get it, and where?"

"It was in Sylvia's mailbox just a few hours ago."

"So it was delivered today?"

"Yesterday. I don't think the mail has run yet today."

"No return address," he observes. "What do you think it means?"

"I was hoping you'd tell me."

"I told you, I didn't deliver it. I've been here, in this cave, for like, weeks. Hardly ever leave." He hands me back the envelope, sinks back down into his chair, directly in the beam of a flashlight that accentuates his dark circles and pasty pale skin. He looks terrible. Worse than last time.

"Have you eaten?" I ask.

"I'm fine," he scoffs.

"That's not what I asked."

"No, I haven't eaten. Not in a little while."

I sit in the chair next to him. "Kid, why don't you just go home? You're gonna have a whole life of living outside of your parents' house. At least there you have food, water, a shower. Television, a nice bed. Trust me, just go home. It's better than here."

"You don't understand."

"Don't I?"

He looks at me.

"My mom and dad barely spoke," I say. "He worked all the time, and she stayed at home. They rarely ever saw each other. She slept on the couch and he slept in the bedroom. I know what it's like to live in a cold, emotionless home... I also know what it's like to live in prison for twenty years and let me tell you, Jesse, your house, no matter what the scenario, is better than prison. Look at me, kid."

He turns his face toward me, his mouth downturned, expression droopy like a basset hound.

"I know about your dad, okay?" I say gently.

His eyes round. "You do?"

"Yeah. I know everything."

"How?"

"I made a late-night visit to that abandoned house at the end of your neighborhood. The one you told me you see your dad go into from time to time."

Jesse's cheeks flare with embarrassment.

"You saw more than you let on earlier, didn't you?" I ask.

He looks down, ashamed by his father's infidelity.

"Hey," I lean forward. "It happens, and it has absolutely nothing to do with you."

"Sometimes I feel like it's my fault their marriage got rocky."

"They are grown adults, Jesse. That's on them—not you."

"Thanks."

"Have you told your mom?"

"No way."

"She'll find out. They always do."

Jesse nods as if this relieves him. "I want her to leave him."

"Hell, me too."

He snorts a laugh.

"Why doesn't she?" I ask.

"She ain't got her own money. The woman hasn't worked a day in her life."

"So she's trapped, then."

"Yeah."

"Just like you are."

He frowns, looks up at me.

"Don't be like your mom, Jesse. Go home, get a job, save up, and get yourself out of that house. Make a better life for yourself. You are *not* trapped. Use the resources you currently have to better your life. Meaning, use your parents' car, use their internet to study, educate yourself, sleep in your comfortable bed so you can get up and be your best self every day. Use them. Screw it. You are in control. Got it?"

He blinks. My point was received, and received well.

"Okay, enough of that," I flick my hand in the air. "Listen, have you seen Detective Stroud around your neighborhood?"

"No… not that I noticed, anyway. Like I said, I haven't been there in a while."

"He drives that big-ass gray truck with deer lights on top."

"I know what he drives—everyone does." Jesse rolls his eyes and I'm glad to know I'm not the only one that thinks Stroud's display of masculinity is absolutely ridiculous. "Why do you ask?"

"I saw him. Last night—late—driving into your neighborhood."

"Late? How late?"

"Around midnight."

Jesse's brow arches. "What's he doing there?"

"Meeting up with your redheaded neighbor."

"What?! Are you serious? Unbelievable—are you serious? Both Detective Stroud *and* my dad are banging my neighbor?" He shakes his head. "God, my dad is an idiot."

I agree but keep my mouth shut.

"I also think that person you saw in the house, that you told Sylvia and I about, is somehow involved. Her name is Crystal Cheri. You know her?"

"No, the name doesn't ring a bell."

"She's passing through town and I think Stroud bribed her not to say anything about what goes on there."

"Do you think she's involved in the letters?"

"To be determined, but honestly, I don't think so."

I regard him closely as a moment passes between us.

"What?" he asks.

"Sylvia's missing."

"*What?*"

"Four days now."

"No shit?"

"Do you know anything about this?"

"No, man. Haven't heard a thing."

"You promise me, Jesse?"

"Yes, I promise."

"Okay, I believe you. If you see her, or hear anything about her—or if any of your caveman buddies know anything—I want you to tell the police, you got it?"

"But—"

"I need you to do this, Jesse."

"Okay..." He nods to the letter in my hand. "But why aren't you calling them? Why aren't you there right now with this letter instead of here?"

"Because they've already accused me, Jesse. They think I'm involved. The entire town thinks I kidnapped her, or worse. I'm a walking target, and Stroud is out to get me—again—and the first thing he's going to do is arrest me for opening someone else's mail, which is a felony. I'll be back in jail, with no shot to redeem myself—again."

"Opening mail is a felony?" Jesse looks shocked, and I'm assuming he's opened a letter or two.

"Yep. It can be considered mail theft, tampering of evidence, etc. I didn't think of it until after the fact, of course."

"You still would have opened it."

"Probably so."

Jesse studies me for a minute. "I heard about you and Detective Stroud."

"What about it?"

"That you guys are some sort of enemies."

"You could say that."

"You really didn't do it? Kill Marjorie Stone all those years ago?"

"No, I didn't. But everyone thinks I did, and they think I'm responsible for Sylvia's disappearance now."

Jesse tilts his head. "You need help?"

"No."

"Are you sure—"

"Jesse. How about you dig yourself out of this mess first," I gesture to the cave, "then you can be my sidekick."

He grins.

"Alright." I stand, look down at him. "Now. Onto business. You're expected at 217 Circuit Street at six-thirty tomorrow morning."

"What?"

"The construction site, behind the liquor store. Six-thirty. Do not be late, you understand me?" I turn, begin making my way out of the room.

"What for?" Jesse jogs after me.

"You've got a job. Digging ditches. Start making your own money so you can change your life. And you're going to want a comfortable bed after a day spent digging ditches, trust me. Go to work and then *go home*, kid."

I duck under a stalactite.

"Rhett."

I turn.

Jesse lifts his chin, pulls his shoulders back. "Six-thirty, sir. Thank you."

"Don't disappoint me. You're taking my job."

"Yes, sir."

He calls my name again as I step down the tunnel. "That letter... those numbers and letters... They're coordinates."

I turn. "What?"

He nods to the letter in my hand. "It's not a password or code for anything, its coordinates for a location."

I blink. He's right. How the hell hadn't I realized that?

Jesse smiles, winks.

"Well, son of a bitch. Thanks, kid."

I dip my chin and jog back to the truck.

FORTY-THREE
RHETT

The moment my cell phone has reception I pull to the side of the dirt road. One bar. Enough to pull up Google maps.

I punch in the coordinates and impatiently wait as the small computer in my hands appears to have trouble connecting.

Where will the coordinates take me? Somewhere local? Or —my stomach sinks—a location I would need a plane ticket for? Where would I get the money? What will be at the location once I arrive? The letter-writer himself? Sylvia? Another clue? My death?

"Come on, come on," I tap the phone against the steering wheel.

Finally, a little red dot pops up on a map.

The location appears to be in the middle of the woods—I zoom out. It's at the base of Black Bear Mountain, five miles out of town.

I tap the "Go Now" button and rows of directions populate the screen.

A rush of adrenaline surges through me. I peel out of the ditch and speed down the pitted road, praying Juan's truck doesn't fall apart along the way.

Thankfully, the rain has receded to nothing more than a light mist.

I am guided deeper and deeper into the woods on a road covered in a blanket of dead leaves. Soon, the forest closes in around me, trees and gangly bushes pushing their way into the path. Big splats of raindrops fall from the treetops, exploding onto my windshield.

I cringe as a branch drags down the side of Juan's truck.

Thirty minutes later, the woods thin and the road comes to an abrupt stop at a barbed-wire fence. Beyond it is a large field that I assume once held livestock. Now, however, it appears to be abandoned. The grass is seven shades of brown, and covered by copses of burr bushes. A large dilapidated barn sits on the edge of the property. The roof is sagging, half appears to be caved in. The windows are boarded up.

I check the map on my phone. X marks the spot.

Huh.

After locking the truck and shoving the phone into my pocket, I realize there is no gate in the fence. So, I climb over the barbed wire, catching a nasty gash on my ankle before landing on the other side.

Withered foxtail weeds tickle my elbows as I cross the field.

It's the first time since being released from prison that I wish I had a gun.

A black crow is perched on the point of the barn's roof, watching me through the mist. I scan the treeline for a gate or any access point for a vehicle, but find none.

My heart starts to pound as I reach the front doors of the barn, one swaying and creaking loudly on its hinges. There is no light on inside.

Ready for whatever might come, I slowly toe open the door and step into a heavily shadowed room. Dust dances in the dim beams of light streaming through rotted walls. A layer of moldy hay covers a dirt floor. Raindrops trickle in from the many holes in the roof. Large rotted beams run just below the ceiling, dangerously unstable. A rope hangs from one.

The smell hits me first. Urine, feces.

Death.

At the opposite side of the barn, a body sits on a mound of hay, legs stretched outward, arms dangling from a rope tied to the ceiling. Her head is bowed, long brown hair snaking over a small, pale face.

Sylvia.

I sprint across the hay, her body slowly coming into focus.

She's wearing a gray nightgown, covered in mud and smears of blood from the lacerations around her wrists where she struggled to break free from the binds. Her gown is up to her waist, saturated in her own urine, revealing veiny, mottled legs spotted with open wounds. Each is oozing, feeding the gnats and flies that are dipping in and out. The wounds remind me of ulcers.

"Sylvia." I drop to my knees and lightly touch her chin.

Her shoulders jerk at the touch.

She's alive.

"Sylvia, Sylvia, talk to me."

I sweep the hair from her sallow, sunken-in face, and tuck the greasy strands behind her ear. The smell of her almost gags me.

She blinks, a pair of bloodshot eyes eventually finding me. It takes her a second to focus. When she does, a soft moan escapes her dry, cracked lips.

"I'm going to get you out of here," I say.

I stand and begin working the rope that binds her wrists.

It is an Arbor knot, known as a noose knot, one that tightens as whatever is on the end of it tries to pull away. It takes me a minute to loosen the wet, swollen fibers. The moment I pull away the rope, her arms drop like dead weight and she collapses onto her side, her face a mere inch from a rotting animal.

A few feet away from the corpse lies a black pillowcase.

I carefully scoop her into my arms and feel for a pulse, a bit surprised when it is strong. Adrenaline, probably.

"Sylvia, I'm going to call 911. You're going to be okay."

Stroking her hair with one hand, I use the other to retrieve my cell phone and call the Thorncrest Police Station.

FORTY-FOUR
RHETT

I am still cradling Sylvia when the cops arrive. It took them thirty minutes. *Thirty* damn minutes because they wouldn't hike once they realized there was no vehicle access to the field. So, instead they called in two ATVs and stretcher.

I have mentally prepared myself to be thrown into handcuffs, tossed into the back of a squad car and taken to the station for questioning. It doesn't happen. All eyes are on Sylvia as the male and female officers jog through the barn. They are covered in burrs and sweat, despite the cool temperature. A medic carrying a massive bag follows a second later.

The silence is shattered in an instant, replaced by rapid-fire questions and excited chatter between the first responders. Boots shuffle against the dirt, kicking hay into the air as they circle around Sylvia. Bags unzip. Someone gags at the dead carcass nearby. Flashlights bounce off the walls, intermittent beams of light flashing against Sylvia's eyes.

Sylvia appears to become agitated at the sudden chaos. Her face squeezes as she shifts her body, grinding her tailbone into my lap. She wraps her arms around me tightly, and buries her face deeper in my chest. The medics and police notice this, which is why I'm not put in cuffs immediately. If I'd been the one to do this to her, she wouldn't be grabbing onto me so desperately.

"Miss Stone," the medic says in a calm, soothing voice as he kneels next to her. He is a young kid; looks no more than twenty years old. Brown hair and a patchy beard on a boyish face. He visually scans her. Once satisfied that nothing needs immediate attention, he carefully tilts her head back and trickles water into her mouth. Sylvia grips the bottle and chugs the contents between spurting coughs and gags.

"That's good. Let her drink," the medic assures me when I attempt to reposition her into an upright position.

"Rhett Cohen, I assume?" The female officer squats next to me. She's an older woman, but reminds me of a voluptuous '50s pinup girl, with bleached blonde chin-length hair, a face caked in heavy makeup, and a look in her eye that suggests she doesn't put up with shit.

I nod.

"I'm Officer Young, I understand you found her like this?"

"That's right."

"Okay, fill me in."

The medic takes Sylvia from my lap, gently leans her up against the wall and begins taking her vitals. The young officer is taking pictures of the scene.

I open my mouth, but hesitate, not sure where to begin.

Just keep it simple, my former attorney's voice whispers in my head. Simple is always best.

"The moment I heard Sylvia was missing," I begin, "I went to her house, looking for her, to see if I could find anything that would help figure out where she was." I decide it best to leave out the fact that I broke into her home using a hidden key I found under her plant. And so, by default, I also left out the disturbing discovery of Sylvia's shrine to me in her nightstand.

"Find anything?" the officer asks.

"Yeah, actually." I begin slowly stroking Sylvia's back, ensuring the officer is aware of the comfort level between us. "I checked her mailbox and found an envelope that looked like the ones she got weeks ago." I pause, waiting for her to chide me for this. She doesn't. "Are you familiar with the case?" I ask quickly.

"Slightly. Fill me in."

"A few weeks ago, someone left four letters on Sylvia's doorstep in the middle of the night. All of them are typed. The first three are of times that Sylvia believes corresponds with her mother's death twenty years ago. The fourth letter contained one of her mom's necklaces and a letter that read *You are next.* A threat, obviously. Officer Marino has the letters stored as evidence at the station and I understand Detective Stroud is lead on the case."

Young nods, narrows her eyes. I can't tell if she has realized that I am the man who was convicted of killing Sylvia's mother.

"What did this fifth letter say?" she asks.

"It gave me coordinates to this location. That's it."

"Do you have it?"

"Yes, it's in my truck."

"Why didn't you call the police when you found it?"

"I don't trust them."

Her thickly penciled brow cocks.

"I don't trust the police," I continue. "I'm Rhett Cohen. The man convicted of killing this woman's mother. Except I didn't."

Her expression doesn't change. She recognized me, I can tell now.

"When Sylvia went missing," I continue, "Stroud told me, point blank, that I was the main suspect. Since then, I've been trying to find her on my own, to clear my name. When I saw the letter, I opened it immediately, without thinking of the consequences, and here I am."

"You're an idiot."

"Not the first time I've heard it, and probably won't be the last."

"So, go back to the story," she says. "You open the letter with the coordinates. Is there a return address on the envelope?"

"No—we didn't get that lucky. So, the coordinates brought me here, I found Sylvia and called you. That's it. That's the story." Minus my visit to Jesse, who I'd made a promise to keep his hideout a secret.

"How did you know about the letters in the first place?" Young asks. "The first ones that were sent?"

"Gossip."

"The necklace wasn't in the gossip."

Officer Young knows much more than she initially led on.

"You're right. I visited Sylvia after I learned about the letters."

"You went to her house?"

"Yes."

"Why?"

"Because I wanted to know who sent them to her."

"Why?"

"Because I believe this can help me find the man who framed me for her mother's murder twenty years ago."

Young tilts her head to the side. "Vigilante justice. Is that what you had in mind?"

"Honestly?"

"Yes."

"I'm not so sure about anything anymore."

"Do you have an idea of who might've framed you— assuming you are innocent of course?"

I hesitate, knowing I need to tread lightly. "I think both Dr. Harris Taylor and Detective Johnny Stroud need to be looked into. They both have their prints all over this thing. It was the doctor's missing son, Jesse Taylor, who was paid by a mystery person to deliver the envelopes to Sylvia. And Detective Stroud is the only person who has been involved in this thing from the beginning, twenty years ago. He knows the same intimate details that were on the letters. I suggest speaking with Dr. Harris first. Ask what he knows."

"Well, I'm afraid we no longer have that option."

I frown. "What do you mean?"

"Harris Taylor had an unfortunate accident recently."

"What kind of accident?"

"He took a tumble down his staircase, at his house, two days ago. His wife, Janet, found him at the bottom of the stairs, neck broken, but alive. He's been airlifted to a trauma center in Burlington. He's on life support."

My stomach drops. I think of Jesse, and how I just saw him. He must not have heard the news that his dad has been injured. Dammit. Poor kid. I'll deal with that after this.

"Was his wife home?" I ask.

"She was. Asleep, she says. Woke to the noise, came out of the bedroom and he was at the bottom of the staircase. And yes, before you ask, she's been questioned."

"Where is she now?"

"By her husband's side, of course."

I take a second to let this new—very interesting—information sink in. I decide that I don't have time to analyze it now, so I continue. "Then question Stroud. He and I have had bad blood since high school. I don't know how, or why he would have framed me... but I think someone needs to question him."

Young shifts her gaze to the medic checking Sylvia over, and appears to be choosing her next words carefully. She dismisses my suggestion to question her colleague and instead says, "The last letter said 'You are next' right?"

"Right."

"So the obvious implication, considering it was sent with her dead mom's necklace is, that Sylvia is next to die."

"Right."

"Well..." Young gestures to the obviously still alive woman.

I nod. It doesn't make sense to me either. Sylvia was taken and left for dead, but not beaten, or tortured, or killed. The threat was not followed through with. Unless....

"Maybe we're thinking about it wrong," I say. "Maybe 'You are next' means something else."

A stretcher is carted into the barn.

Young jerks her chin. "Come with us, will you? I'd like to ask you some more questions and we could use the extra help getting her across the field."

"Do I need to get a lawyer for these questions, Officer Young?"

"Listen. I didn't think you did it back then, and I don't think you did this now."

I can't hide my surprise.

She continues, "Your case wasn't fair. Your lawyer was crap, Stroud hated you, and the jury was hand-selected by him and him alone—though you didn't hear that from me. You did not receive a fair trial. Hell, everyone knows." She stands as the officer readies the gurney. "More than that, I just didn't peg you as the type. Call it a gut instinct."

"Thank you."

She dips her chin, "Now, help us."

Together, we lift Sylvia onto the gurney.

"You guys ready?" the medic asks.

I nod.

"*Left, right, left, right...*"

"Where did you guys park?" I ask as we maneuver out of the barn.

"Next to what I assume is your truck."

"You couldn't find a gate either?"

"Nope."

I frown. "Then how did whoever did this get in?"

"Carried her?"

"That's a hell of a carry, especially considering the rusty barbed-wire fence."

"We'll check around for tire tracks after we get her loaded."

I nod, but something doesn't feel right.

Sylvia's eyes open.

"He didn't do this," she whispers in a gritty voice. "Rhett didn't do this." Her eyes dart between the officers, panic flashing.

I close my eyes and exhale with relief, feeling a million pounds lift off my shoulders.

Officer Young lightly strokes her forehead. "Don't you worry about that right now, sweetheart, let's get you to the hospital and then we'll chat. You rest, dear. Just close your eyes."

As we carry the stretcher across the field to the ATV, I hear Officer Young doling out orders into the radio attached to her chest—

"*...and lastly, we need to do a rape kit...*"

My stomach sinks.

FORTY-FIVE

RHETT

I follow the ambulance to the hospital, trying to fit this new piece of information into a rapidly growing puzzle.

I know, in my gut, that Harris Taylor didn't fall down his stairs. He was pushed. But by whom? His wife? Did she find out about his affair with their neighbor, Gloria?

Or was it Gloria herself? Did she emotionally snap after our tussle in the woods? Did she try to kill Harris to ensure her dirty secret would never come to light?

Or, was it Stroud? The detective (being the detective that he is) found out that his side-chick, Gloria, was also having sex with Harris and got jealous—so jealous, he tried to kill the man. This is not too difficult to imagine considering Stroud's fragile ego.

I shake my head, feeling the twinge of a headache. I force myself to refocus on the main issue at hand. Who tied Sylvia in a barn and left her for dead? And why not kill her right away?

One name enters my brain, and to my surprise, it is not Johnny Stroud.

Jesse.

Jesse Taylor is a link that ties everything together.

1. Jesse delivered the letters to Sylvia, beginning this whole mess.

2. Jesse suggested we visit the abandoned house at the end of his neighborhood. There, Dr. Harris, his dad, caught us watching him have sex with the neighbor. *Then* Stroud caught us sneaking out. Coincidence? Did Jesse set us up?

3. Jesse's dad mysteriously falls down a staircase and is currently clinging to life on ICU.

Jesse.

Everything links to him.

I need to go back to the cave after Sylvia is taken care of.

Once inside the hospital, I'm asked to remain in the waiting room while Sylvia is examined by a doctor and interviewed by the police. For an hour, I pace the corner of the room, listening to a baby scream for its bottle, watching a skeleton of a man suck chocolate pudding through a straw, and a young couple with matching American flag tattoos argue about money while draining the vending machine.

Officer Young finally emerges, but offers no update on Sylvia. Instead, she pulls me into a small room just past the *Do Not Enter* doors. Inside is a plastic table and matching chairs that remind me of the interview room at the police station. Here, she questions me again, this time with a small recorder on the table. This time, she asks for alibis. I tell her that the night Sylvia went missing I was sleeping at the construction site, which I am sure is in full view of the security cameras outside the liquor store, and/or any of the surrounding buildings. The crew can vouch for me the next morning. It's more than enough, and this should make me feel good, but it doesn't. Once you've been wrongly convicted you realize how messed up the justice system truly is. If someone of power wants to nail you, they will. Alibi or not.

I keep waiting for Stroud to come striding in, cuffs in hand, a wad of chewing tobacco in his mouth.

He never shows.

This surprises me.

Something else that surprises me is that I am the only person waiting to hear of Sylvia's condition. She has no friends, no family.

I called Billy on the cell phone he'd given me, and asked him to keep me up to date if and when the gossips learn about Sylvia's rescue.

Around one in the afternoon the doctor enters the waiting room, and motions me into the same room where Young questioned me.

We stand, facing each other, awkwardly close in the small room. He's a large man, a few inches taller than myself, with a head of gray—gray hair, gray beard, gray eyes, and bushy gray eyebrows. His skin even has a grayish tint, suggesting he is long overworked.

"Mr. Cohen, I'm Dr. Mansfield."

"Pleasure to meet you." We shake hands.

"Miss Stone is stable, resting now."

"Is she okay?"

"Yes, she's got a few cuts and bruises but is otherwise healthy. The lacerations around her wrists didn't need stitches. We cleaned and bandaged them up; they should be fully healed in a week or so." He frowns. "Her legs, as I'm sure you saw, are riddled with infected bug bites."

"Bug bites?" I frown. "They looked a lot more serious than that."

"Yes..." A line creases his brow. "Under her toenails we found pieces of scabs and skin from where, it appears, she scratched the bites open with them."

"With her own toenails?"

"Appears that way, yes. We took a sample of the skin for

forensics—to confirm it doesn't belong to whoever tied her up—but it appears that's what happened. She scratched them open, cutting into her skin."

We stare at each other for minute.

He clears his throat. "Anyway, we've cleaned and bandaged each of them. She'll have a round of antibiotics to take and I've prescribed painkillers as well. Other than that she just needs lots of rest, food, water, and likely therapy when she gets around to it."

"Did you run a toxicology scan on her?"

"Yes, her system is clean of drugs and alcohol. Also, there appears to be no sign of penetration, forced or otherwise, in or around her anus or vagina. No contusions or anything to lead us to believe she was sexually abused. Or physically, even."

"Not even physically?"

He scratches his head. "Right. No sign of struggle, from a medical perspective anyway, but that's for the police to figure out."

"How much water should I make sure she drinks?"

"Actually, according to the urine sample, she's not dehydrated." He frowns again. "But make sure she drinks and eats with these pills regardless."

Not dehydrated? How is that possible?

"Can I talk to her?" I ask.

"Officer Young is speaking with her now. Let me see if she's finished up, and then yes, she's all yours. As long as her vitals hold up, we'll release her in a few hours—before words gets out that she's here."

FORTY-SIX

RHETT

I'm pouring my fourth cup of tepid waiting-room coffee when I hear—

"Rhett!"

Jesse rushes me, eyes wide, a child-like worry on his face.

"My dad," he hisses. "He fell—he fell and he's not okay."

"I know." I set my coffee on the windowsill, grab his elbow and pull him to the corner, away from the prying eyes of the other people in the waiting room. "Officer Young told me. What are you doing here?"

"I had to see you—I knew you'd be here because I heard about Sylvia. Anyway, you remember you told me you saw Stroud in my neighborhood at midnight two nights ago?" The words tumble out breathlessly, hyper, uncontrolled. "And that Stroud was also seeing my neighbor? That's when it happened, dude."

"When what happened?"

"When he fell down the stairs!"

"You don't think he fell, do you?"

"No, man. No." Jesse leans in, his face flushed with anger.

"Stroud found out about my dad and Gloria, and he tried to kill him. I know it."

"Lower your voice. How do you *know* it?"

"I just do, alright?"

"Jesse, are you sure it wasn't your mom?"

"Yes."

"Are you sure, Jesse? Think about it. Your mom finds out about the affair. Gets pissed. Remembers she has a lot to inherit if her husband dies..."

"My mom would *never*. She's crazy but not that crazy. It's Stroud, dude. I know it... Jesse begins shifting his weight back and forth like a tweaked-out druggie. "I'm telling you—Stroud found out about Gloria and my dad, drove to my house, and tried to kill him."

"That's a huge accusation, Jesse." I grab his shoulders, force him to still—to *hear* me. "You do *not* want to go around accusing the town detective of attempted murder unless you are absolutely, unequivocally sure he is at fault."

"He tried to kill my dad, Rhett!"

Heads turn in our direction.

I glance at the security guard chatting with the receptionist, then refocus on Jesse, my patience cashed out. "Get ahold of yourself, kid."

"This guy needs to fry, man. For what he did to you, for what he did to my dad."

Jesse's loyalty makes me uneasy—and also makes me feel protective of him.

He jerks out of my hold. "I'm going to fix this, Rhett."

"No, Jesse, you need to stay out of this. How did you get here, anyway? I'm assuming you're no longer hiding."

"No. I left the caves after you came by. Decided to take your advice, go home, and start that new job tomorrow. I stopped by a diner on the way in and that's where I heard about it. I had no idea my dad was in ICU. I—I wasn't going to do anything. Told myself I didn't care, but..." He drags his fingers through his greasy hair. "But I do, man. I do."

"How did you get here?"

"On some random bike I found in the woods after I left the cave."

"Where in the woods?"

"Abandoned in a ditch at the bottom of Black Bear Mountain. Listen, I've got stuff to do..."

"Jesse—" I call out, but he's already storming out the door.

On the television mounted in the corner of the room a red *Breaking News* banner is flashing...

I let Jesse leave and walk over to the television, expecting the headline to read: *Missing woman Sylvia Stone found.*

The security guard sends me the side-eye as I grab the remote and turn up the volume.

A young brunette is reporting in a ditch next to the interstate. Her eyes are laser-sharp, her face a little pale. She's mid-sentence.

"*...woman was found beaten to death on this very access road that I am standing on right now, along Interstate 314, just past mile marker twelve. Her identity was confirmed by the Tennessee driver's license found in her purse. Please take a look at your screen. If you recognize this woman or know anything about her, you are asked to contact authorities immediately...*"

A picture of Crystal Cheri's face fills the screen.

FORTY-SEVEN
RHETT

Sylvia is sleeping when they finally allow me inside her hospital room. I pace the edge of the bed, one eye on her, the other on the door. I expect Stroud to arrive any minute.

He doesn't, and as each hour passes I grow increasingly curious. The detective should be chomping at the bit to talk to Sylvia and find an angle to arrest me. Why isn't he? Where is he?

The hospital room is tiny and dated. The paint is peeling, the floor stained. A dead fly lies in the windowsill. I wonder how it died upside down, and then I wonder how long it's been there and why someone hasn't disposed of it. I grab a tissue, carefully pluck the carcass from the sill, toss it into the trashcan.

The afternoon has turned a gloomy gray, and also cold, based on the coats and scarves that the elderly couple shuffling across the parking lot are wearing. The man is wearing a newsboy cap and reminds me of my father. George Cohen died sixteen days after my conviction. My mother, Cici, two years later, of cancer. I wasn't allowed to attend either of their funerals.

A few feet from the couple, a woman paces the sidewalk,

sucking a cigarette, her head bowed against the frigid wind. Brown leaves spin around her feet. Her sneakers are untied. Next to her, a handicapped child sits slumped in a wheelchair, asleep. I am suddenly struck with an overwhelming sense of melancholy. Why is there such pain and sadness in this world?

Why does being out feel so much like being in?

I close my eyes and remind myself of my dream of a cabin, somewhere deep in the woods, cut off from the world. A place of my own, surrounded by trees, dogs, and countless sunrises. I turn away from the window.

You'll do it, Rhett. Just get through this first.

Around seven in the evening, Sylvia wakes.

Her eyes find mine immediately. I hurry to the side of the bed.

Sylvia turns her head, her brown hair fanned over the pillow like a spider's web. She opens her palm. I slip my hand inside hers.

"I told them it wasn't you," she whispers, her voice scratchy.

"I know you did, thank you. Are you okay?"

She nods, but squirms uncomfortably under the sheets. The IV connected to her arm beeps angrily.

"Do you need another blanket?"

"Yeah... one of those heated ones. Please."

I page the nurse and we wait silently until the blanket arrives and the door is closed once again.

I stretch the heavy, warm fabric over her legs.

"Sylvia, is there anyone you want me to call for you?"

Her face hardens. "There is no one to call."

"How about any friends?"

"I don't really have any, Rhett," she snaps.

I inhale, chiding myself, hoping it wasn't obvious that I want to hand her off to someone else so that I can get the hell out of here. I don't want to be any more involved with Sylvia than I have to be. I don't want to be the one to handle her recovery.

"I'm sorry," I say.

"No, it's fine." She takes a deep breath. "I'm sorry I snapped. It's just that every nurse who's walked in here has asked me the same questions. Who can I call for you, darling?" She snorts a laugh that sounds like it hurts. "The only person I can think of is Ginger, my hairdresser."

"Do you want me to call her?" I say, far too eagerly, and again, wince.

"No, I don't want you to call my *hairdresser*, Rhett."

An awkward moment passes between us.

"Sylvia, do you—can you talk about it? About what happened?"

"Yes... I've already told the cops everything..." She folds her hands over her stomach as if settling in for a long talk. "They told me how you found the letter in the mailbox—my God, thank you."

"Just good luck is all. Can you tell me what happened?"

She nods, begins. "It was the night we went to the abandoned house, the night we saw Dr. Harris Taylor doing... you know."

"The neighbor, yeah. Did you tell the cops what we were doing there?"

"No, I didn't tell them any of that. Just that I was at home when it all happened. They didn't even ask how I'd spent the day and first half of the evening."

Sloppy police work.

"So," she continues, "after I dropped you off at the construction site, I went home. I was in the kitchen, pouring a glass of wine, when out of nowhere, someone pulls a black bag over my head."

This must have been the black pillowcase I noticed in the barn.

"How did they get in?" I ask.

"I'm sure I left the front door unlocked. I'm bad about leaving it unlocked until right before I go to bed."

"That must change."

"I know. Hey—how's Shirley? She's okay, right? The officer told me they saw her when they checked the house."

"Yes, she's fine."

Sylvia exhales. "Good. Anyway, after they bagged my head, they shoved the barrel of a gun in my neck and tied my hands behind my back. Then I was dragged out the front door and into a car."

"Did you scream?"

"Of course I screamed. I tried to fight but there's not much you can do with your hands behind your back. I couldn't even walk upright."

"Did you see the person?"

"No."

"Do you know if they were a man or woman?"

"They never spoke."

"Not a single word?"

"No." She begins smoothing the blanket in short repetitious strokes. "Anyway, they drove me out to the middle of nowhere—I could tell we were going into the woods from the bumpy road and the smell in the air. Then I was forced into the barn, gun at my back. I was connected to a rope, and that was it."

"And then they left?"

"Yep."

"How did you get the bag off your head?"

"I used my mouth. Kept yanking it with my teeth until eventually it was repositioned enough where I could shimmy it off."

I stare at her for a long minute.

The door opens and a nurse hurries in with discharge instructions.

FORTY-EIGHT
RHETT

Ten minutes later, I'm wheeling Sylvia Stone to my truck. Twilight glows blue around us, the setting sun nothing but a thin line of orange on the horizon.

I open the passenger-side door, scoop Sylvia into my arms. She's wearing an oversized blue T-shirt with the hospital logo and baggy shorts, given to her by the nurse. I carefully sit her on the seat, my eyes grazing the bandages on her legs.

"Good?"

"Good," she nods.

I shut the door, return the wheelchair, then slide behind the steering wheel.

"Nice truck," she grins. She has laid back the seat, her head resting against the torn leather.

"Only the best for you." I turn the engine, click on the lights, and pull onto the road.

"Whose is it?"

"Someone I work with at the construction site. It's on loan." *Used* to work with.

Sylvia turns her face to me, the light from the streetlamps

highlighting her pale skin. "Thank you, Rhett. You literally saved my life. Thank you."

"I just checked the mail, that's it."

"Exactly. Why didn't the cops check my mail? Seems so obvious to check a missing woman's mail. Right? Did you talk to Jesse?" She's wondering the same thing I did when I found the letter—did Jesse deliver it, as he had the others?

"I did, and no, he had no part in this letter. He's been in the cave for the last few days and hasn't left. Whoever sent it, did so through the mail system." I pause. "There's something else..."

"What?"

"Crystal Cheri's body was just found..."

Sylvia's eyes round in horror. "Dead?"

I nod.

"Where?"

"In a ditch on the side of the interstate."

"Oh, my God. Who did it? Do they know?"

"I don't know. I just saw it on the news. That's all I know."

Sylvia sighs deeply, closes her eyes. "What the hell, Rhett? What the *hell?*"

I don't respond because the truth is, I'm still having trouble wrapping my head around it.

A minute later, her eyes are still closed. I can't tell if she's asleep or not, so I do my best to stay quiet. After picking up her prescriptions, I drive to her house, slowly over the dirt road so as not to wake her.

As my headlights round the corner, the scene unfolds in front of me.

I hit the brakes, jostling the cab.

A row of red brake lights lines the road in front of Sylvia's home. Voices carry on the wind. Flashlights bounce off the trees, the torches blurred by a cloud of cigarette smoke hanging over a crowd. There are at least two dozen people, some crowding the driveway, some leaning against the vehicles.

"*Shit.*"

Sylvia lifts her head off the seat, blinking. "Where are we?"

"Your house."

"*What?* Who are all these people?"

"Media. Reporters. It must've gotten out that you were found."

Her jaw drops. "You're not serious."

"Yes—your disappearance has been all over the news."

I stare at the line of cars and media vans, contemplating what to do. I begin mentally counting how much money I have so that we could get a hotel room somewhere far away from this mess. It's all I can think to do.

"Drive, Rhett," Sylvia demands, her eyes narrowed in defiance. "They're not chasing me from my damn home."

"Are you sure?"

"Yeah. Take me to *my* house."

I dip my chin. I admire the grit. "Okay then."

I lock the doors and slowly drive down the center line of the usually quiet dirt road, now packed with vehicles. Wild-eyed faces swarm the windows, pointing flashlights. The cab of the truck turns into a dizzying discotheque of bouncing light.

"*It's them, it's them!*" someone shouts, triggering a rush of questions and accusations. A dozen voices begin screaming at us all at once. A hundred little knuckles tap the windows. Someone pounds on the hood.

The noise is almost deafening, triggering my fight or flight response.

All I can think is: *Don't run over anyone, don't run over anyone...*

I turn into Sylvia's driveway and slam the brakes. "Stay here."

I push out of the truck.

"Rhett—"

I slam the door.

I'm blinded by a blast of camera flashes. I shield my eyes and yell over the noise. "The cops have been called. If one person sets foot on this property, they will be arrested for trespassing and harassment."

With that, I turn and stalk back to the truck while a dozen questions are hurled in my direction.

"*Mr. Cohen, is Sylvia Stone pregnant with your baby?*"

"*Is she okay?*"

"*We heard she was stabbed like her mom. Can you confirm?*"

"*Can you tell us the location of the barn where she was found?*"

"*Was there another letter?*"

"*Did you kidnap her?*"

"*Why don't you go back to jail where you belong?*"

I hit the gas, kicking rocks into the air as I speed down the driveway.

Sylvia is balled in the floorboard, sobbing.

I skid to a stop at the front door, jump out and jog around the hood, ignoring the screams and shouts. Sylvia lurches into my arms the second I open the door and shoves her house key into my hand. Cradling her like a baby, I kick the truck door closed, hurry onto the porch. Seconds later, we are finally inside the house.

I gently lay Sylvia on the couch, and stroke her head. "You okay?"

She sniffs, nods.

"I'm going to check the house and then call the cops; they'll send someone out here."

I hurry from room to room, pulling the shades, ensuring there is no clear view inside the house.

Shirley takes no interest in greeting Sylvia and instead, follows me through the house, the wrinkled ball of skin meowing for attention, totally oblivious to the tension in the air.

Once I'm certain the house is secure, I call Officer Young and demand she handle the crowd outside.

Sylvia is sitting up when I return to the living room. Her face is red, jaw clenched. Her fear has turned to anger.

"I cannot believe this, Rhett," she seethes.

"I can." I grab the bag of prescriptions, sit next to her, and begin laying them out. Shirley jumps onto the couch, then onto the armrest, and curls into a ball.

I study the instructions on each bottle. "It says you need to eat with these. I'll be right back."

"Will you turn on the TV?"

After clicking on the television and turning up the volume to drown out the noise outside, I search through the kitchen cabinets, eventually settling on a can of chicken noodle soup. The cure-all, right?

I pace the kitchen as the soup heats. My stomach is in knots. It feels like this is all happening again. So eerily similar to the weeks leading up to my arrest for Marjorie Stone's murder.

I grip onto the sides of the kitchen sink and bow my head.

Inhale, exhale.

I cannot go to prison again.

Inhale, exhale.

Please, God, I cannot go to prison again.

A sickening panic of desperation sends a rush of tears to my eyes. Fucking *tears*. I feel like I am spinning, that nothing is in my control.

I feel like I am going to throw up.

My mother's face flashes behind my eyes. The pain, disappointment, the sheer horror on her face when the verdict was read and I was pulled out of the courtroom. I remember my father's face, eyes wild with fear, face mottled with rage.

I remember what they were wearing and think about it often. Silly, isn't it? They'd dressed up for the delivery of the final verdict. My mother was wearing a dingy, moth-eaten blue dress (her "nice" dress), and a pair of scuffed flats with a hole in the side. My father wore the only suit he owned. The one he wore to weddings or whatever, and the one I wore to my high school graduation. He looked as uncomfortable as ever in it. My court-issued attorney (we had no money for a respectable lawyer) was wearing a navy suit that looked like it cost more than our family car.

I remember thinking I would never have the chance to offer my parents a better life. To buy them better clothes, a better car, healthier food. I remember feeling so guilty that I was the cause of so much stress in a life already filled with insurmountable debt and depression.

My mother visited every week. My father didn't visit once.

Then, he died.

I'll never forget the final visit from my mother. She was wearing a pink beanie someone knitted for her from the church. It didn't fit quite right, sitting crooked on her pale, bald head. Tiny strands of gray hair poked out above her ears, the few that remained after the chemo. She was jarringly skinny. Long veiny fingers pressed against the glass as milky, tired eyes stared into mine. She was wearing the same blue dress that she'd worn to the trial and pink lipstick, as if she'd made an effort before coming to see me. I, on the other hand, had just been involved in my latest scuffle, and was sporting a black eye and busted lip. I was so embarrassed for her to see me like that.

She died three days later.

My fists clench around the sink and I have to force myself not to release a bellow of agony.

The soup begins to boil, pulling my attention. I look at my distorted refection in the window above the sink, and tell myself to get it together.

One thing at a time.

I go through the motions of piecing together a meal. Soup in bowl, water in glass, add ice. Napkin, spoon, tray.

As I step in the living room, blue and red lights reflect against the curtains.

"Thank God," Sylvia murmurs. "The cops are here."

I set the tray on her lap, sit next to her. We stare at each other for a moment, listening to the noise outside, unbelieving of the situation we have found ourselves in.

I look away, stomach churning once again. "Eat, please. It's time to take your pain pills."

We shift our attention to the television just as a headshot of each of us fills the screen. The headline: *Local woman found.*

I quickly change the station to the weather channel, and turn up the volume.

We sit in silence, Sylvia, Shirley, and I, for six rounds of *Local on the Eights*, staring blankly at the television. The noise outside finally fades. The road empties of vehicles. My focus begins to waver and I realize how tired I am.

FORTY-NINE

RHETT

At one o'clock in the morning, Sylvia falls asleep on the couch.

I retrieve a pillow and blanket from her room, and cover her up.

The light of the television flickers over her face. Shadows circle her eyes, giving her a ghostly appearance. I look down at the leg she kicked out of the blanket immediately after I covered her.

Six bandages.

I imagine her ripping open her own skin—with her own nails nonetheless.

Who would do that?

I think about my longest stretch in the hole in prison. Six days. Six days caged in a small black room, hardly tall enough to stand in. No light. Total darkness for 144 hours. I had to feel my way to the bucket in the corner meant to serve as a toilet. I was allotted only enough food and water so not to die. The water tasted like dirt, and the food came in the form of a squeeze gel pack. Rats dipped in and out of the room. Centipedes as long as my finger crawled up my legs. I was bitten several times. Hurt like fire. Yet, even in that kind of environment, I never once considered slicing myself open with my own nails.

I quietly push myself off the couch, walk to the window and stare into the darkness.

Sylvia said her abductor dragged her out of the house and into a vehicle... but there were no drag marks found on the ground.

She said she was pouring a glass of wine when her abductor pulled a pillowcase over her head. Yet, her wine glass was found upright on the table, the bottle sitting next to it. Wouldn't she have dropped the glass, and/or the bottle, startled by the confrontation? Shouldn't the glass be in a million pieces on the floor?

The doctor said Sylvia's tests indicated that she was not dehydrated—despite having her hands tied to a barn wall for three days. Did someone care for her during her captivity? Give her water? If so, why hadn't she told anyone?

And lastly, why was Sylvia's life spared? Why did her abductor guarantee her discovery by sending a letter with her location? Whoever did this wanted her to be found. Why?

I turn from the window, stare at Sylvia.

I study the heavy rise and fall of her chest, the jerk of her arm as she dreams. I am aware of that feeling once again, that red flag in my gut that screams at me every time I see her. Something is off with this woman.

Her story doesn't add up.

Sylvia Stone is lying. I am as sure of this as my next breath.

Why? To what end?

Is she lying *for* someone?

Is she protecting someone?

Who?

A crazy thought enters my head—

Is Sylvia protecting *me*? I recall her first words to the

responding officers: *"He didn't do this."* Sylvia went on to repeat this proclamation many times over the course of her treatment.

I look to the staircase that leads to her bedroom, where a shrine to me lays hidden in her nightstand.

Have I missed something?

FIFTY

RHETT

It is 8:47 p.m., the coldest night of the season so far.

Sylvia has slept for over twenty-four hours, waking only a handful of times to eat, drink, and take her pain pills.

Sometimes I wonder if she is actually awake, only pretending to sleep.

The story has exploded. The daughter of the brutally slain Marjorie Stone is recovering from being kidnapped in the arms of the man convicted of killing her mother—the same man she herself testified against during the trial. It's a real-life soap opera and the entire nation is drinking it up.

You can't turn on the television without seeing my face.

The crowd outside Sylvia's home has doubled, despite Thorncrest PD's occasional drive-bys. I feel like I'm trapped in a fish bowl, prying eyes watching my every move from all angles.

I don't dare leave. I will be followed, and besides, where would I go? Also, I've realized that staying by Sylvia's side looks good on me. Appearance is everything, after all—why would I have kidnapped her in a quest for revenge, then stay by her side and nurse her back to health? Makes no sense, right?

Then again, at this point, nothing does. Especially why Detective Stroud *still* hasn't shown up to interview Sylvia about her kidnapping.

I'm growing increasingly uneasy, that feeling right before a severe thunderstorm hits. Like something building, soon to erupt.

I'm peering at the crowd through a slit in the window when my cell phone buzzes from the fireplace mantel. I'd almost forgotten I had it.

"Hello?"

"Rhett, it's Billy. How're you holding up?"

"Holding up's about it."

"I heard the crowd outside her house has doubled since last night. You still there?"

"Yeah."

"You're welcome to come to my house if you need to, or come back to the shop and hang out in the office if you just need to get away."

"Thanks, but I'm alright. What's up?"

"Gossip. Dr. Harris Taylor is awake."

"Is he talking?"

"Oh yeah. Says he didn't fall. Claims he was pushed down the stairs—and get this: Says he didn't see the guy's face but remembers seeing a glimpse of a Celtic cross on the guy's arm who pushed him."

My jaw drops. "Detective Stroud."

"Yep. Here's the deal though: Chief Allen isn't going to arrest Stroud on that alone. Lots of people have cross tattoos and what's to say Harris's memory is correct—that's what they're saying. My thoughts? I don't think the chief will even question Stroud. Those two are thick as thieves."

I agree, and this is exactly why the chief needs to find out that Stroud has been having sex with his brother's fiancé.

Billy continues, "Dr. Taylor's wife, Judy—"

"Janet."

"Janet, right. She's got an attorney flying down from New York. I guess they're still looking at her as a potential suspect because she was home and all. It's going to be a circus, man."

"It already is a circus."

Just then, a knock sounds from the back door.

"Billy, I gotta go. Thanks for calling—keep me updated."

I slip the phone back onto the mantle and hurry across the house, ready to send my fist into the nose of the reporter who's had the balls to creep onto Sylvia's property.

I swing open the door.

Jesse rushes in, winded, face beet red from the cold air.

I quickly shut the door behind him. "What the hell are you doing here, son?"

He doubles over, gasping for air.

"You okay? What's going on?" I guide the kid to the kitchen table, glancing over my shoulder to ensure Sylvia is still asleep.

Jesse collapses into the chair.

I squat at his feet. "We need to be quiet, she's sleeping—what's going on?"

A bead of sweat rolls down his face. "I ran here. Parked the bike I found about a mile east." He's sucking in air as he's talking. "Didn't want the media people to see me."

"Sit tight." I rise, fill a glass of water, hand it to him. I watch as he chugs it in one go.

Jesse licks his lips, takes a deep breath, then looks up at me. "I need to talk to you."

"So talk."

"You heard that my dad is awake?"

"Just now, this very second in fact. I know that he says he remembers a cross tattoo on the guy who pushed him."

"Stroud."

I nod.

A wry smile crosses Jesse's cracked lips. "I got him, man. I got him."

"What do you mean you *got him*?"

"Well, I told the cops that *I* saw Stroud in my neighborhood the night my dad was pushed—didn't want to get you in trouble."

"Good. And?"

"And of course they didn't believe me. So I camped out last night, right there at the police station, refusing to leave until someone took me seriously. Finally, that woman officer—Young—pulled me back for another interview. I told her to check Stroud's cell phone GPS, to pin his location for the night my dad was pushed." His smile grows. "She got a warrant from the judge to access the records, dude, and guess what—he was *there*. Right around midnight, just like you said. He was there, at *my house*. He did it. Tried to kill my dad for fucking his girlfriend. They've got a warrant out for his arrest. Attempted murder, dude. We got him."

I blink, processing. Between this and the fact that Harris saw a Celtic cross on the man's arm who pushed him, the chief will have to interview Stroud. I can't fight the smile. "Nice work. You got him, Jesse. *You* got him—You're a hero."

He smiles, and I realize that's exactly what this is about. Jesse might not like his dad very much, but deep down, he loves him.

"I'm proud of you," I say.

"That's not all. I guess they traced his movements over the last few days and Stroud was in the same location that that Tennessee girl's body was found. Crystal Cheri. They think he's connected. They're going to dig in."

Relief swells in my lungs. Stroud killed Crystal Cheri because she knew about his dirty little secret. This also explains why he's been MIA. Stroud's been on the run.

Jesse inhales deeply, sitting a bit taller. "Doc says he thinks my dad is going to be okay."

"That's great news."

"Yeah," he nods, meets my gaze. "I want to thank you... for everything."

"I didn't do anything, Jesse. I just gave you a little push."

"A kick in the ass, more like. And I needed it. Thank you."

I dip my chin.

"I started that job you gave me and have moved back into my house. I'm going to save money, just like you suggested, and then get out."

"Good."

He exhales deeply. "Anyway, I'm sorry this doesn't solve all that," he gestures to Sylvia on the couch. "You know, who wrote the letters, who kidnapped her..."

"Yeah about that... so I'm assuming the GPS tracking didn't happen to show Stroud anywhere around the barn where Sylvia was held?"

"No." Jesse solemnly shook his head. "I asked about that specifically. He had no part in that."

Of course he didn't. Because that would have been too damn easy.

So who kidnapped Sylvia? Stroud didn't, and Dr. Taylor didn't... so *who*?

Jesse stands. "Anyway, I need to get back. I just wanted to tell you all this."

I put my hand on his shoulder. "You did good, Jesse."

"Oh, and, um, one more thing. I wanted to let you know..." He shifts his weight. "I've decided what I'm going to do with my life after I get back on my feet."

"Yeah?"

"I'm going to be a cop, work up to be a detective."

My smile widens. "Good. That's real good, Jesse. Go for it."

"I will."

I watch misfit Jesse Taylor sneak out the door and disappear into the night, into his new life.

I turn, lean against the living room doorframe, and stare at Sylvia. Though I'm relieved Dr. Taylor is going to be okay and that Stroud is going to get what he deserves, I can't help but feel I'm farther away than ever from figuring out who framed me.

A small meow whispers from the across the room.

I spot Shirley sauntering up the staircase. The cat looks back at me, then disappears into Sylvia's room.

For some reason I can't explain, I feel like the cat is leading me.

One more look, I think.

Just one more look around...

FIFTY-ONE
RHETT

I slowly take the stairs, two by two, carefully releasing my weight so that the warped wood doesn't creak and wake Sylvia.

Shirley weaves in between my feet on each step, a dangerous game that gives her far too much pleasure.

After one final look over my shoulder, I step into Sylvia's bedroom.

Shirley meows loudly. I shoot her a look, then click on the lamp on the nightstand.

I open the bottom drawer and begin filtering through the shrine of me. This time, I study each photo, each newspaper clipping, each printout, looking for some sort of clue or link to each one. Trying to find whatever it is that I know I'm missing here.

After checking to ensure Sylvia is still asleep, I resume my snooping.

Her closet is a mess, but appears to hide nothing nefarious. Her bathroom, same. I check under the bed, under the mattress, inside the pillowcases. Same with the loveseat in the corner. I even check under the potted fig next to the window.

Nothing.

I make my way to the small bookcase that sits next to the dresser, which I'd also checked through. Agatha Christie, Gillian Flynn, Karin Slaughter, Lisa Jackson, Stephen King, Nora Roberts. A dozen more murder mysteries and horror novels. I look for a diary or journal, but don't get that lucky.

I glance up at the doorway, darkened by shadows. Shirley is sitting in the hall, in the middle of the pool of light coming from the room. A spotlight on her pale wrinkled body.

We stare at each other for a moment and, again, I get the weird feeling she's trying to tell me something.

My eyes rake over her body, her round, plump belly. I suddenly recall the mounds of cat food and massive water bowl that lined the floor when I broke into the house shortly after Sylvia went missing.

I frown...

That's *extremely* convenient, isn't it?

The day Sylvia goes missing, a perfectly adequate week-long supply of food and water is laid out for her cat.

"Talk to me," I whisper to Shirley. "Tell me what happened."

She flicks her tail, but doesn't move.

"Fine."

Fisting my hands on my hips, I step back from the bookcase, my heel creaking on a very bendy floorboard. I move off the board and study it.

It stands out, visually. The single slat of wood appears different from the rest, like a piece of a puzzle that doesn't quite fit correctly.

I kneel down, finger the edges.

They're loose.

I pause, listen over my shoulder. When I hear nothing, I gently pry open the slat.

A wide, skinny wooden box sits on the subfloor between two parallel support beams.

I carefully lift the box from its hiding spot, my pulse racing, as if my body knows the significance before I do.

Inside is a journal. The pages are faded and worn, indicating it is very old. I flip open the leather flap. The inside cover reads: Marjorie Stone.

It's her mother's journal.

The blood begins rushing through my ears.

I set aside the journal and go through the rest of the box.

There is a stack of long, thin envelopes exactly like the ones that contained the letters. Underneath, a clear baggie full of jewelry—the same jewelry that was reported stolen the day Marjorie was murdered—presumably stolen by the man who murdered her: me. And tucked under the bag, is a folded black ski mask—the same mask worn by the person who paid Jesse Taylor to deliver the letters.

FIFTY-TWO
RHETT

It's morning. I have stayed awake all night, motionless at my perch on the edge of the couch where I have done nothing but watch Sylvia sleep. Clutched in my hand is a small gold band. It is her mother's wedding band, part of the jewelry that was reported stolen the day Marjorie was killed. Sitting next to me, on the coffee table, is her mother's journal that I have read cover to cover.

The woods around the house are beginning to lighten, the early morning sun soon to breach the mountaintops.

Sylvia's eyes flutter open, lock on mine.

She doesn't move.

My fist squeezes around the ring.

We stare at each other for a minute.

My face gives it away. She knows.

Without a word, I rise from the couch, walk into the kitchen, and start the coffee that I'd set hours earlier, preparing for her to wake. Preparing for the conversation we must have.

I am not calm, cool, nor collected. My stomach is on fire.

Gripping the edge of the counter, I lean forward and stare mindlessly out the window as the coffee brews. A dense fog swirls above the forest floor, weaving through the gnarled tree trunks. I watch a crow swoop off a branch, disappearing into the treetops.

I feel her before I see her.

My body tenses.

It's time.

I push away from the window, pull two mugs from the cabinet.

Sylvia says nothing as she meets me at the coffee pot. In her hand is her mother's journal. She stops next to me, the tension so thick between us you could reach out and grab onto it.

We don't look at each other.

I fill the mugs, hand her one, keep one for myself, then lean against the counter.

She mirrors this stance, leaning against the counter on the opposite side of the kitchen. She's set the journal behind her.

The coffee cup in her hand is trembling, just slightly.

I open my palm.

Sylvia stares at her mother's wedding band.

There is no question anymore. None in my heart and soul. I know—and she knows I know.

Our eyes meet.

"It's time to talk, Sylvia."

She continues to stare at me, her mind racing. I realize that, ironically, mine is suddenly completely clear. For the first time in twenty years, I feel like I am exactly where I am meant to be, at the exact moment I am meant to be there.

"Talk," I repeat.

"What do you want me to say?" she says, indignant.

"For starters, I want to know why you killed your mother, and why you framed me for doing it."

Though she's making an effort to keep her expression neutral, her entire body begins to shake. Like an earthquake, a slow rumble at first that turns violent. It reminds me of the time she vomited on the witness stand.

I watch tears gather in her eyes.

I watch her face soften with defeat.

I feel a sick sense of victory in that moment.

"I need you to forgive me," her voice cracks while piping hot coffee spills over her shaking fingertips.

I don't rush to her side. Sylvia Stone is a liar. She is manipulative. She is unstable.

She is a loose cannon.

"Forgive me," she demands.

"Sylvia," I say calmly. "You're sick."

"You think I'm sick?" The coffee is now a steady stream over the tip of her cup. Her cheeks heat with anger. "How dare you say that. You have no idea what I've been through." The cup drops from her hand and shatters on the tile floor. "How *dare* you, Rhett."

"Sylvia, stop deflecting." I remain calm. "There is no going back now. I know what you did, and I want to know why you did it."

She pushes away from the counter, a swinging pendulum of emotions. Snarling anger and spurts of sobs. She begins pacing, manically raking her fingers through her greasy hair, her bare feet stepping on broken shards of the cup. She doesn't notice.

"I've given you *everything*," she snarls. "I've helped you, taken care of you. It's because of me you're not back in jail. I've given you *everything*—and risked *everything*." With a growl, she viciously jerks a clump of her own hair. "My God, what the hell is wrong with me?"

Yes, this woman is very, very sick.

I step forward, gently grab her elbow and guide her off the broken pieces, now speckled with her blood. Still, she doesn't seem to notice that she has shredded the bottom of her feet.

She swats away my advance. "Do you have feelings for me or not?"

I blink, the question catching me off guard. "I don't have feelings for you, like that, no, Sylvia, I don't." I step forward again. "Sylvia, you're cutting the bottom of your feet—badly. Come here. Please, come here, please."

She shoves me backward. "What is so wrong with me? What is *so wrong* with me?" She begins screaming the question, over and over and over, tears streaming down her cheeks.

What is wrong with me? What is wrong with me?

"Sylvia, stop!" I yell, my adrenaline spiking. I hate the noise, the screams. "Stop, I—we—need to get you help."

Her eyes flare, bugging out of her skull. Her face contorts with madness, reminding me of a creepy cartoon character. "My mom never loved me either, do you know that? She *beat* me, Rhett. Physically abused me. It started with slapping me and my sister across the face, almost daily. But then she started getting harder with me. After Anna died, it got worse. She'd be drunk—she would drink a box of rosé for breakfast and I would be on the floor curled and in pain by noon. When she sobered, she wouldn't remember a single moment of it." Her eyes are wild, unnerving. "But you don't believe me, do you? Because she was nice to you, nice to everyone. The bitch found God." She snorts. "Un-fucking-believable, isn't it? Beats her child, then one day, just..." She snaps her fingers in the air, "Finds God and, *boom*, quits drinking and decides she wants a real relationship with me. Decides to become a totally different person."

"Is this why you killed her?"

"I killed her for you! Don't you see that? I did it for you."

"You're a liar. You're lying and you're not making any sense. You didn't kill her for me. You framed me."

"*Before* I knew you—and I've spent every day regretting what I did."

"Bullshit. You're lying. Why did you kill your mother?"

She explodes. "I killed her because she deserved it, okay! People who beat their children don't deserve to live."

"Bullshit, Sylvia! Why did you kill her?"

"Fine! I killed her for money, okay?" Spittle flies from her lips. She's completely unhinged. "Money! She told me the week before that she was giving her savings—*my inheritance*—to support the construction of a new church in the area. I couldn't believe it. This woman who beat me was becoming a huge hero in the community—while cutting me out of my inheritance. She was the liar, Rhett, not me."

"So you wanted to kill her before the money went away, so you could get your inheritance. Okay, revenge, greed, fine. I get it. But why frame *me* for it, Sylvia? *Why me?*"

"You showed up!" She flings her arms into the air like this should be completely obvious to me. "I didn't realize she'd hired someone to do her cabinets—it was the perfect opportunity. That, coupled with the recent break-in's that were happening. It was perfect."

I think of the way she looked at me when she saw me, how her gaze lingered on the kitchen knife when I picked it up.

My jaw drops. "You are *kidding* me."

"I'm sorry, okay? I told you I'm sorry."

I snort. "Sorry. You're *sorry?* Jesus, Sylvia." I shake my head. "But the letters... you wrote them, right? That was you."

"Yes," she snaps—again like why am I asking the obvious.

"*Why, though?* Why start everything up again, twenty years later?"

She turns away.

I want to grab her hair and pull her backward, but I don't. I stare at her, as she stares out the window, her back to me.

"Remember I told you I was offered a book deal when my mom was killed twenty years ago? I turned it down because I'm an idiot. Now, here I am—got laid off from my job—no money, no inheritance, no life, no nothing. I have two credit cards that have been sent to collections, and my water was about to be turned off. I thought the letters, everything, would reignite the case and set me up to revisit the book deal. So, I made a plan. I went to the pool hall with the letters—I knew that's where all the addicts hang out. I waited for one to come out, to offer them money to deliver the letters. Jesse walked out."

I shake my head. "So *I* was in the wrong place at the wrong time, and *he* was in the wrong place at the wrong time."

"Listen—" she turns and steps toward me.

"No." I hold up my hands. "You are not done talking until I understand *everything*. What was the deal with the barn? Why fake your own kidnapping? Why pretend someone took you?"

"You pissed me off when you told me we—whatever was between us—was through. That we were over, after everything I've done for you. So, I faked the kidnapping," she lifts a finger, "one, to keep media interest, and two, to get back at you for leaving me."

I can't even speak. The woman is completely sick in the head.

She continues, scrubbing her hands over her face. "Also, they found a half-print on the pendant that I put in the fourth envelope. I didn't realize at the time, but it must be mine from when I took it off her after I killed her. It was only a matter of time until they figured that out. I needed something to distract them. So I mailed myself the final letter, took my bike, and rode to a barn I saw one time on the news, for sale. That's it. Done."

The anger boiling inside me bubbles over. "Do you realize how close I am—was—to getting accused for it? Do you know that, Sylvia? I am one mistake from going back to prison for life. All for a book deal? For validation and money?" I lunge across the kitchen, grab her shoulders, shake her violently. "You—you are *crazy*."

"I am not!"

"You killed your own mother," I screamed back. "You

fucking framed me and sent me to jail for twenty years." I squeeze her shoulders, digging my nails into her skin. "And you killed your sister, didn't you? You pushed Anna that day at the city pool, didn't you? Your mom says so in the journal. That's why you took it and hid it in your room. You killed her, didn't you?"

I watch as Sylvia's face drops. She looks out the window, and her body stills as she slips into a memory from long, long ago.

FIFTY-THREE
SYLVIA

Twenty-Six Years Earlier

I wade into the deep end, pushing my way through the swimmers. The city pool is the most crowded I've ever seen it. I'm grateful for this because no one is taking notice of the swimsuit Mom bought me (and forced me to wear). It's at least one size too big, and has a stain on the side. I have no doubt she bought it from the discount bin. Because everything we own comes out of the discount section.

I dive under and breach dramatically, smoothing the hair out of my face. I'm trying to catch the lifeguard's attention. The one my sister is so obsessed over. The thing is, Anna wouldn't have even noticed him if I hadn't blurted my crush on him. Stupid, stupid, stupid.

I've done, like, a hundred dives and twirls in the water, and still, he hasn't noticed me.

But he has noticed Anna.

I *hate* her.

I hate my twin sister so much. It's not normal, I think, but I can't help it. I've wanted to tell my mom so many times, but instead of listening, I know that she would just freak, call me mean and ugly, and tell me not to say things like that. Anna is her favorite, after all. Always has been.

I feel unusually angry as I swim back to the shallow end and stalk out of the water.

Why is everything always about Perfect Anna? Somedays it feels like the entire world revolves around Perfect Anna.

My jaw clenches as I weave through the crowd cluttering the side of the pool. I'm imagining walking up to my sister and just straight-up punching her in the face. That would definitely get the lifeguard's attention—and also my mom's. Then maybe we could finally talk about my feelings.

When I reach Anna sitting on the edge, I notice her bite-free legs, dangling in the water. (Mine are currently covered with like ten chiggers). No matter how many times Anna and I played in the woods while growing up, I was always the one to get a million nasty bug bites and Anna wouldn't get a single one. Not one! How is that even possible? Even the bugs thought she was too perfect to bite.

My gaze sweeps up her body to her arms—and that's when I snap. A rush of anger so hot shoots through my veins that it feels like my skin in burning.

Her arms are flawless. Pale and soft. Not a bruise on them. Not *one*. My arms, on the other hand, have a line of four tiny bruises around my bicep. My mother's fingerprints from when she dragged me across the house two days ago.

Anna has none.

None.

She has never had a bruise in her life.

Mom never hits her like she does me. The worst Anna ever gets is a slap in the face. And I don't even think Mom hits her that hard.

My heart is roaring as I stare at my sister's perfect, perfect, arms.

"Anna," I say, forcing a smile.

She looks up, smiles widely. "Hey!"

"I'm ready to give you those swimming lessons now."

"Really?" she squeaks, then glances up at the lifeguard. She's probably thinking it's the perfect opportunity to snag his attention.

"Yeah. Come on."

Anna hesitates, worry pulling at her face. She's scared of the water.

"Oh, stop it, you big baby. Come on. You're, like, the oldest person here who can't swim."

She nibbles her lower lip. "Okay, okay, just don't let me go."

"Of course not."

My adrenaline spikes as I glance over my shoulder at Mom, scrubbing away in a notebook. When I'm certain she's not watching, I slide into the water. While holding Anna's hand, I slowly coax her into the deep end.

There are kids all around us, so much so that we can't even move without bouncing off another swimmer. They're kicking, giggling, diving in and out and creating tons of waves.

The only memory I have of the next two minutes is the feeling of Anna's hair floating through my fingers, and tickling my skin, as I held her under.

FIFTY-FOUR
RHETT

Present Day

When Sylvia blinks out of her trance, she refocuses on me. Her eyes are wet, her chin quivering with madness. "Yes, I killed her. And I have never spent one second regretting it."

I release her like she's a venomous snake. "I'm calling the cops, Sylvia. You are a murderer—I'm calling the cops." I grab her phone, which is sitting on the counter.

I hear the *whoosh* of a blade being pulled from a knife block.

I freeze, my back to her, my hand wrapped around the phone.

"Don't you even think about touching a single button on that phone."

I slowly turn, but not before pressing the Emergency button.

I look at the knife in her raised hand, the point just feet away from my beating heart. "Sylvia, you need help." I release the phone on the table and raise my palms. "Don't do this. Set down the knife."

She begins to cry, teetering on the fringes of a complete

mental breakdown. "I don't need help. I need someone I can count on. Don't you get that?"

"Let me get you help, okay?"

Keeping my eyes on hers, I reach back for the phone.

She lunges forward.

I stumble backward, the tip of the blade nicking my collarbone.

The kitchen table teeters, the chairs topple over.

"Sylvia, stop!" I plead, stumbling over a chair.

Her eyes are wild with madness. She comes at me again, again, slashing the knife through the air, trying to hit any part of my body she can. I scramble over the chairs, over the table, but am backed into the corner.

Sylvia closes in.

There is no escape.

I lunge forward, throwing my full weight onto her. We tumble over a chair, the knife still in her hand. We crash onto the tile floor, hitting hard with a thud.

Then, everything just... stops. The movement, the sounds. It's eerily quiet.

I rise off Sylvia's torso. Her eyes lock on mine, so wide that her pupils are like little pinpricks. She opens her mouth, a pained gasp escaping.

"Rhett..."

I realize then something is very, very wrong.

I scramble off her body, kick the chair out of the way. It comes away red with blood.

"Sylvia," I drop to my knees, sliding on the growing puddle of blood beneath her. "Oh, *shit*, Sylvia."

Then I see it.

The hilt of the knife, the blade buried in her chest.

FIFTY-FIVE

RHETT

I'm sitting on the front steps.

My head is in my hands. A cell phone at my side, the wooden box beside one foot, the nightstand drawer at my other.

A dead body in the house behind me.

I listen to the wail of the siren. Distant at first, then louder and louder.

I look up just as the tip of the sun emerges from the mountaintop. Swords of gold, spearing through pink clouds. The pinkest I've ever seen.

My eyes remain on these clouds as the police cars skid to a stop at my feet. As the noise erupts, as three guns are pointed at my face.

I don't speak as I am thrown to the ground, my hands pulled behind my back, handcuffs secured around my wrists.

My gaze meets the rising sun once again as I am dragged to the police car. As a hand is placed on the top of my head. As I am pushed into the backseat.

The door slams.

I bend over, peering through the window, finding the light once again.

Silence engulfs me, confinement closes in. Freedom escapes me, once again, yet the sun continues to shine.

There is always the sun.

EPILOGUE
RHETT

Not a day goes by that I don't think of Marjorie or Sylvia Stone. Not a day that I don't awaken to flashbacks of the final day of Sylvia's life. Of rolling her over and seeing the hilt of the blade buried in her chest.

Following the discovery of Sylvia's bloodied body in the house where I had been sitting on the front steps, I spent a week in jail, arrested under the assumption I had killed Sylvia. The media coverage was unlike anything anyone had ever seen. The town accused me before I'd even been assigned a lawyer. Despite the world wanting to lock me away again, the evidence spoke for itself: the jewelry stolen from Marjorie's home the day of her murder, the ski mask, the journal, the shrine to me. Combining all that with the autopsy and forensic analysis of the blade that Sylvia had fallen on (and the lack of my fingerprints on the hilt—ironic, isn't it?) I was released from county lockup.

My court-issued therapist has suggested (countless times) that I see a psychiatrist who will medicate me for what she has diagnosed as severe PTSD.

I have respectfully declined (countless times).

I don't need pills. I need solitude. Peace will come eventually. Until then, I will take each day, each moment as it comes. Piece by piece. I will be grateful. I will be fully present. I will be myself, whichever version of me decides to wake up that day. Sometimes he is complacent, sometimes he is angry, sometimes he wakes in the throes of a panic attack. Sometimes he is still drunk from the night before.

Sometimes he hasn't slept at all.

Today is one of those days.

It is morning now. I'm sitting on the rocking chair that I finished making last night—or was it two nights ago?—on the deck that connects to the two-room cabin that I built from the ground up.

I have watched the sun set, the rising of the moon, the awakening of the stars, and now, the rising of the sun once again. Today she is exceptionally beautiful, her beams spearing like swords of fire through the mountains in the distance. The birds revel in her reappearance, welcoming her with song and dance. The wilderness around me is a symphony of sound and movement. Life. It is all around me. It is truly a beautiful morning.

I close my eyes and inhale, reaching down and scratching between Tucker's ears, asleep at my foot. He lifts his head, rests his graying chin on my knee.

A rare smile catches me.

I adopted Tuck the day after I was released. I walked into the shelter with one single question: which dog has been here the longest? The moment I met Tucker, I knew we'd both been waiting on each other. Tuck was surrendered to the pound when his owner, a retired veteran passed away. He's fourteen years old. Tuck's breed is a bit of mystery. The vet thinks he's a mix of shepherd, hound, and collie. As I was paying the adoption fee, I learned he was scheduled to be put down the very next day.

Tuck suddenly turns his head, releasing a grunt (the closest thing to a bark he can muster these days).

I squint at the truck pulling up the driveway. I glance at my watch. Right on time.

Tuck's tail wags wildly as Jesse climbs out of Juan's beat-up truck. Yep, Juan's—the same one I was given when I needed it the most. After paying Juan for it, as I'd promised, I gave it to Jesse.

Passing it forward.

I smirk at the circles under Jesse's eyes when he lumbers up the porch steps.

"Rough night?"

"Rough week." He yawns. "I don't understand why I have to learn so much legal stuff to become a cop."

"Test Friday?"

"Yep."

"Then more weapons training?"

He smiles, a sparkle in his eyes. "Yep."

Jesse's favorite part of police academy thus far is weapons training, naturally.

Together we lift the two-by-fours out of the bed of the truck.

For the last six months, Jesse has been coming over three days a week to learn basic carpentry skills. Something he can do on the side to help pay for the apartment he just rented. Together, we make and sell woodworks at the farmers' market, and he's even picked up a few clients to do things around their house. I'm proud of him.

"Let's get this porch swing finished and then we'll go hit the shooting range and get ready for next week," I say.

As I stack lumber in Jesse's arms, he squints at me. "So, have you heard any more from that lawyer?"

"You mean Eva?"

"Yeah the super-hot lawyer lady who tells you she could get you over two million dollars for being wrongfully convicted?"

"I think I have a voicemail from her."

"Dude." Jesse scoffs. "Call her."

I shrug, and we switch gears to the academy.

As Jesse drums on about class, and we settle in behind the saw bench, my face lifts to the sky. The sun finds me, once again, peeking through the thick canopy of leaves.

I smile.

Maybe I should return that call.

A LETTER FROM THE AUTHOR

Dear Readers – let's stay in touch!

Sign up here to hear about my new releases with Storm:

www.stormpublishing.co/amanda-mckinney

Sign up here to be included in my personal newsletter:

www.amandamckinneyauthor.com/contact

If you enjoyed *When I Disappear* and could spare a few moments to leave a review that would be hugely appreciated. Even a short review can make all the difference in encouraging a reader to discover my books for the first time. Thank you so much!